*He Nuzzled his Mouth
Against her Neck, Sending Shivers
of Heat Down the Bare Flesh
of her Chest and Arms.*

"You see, you can do anything you want to do, if you work hard enough at it." He reached around with his free hand and tipped her chin up so that he could look into her eyes. "You can have anything you want—anything at all. Do you understand that? You just have to decide what it is you want."

They looked into each other's eyes for a long moment, and then Keith bent to kiss her again. But this time the kiss was not tender. It was full of longing, and so deep that it took Avis's breath away. With a sigh, she nuzzled closer to him, feeling herself slip blissfully into a state of half-exhaustion, half-arousal.

Dear Reader:

Nora Roberts, Tracy Sinclair, Jeanne Stephens, Carole Halston, Linda Howard. Are these authors familiar to you? We hope so, because they are just a few of our most popular authors who publish with Silhouette Special Edition each and every month. And the Special Edition list is changing to include new writers with fresh stories. It has been said that discovering a new author is like making a new friend. So during these next few months, be sure to look for books by Sandi Shane, Dorothy Glenn and other authors who have just written their first and second Special Editions, stories we hope you enjoy.

Choosing which Special Editions to publish each month is a pleasurable task, but not an easy one. We look for stories that are sophisticated, sensuous, touching, and great love stories, as well. These are the elements that make Silhouette Special Editions more romantic...and unique.

So we hope you'll find this Silhouette Special Edition just that—*Special*—and that the story finds a special place in your heart.

The Editors at Silhouette

SERL-7/85

JILLIAN BLAKE
Water Dancer

Silhouette Special Edition

Published by Silhouette Books New York

America's Publisher of Contemporary Romance

SILHOUETTE BOOKS
300 E. 42nd St., New York, N.Y. 10017

ISBN: 0-373-09256-3

First Silhouette Books printing August 1985

10 9 8 7 6 5 4 3 2 1

America's Publisher of Contemporary Romance

Printed in the U.S.A.

JILLIAN BLAKE

is a voracious consumer of all types of fiction from the ridiculous to the sublime. Lately, it seems she's been finding something to write about in everything she sees and does.

An ex-dancer with a five-year-old daughter and a husband who is a dedicated jazz musician, Jillian leads a busy and happy life in Cambridge, Massachusetts.

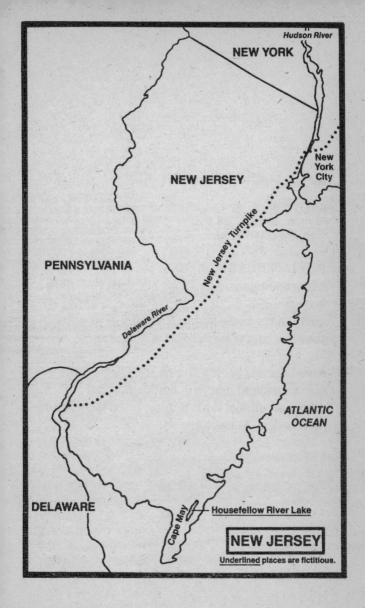

Hudson River

NEW YORK

NEW JERSEY

New York City

New Jersey Turnpike

PENNSYLVANIA

Delaware River

ATLANTIC OCEAN

DELAWARE

Cape May

Housefellow River Lake

NEW JERSEY

Underlined places are fictitious.

Chapter One

M onday, May 12

When I first found out that my foot injury might really prevent me from ever dancing lead roles again, I went into hiding. Not literally, because I would never—not for all the world—let my fellow dancers or the company administrators see how devastating the prognosis was for me. After all, injury or no injury, I was still Avis Considine, prima ballerina of the National Ballet, and I didn't get *this* far at age 28 by collapsing into tears for all the world to see!

Sweat poured down Avis's forehead and stung her eyes. She could no longer read the handwritten pages; her vision was dimmed by the sweat and the intense dry heat of the sauna. She dropped the sheaf of papers on the slatted bench at her feet and stretched out full-length on the hot oak boards of the upper berth.

She had gone into hiding, all right, Avis thought grimly, throwing one arm over her face and shutting her eyes. But it had been an emotional hibernation. She had nursed her pain and shock privately, retreating into a world of proud silence that most of her fellow dancers took to be a sign of inner strength. Very few of them knew that it was Avis's only protection against utter desolation. Dancing was her life, and she was afraid of having no life left at all.

Fortunately, one of her closest friends knew better, and cornered Avis in her studio apartment one afternoon, demanding that she admit the extent of her pain and fears. Beth Keane was seven years older than Avis and already relegated to character roles in the classics like *Swan Lake* and *Nutcracker*. It was she who had convinced Avis to express her feelings of depression and anxiety, who warned her that to keep silent was to let the fear fester and become even more ugly than it already was. "We're survivors, you and I," Beth had said, "we didn't get to the top without a lot of control and a lot of sacrifice. But the time comes when you have to relinquish a little of that control. It's that, or go crazy, Ave. Believe me."

It was Beth who had convinced Avis that, if she didn't want to confess to a friend, then she should try to confess to a sheet of paper. That was how her journal had been started, and, now that she was doing little besides her daily regime of physical therapy, she had plenty of time to write. In fact, it had begun to take over her life, much the way daily classes and rehearsals had occupied the days, months, and years before her injury. That was the way Avis worked: She immersed herself completely or not at all.

The timer went off on the wall of the sauna, and Avis opened her eyes and got up slowly from the bench. Beth had been right, she decided. If she hadn't had the journal, she might indeed have gone crazy by now.

When she first had walked into the Sportscape Club, Avis had hoped to find some solace. After all, she figured, a gym dedicated to the body was much like a dance studio, and the very act of standing in that hot, intense, and familiar environment was sure to make her feel at home. If she couldn't be in the studio, the Sportscape Club would be the next best thing.

But now, as she stepped outside the sauna and stood for a moment to let her body adjust to the relatively cool air, she realized it was not the same. She was standing in a large low-ceilinged square room with pale grey walls and carpeting. The effect was supposed to be soothing, but it was belied by the gleaming chrome and blue vinyl of the exercise machines that surrounded it like military sentinels, and by the men and women making a tremendous effort to push and pull against the unremitting bars and pulleys that built their muscles for them.

The entire scene was multiplied by the mirrors that lined two of the walls. This was the only feature that had been familiar to Avis when she first had come to the club a month ago. She knew mirrors well; she had grown up in front of them. But, in her experience, mirrors had always reflected worn wooden floors and large, multipaned windows with the grimy outlines of New York City silhouetted between their peeling frames. The mirrors had reflected dancers, bending and stretching and twisting their bodies to new limits, flying across the floor in a continuous, graceful tapestry of movement and music.

It had been a beautiful sight, even on the darkest, dampest winter day, and Avis still could not get used to the sight of the antiseptic gray walls and the mechanical contraptions that glittered in its place. She especially could not get used to the fact that the people in the Sportscape Club groaned and grunted and sweated and strained not to achieve a beautiful arabesque or a triple pirouette, but only for the sake of the exercise.

There seemed no point in it. But Avis had spent her life sweating and straining in the pursuit of beauty and art, and she knew she was biased—she was a professional dancer. And she was honest enough to admit that part of her discomfort in the Sportscape Club had to do with the fact that she herself might soon be facing a future much like these men and women. Her body would always be sleek and well-tuned, like a fine engine on a very expensive car. But to what purpose, if she couldn't make it do beautiful things?

She glanced down at her bare feet. They were long and narrow and shaped like cashew nuts—a firm, round heel; broad, flat toes; and the high arch which had been the envy of all the other female dancers. It had been that bridge-span arch that, only a month ago, had been her undoing. She had been working every night, with solo and featured roles in three out of the four pieces on the company's spring program. And she was rehearsing during the day for a new solo that the resident choreographer was "putting on her"—creating especially for Avis's considerable talents.

It had not been an unusually hard schedule, but for many reasons it had been an unusually tense one, and Avis had been having difficulty sleeping. The combined stresses of being overworked and fatigued had made the sudden injury—really just a simple sprain resulting from a missed step—much more serious. The entire left metatarsal was badly bruised, and even now, a month later, underneath the support bandage that Avis wore, the foot looked curiously deflated, as if all the air had been let out of her buoyant arch.

Avis sighed and forced her eyes to travel up her body with professional disinterest. She was wearing a black maillot leotard that fitted her so well it looked as if she had spent her life in it. In a sense, she had; she'd been wearing dance clothes for so long that sometimes, dressed for a rare evening away from the State Theater where she had been performing for twelve years, she caught a glimpse of herself in the mirror and was startled by the image of herself in street clothes.

The leotard was cut modestly enough, but it would have been clear to even the most casual observer that the woman who wore it was in superb physical condition. Avis was small and compact, but her long legs gave the illusion of height; admirers, when they met her backstage after a performance, invariably exclaimed, "How tiny you are!"

She knew herself intimately enough to know that she was small, but hardly tiny. Her broad shoulders, which aided the graceful allure of her arm movements on stage, were a source of constant annoyance. Her skin was dark and smooth, rippling over well-shaped thighs and gently rounded calf muscles. Her hair was dark and sleek, too, and even now, when she no longer had to do so, Avis wore it in a taut coil at the back of her small head.

The human body was a beautiful thing, with what it could do with flesh and bones and muscle. She looked back up at the men and women straining against the weights and pulleys, and she smiled. Getting depressed was not going to help any; she knew that from years of dealing with less serious injuries. She had to heal as quickly as possible and get back on stage, despite the grim prognosis that the company doctor had warned her about. She could save her tale of woe for her journal. The thing to do was to get on with her life.

Still smiling, Avis strode across the exercise room toward the pool. The machines, thank goodness, were not for her use. It would be redundant to try and build up muscles that had developed so splendidly after years of training. And she had no intention of building up anything other than her dancing muscles. After all, she *was* going to be back on stage in a matter of weeks.

Her regimen, prescribed by the company doctor and

the physical therapist, included heat and water therapy, gentle massage, lots of rest—and swimming. Swimming, Dr. Grey had told her, was the most beneficial form of exercise. He had looked severe as he said this, as if he was warning Avis not to mention dance as another contender in the beneficial exercise department. Swimming toned all the muscles of the body without straining the injured areas. It involved all the muscle groups, thereby lessening the strain on any one particular muscle as dance was likely to do. And if Avis was conscientious about her therapy program—all of it—Dr. Grey allowed that she might conceivably be back on pointe at the end of two or three months.

Avis, of course, had other ideas. To be out of circulation for two or three months meant losing the solo Laurence Lessine was "putting" on her, and her seniority for other, more classical roles as well. The company had a brief summer season at an open-air theater in Central Park, and Avis was determined to be back in her Nicolini pointe shoes by then, even though "then" was only two weeks away.

So she had demurely consented to all that Dr. Grey prescribed, and conveniently neglected to tell him that, instead of doing ten laps a day in the Olympic-sized pool, she was up to forty, and counting.

The pool at the club was considerably more appealing than the exercise room. It had a high-domed ceiling covered with old wooden paneling that smelled like a rain forest—damp and smoky-sweet. There were windows in the pool room, and, although they looked out onto nothing more stimulating than a brick apartment building across the street, they provided a familiar sense of home to Avis as she swam.

She also liked the pool director. He was an elderly man who had obviously once been a powerful swimmer himself, even though his barrel-shaped torso now sagged with age. He moved slowly from his cluttered desk to the pool area, and seldom came in the water unless he absolutely had to while teaching. It was during those times that he underwent a remarkable transformation. Water-borne, he became sleek and agile as a seal, his nearly bald head cutting through the blue-green water without a trace of wake. Watching him, Avis thought that, if she had chosen to dedicate herself to a sport over an art, it would have been swimming.

She was cut out for it. Her powerful shoulders made her stroke long and sure, and her light weight enabled her to skim the water like a skiff. She enjoyed the rhythmic cadences of the sport, and found it easy to lose herself in the hypnotic momentum of stroke and breath. Only Dr. Grey's warning about the dangers of fatigue and muscle strain made her stop at forty laps.

Today, though, the coach was not in evidence. Avis looked at the desk and around the perimeter of the pool, but could not see Tom Miller anywhere. She recalled that he had mentioned taking some time off, and felt a stab of irritation. She and Tom liked each other, took each other seriously, and she had looked forward to her daily desultory conversations with the man. She also needed his encouragement and pointers if she wanted to continue on her rapid-recovery course; it was Tom who had suggested that she accelerate her swim therapy, although Avis had been all too eager to comply.

But Tom was not there, and neither was the young boy who sometimes came in to help him out. There was no one in charge, it seemed, and the only other person in the room was a man who was swimming laps in the far lane of the pool.

Shrugging, Avis dropped her towel and slipped out of her rubber sandals. Perhaps Tom was just out for a cup of coffee. She went over to the corner of the room nearest her desk to begin her warm-up stretches. She would have loved to talk to Tom today. Over the four weeks they had developed a friendly, jocular intimacy, but Tom could be counted on to listen sympathetically when Avis went through her frequent bouts of anxiety over her future. She sometimes thought he understood her better than many of her dancer friends did.

Avis's stretch routine never varied. It was an abbreviated version of the ballet barre warm-up she had done for more than half her life, and it always put her in a quiet, meditative state. Holding on to the edge of Tom's desk, she did a series of gentle pliês, bending her leg at the knee and thigh with her feet turned out in a wide second position. Then she dipped her back forward, releasing one vertebrae at a time until her head rested comfortably on her knees. This was followed by a backbend of equally dramatic proportions.

As she leaned back, her head parallel to the backs of her knees and her free arm stretched in an arch over her head, she caught a glimpse of the man in the pool. He had not stopped to watch Avis's contortions, as so many other athletes did, appalled and astounded by her pliability. He had not even missed a stroke. His stroke, she noticed, was powerful—not fast, but steady and strong, like a metronome's relentless beat. Probably just another jock in doing laps, she decided. But what was he doing here on her pool time?

She straightened up, then lifted one leg easily onto the window ledge behind Tom's desk. With a single supple motion, she bent her torso like a reed over her leg, first from the side, then facing forward, so that her body lay against her thigh. She repeated the ritual with the other leg, careful not to put too much weight on her injured metatarsal as she stood. Stretching, she hummed a melody under her breath, vaguely classical but in perfect three-quarter time. Her body moved like a blade of grass fluttered about by the wind.

Her entire stretch program took almost twenty minutes, during which she forgot all about Tom's absence and the presence of the man in the pool. But after she had finished, just as she was getting ready to dive into the water, she heard a voice.

"I wouldn't dive in if I were you. Pushing off from the side of the side of the pool like that puts too much pressure on your metatarsal. And on your hip joints. Bad for the turnout, you know?"

Avis had to catch herself to keep from falling into the pool, so startled was she by this little speech. She had forgotten about the man, who had stopped swimming—apparently a while ago, judging by his nearly dry body—and was sitting on the opposite edge of the pool, watching her calmly.

"What do you know about turnout?" she inquired tartly. Something about his smug, self-assured tone made her bristle. Who was this guy to tell her, a professional dancer, about turnout? Avis was so taken aback that it never occurred to her to wonder how he had known she was a dancer in the first place.

But the man simply smiled and answered the question she had not asked. "I assume you're Tom's ballerina client. He told me all about you." His eyes narrowed appealingly. "The turnout was a lucky guess." Even from across the pool, she could see his eyes flick over her body, poised for flight. "You are Avis Considine, the dancer, aren't you?"

"Who are you?"

The man got to his feet quickly, and Avis was surprised at his size. He was big and burly, with a sandy beard that nearly obscured his face. He looked more like a football player than a swimmer. But she remembered the ease with which he had cut through the water. He was a swimmer, all right, just as Tom had been. Good swimmers transformed themselves in the water, just as good dancers transformed themselves on the stage.

"I'm Keith Harding—Tom's temporary replacement. He told me all about you, Miss Considine." The man moved closer to Avis and noticed her expression. "Didn't he tell you about me?"

His face bore some concern, and Avis noticed that he had deep-set, ocean-blue eyes. "Tom . . . no, he didn't even say he was leaving, for sure. What's wrong with him?" Now it was her turn to show concern.

"Nothing, really. He was due for a vacation, and his doctor has been telling him to take it easy for years now. I guess he just figured it was time." The man looked more closely into Avis's dark eyes. "Really. There's nothing wrong. He'll be back in a few weeks, on a part-time basis."

Avis wondered if he would have told her if there had been something seriously wrong with Tom, and then decided that Keith Harding did not look like the type to pull any punches. He looked like a jock, but there was something about his eyes, something wise and serious that belied the usual jock image. Besides, he was smiling at her with real cordiality.

"And you're his replacement here?"

"I'm it. Tom filled me in on all his physical therapy customers. He was particularly concerned that I get to work with you."

"What exactly did he tell you about me?" Avis inquired coolly. She disliked being thought of as in need of physical therapy, and she doubted that Tom had described her as just another customer; Tom was always kidding her about her unattached state. It was not beyond reason for Avis to assume that Tom had considered the possibility of a match between Avis and his replacement. He was a mischief-maker.

Keith was looking at her as if he knew what she was thinking about Tom, and Avis felt immediately disloyal. "He just said that you were a dancer with the National Ballet, and that you had seriously injured your left metatarsal about a month ago. He told me that you planned to be back on stage in two weeks."

Avis was still feeling slightly defensive. She was uneasy with the fact that he knew so much about her, and she so little about him. She lifted her chin slightly as she spoke. "And I guess you think that's an unrealistic goal, is that it?" She saw her accelerated training program disappearing before her eyes.

Keith shook his head. "He also told me that you're the best natural distance swimmer he's seen in years. And Tom should know. He was the best once himself."

All this information was so unexpected that Avis forgot to maintain her cool. "He was? He said that about me? Really?"

Keith's smile broadened at the sight of Avis's incredulity. "Honest. That's what he said."

Avis's eyes gleamed. "Does this mean I can keep to the rehab schedule Tom and I worked out?"

Keith shrugged and took a step back. "Get in the water, and let's see what you can do."

With a brilliant, grateful smile, Avis stepped to the edge of the pool. She had almost left the deck when a powerful hand reached out and drew her back, almost pulling her off her feet.

"I told you, no diving," Keith said firmly. "Doctor's orders." Then he released her arm so that she could slip into the pool, but not before he smiled. The dazzling after image of that smile followed Avis all the way into the water.

Chapter Two

Tuesday, May 13

I'm determined to get back on stage in time for the summer concert. Laurence will never save the new solo in the fall concert for me if I'm not back in the repertory by then. I know exactly how he operates, that snake! I'm sure he has his eye on a possible replacement for me already.

But he won't get a chance to use her, whoever she is. I'll be back by then, I'm sure of it. Everything depends on my being there. Therefore, everything depends on my therapy regimen. I must dedicate myself to swimming with the same intensity I dedicate to learning a new dance. I can even think of it as a new kind of choreography to learn. It's endurance that counts—that and concentration.

I just hope this new coach is up to the task of teaching me. He seems like a pretty good teacher, and I can tell he swims like Poseidon, the god of the ocean. He even looks a bit like that Greek god type.

But I've learned to be aware of the godlike in a man. After all, Laurence was the god of dance, as far as I was concerned. And look where he got me. Nowhere I wouldn't have gotten by myself!

Avis swam far more than forty laps that afternoon. As a matter of fact, she lost count after fifty-five. The only thing she remembered was the rhythm of her stroke, so much like the meditative cadence of her stretch routine. Stroke and breath, stroke and breath . . . after a while, there was a musicality to her motion in the water that she had never realized. The sheer monotony made the movement as graceful as an adagio.

She remembered seeing Keith, too, at odd intervals during her swim. He did not stand in one spot while she swam, as Tom did, so that she could count her laps by the number of times she passed his watery image. He seemed to be moving slowly around the edge of the pool, although his eyes never left her body. Avis was aware of his scrutiny even when she could not find him on her breath count, and it made her feel curiously at ease in the water, as if the intensity of his attention was buoying her up.

Finally, Keith had to dive in and get her. She felt rather than heard the splash as he dove in the pool, and then she felt the push of the water as he made his way toward her in eight feet of water. She intended to stop swimming, thinking that was what he must want her to do, but somehow she couldn't get her arms and legs to obey. So she just kept on stroking, waiting for him to pull her up short.

But he didn't. Instead, he fell into place beside her and adjusted his more powerful stroke so that he kept in perfect tandem with hers. She pulled her head out of the water, but he just smiled and shook his head.

"Keep on going," he said, his voice very close to her ear. "But try and slow your stroke down to match mine." His beard glistened with water, and Avis smiled and nodded to show that she understood.

He began to swim very slowly, so slowly that Avis

thought she would sink to the bottom of the pool. But she soon caught the rhythm of his pace, and, the minute she did, she realized how tired she was. Her arms began to ache and her legs felt like lead pipes. Every stroke seemed to take hours to complete, and every breath felt as if it was never going to come.

She lasted only three more laps, and then stood up in the shallow end of the pool. "Stop," she gasped. "I . . . can't swim another stroke."

Immediately Keith was on his feet beside her. He did not seem surprised or disappointed that she had stopped, but only smiled as he took her elbow and led her to the side of the pool. He had to lift her bodily onto the tiled ledge.

"How far did I go?" she asked. But Keith did not answer her. Instead he lifted her foot out of the water and examined it closely.

"You shouldn't be swimming with this thing on," he said, touching the ankle-support bandage she wore. "It only slows you down."

Avis was surprised by this remark. "But Dr. Grey said I should wear it all the time, even in the water." She saw Keith's slight frown and felt a twinge of annoyance. "Besides, I'm not here for speed swimming. I'm here to get strong so I can dance again, remember?"

He stopped examining her foot and looked up at her. Standing in the water before her, his eyes were level with hers, and she was struck again by their depth and complexity. They were sea-green, but flecked with gray, like the sea on a threatening day. His brows were thick above them, like heavy clouds, and his cheekbones were high and wide. Only his generous mouth and witty smile saved his face from severity. He wasn't smiling now.

"You want to dance again soon, isn't that the general idea?"

She had to fight back irritation. Once again, he seemed to be talking down to her, patronizing her with that half-amused glitter in his eyes. She knew damn well that speed was of the essence—she wasn't some half-baked amateur just in this for the fun of it! She glared at him for a moment, wondering why he seemed to enjoy needling her. Was it because he had no respect for what she did? He probably had never even seen a ballet before, much less a real live ballerina.

Still, she could not risk alienating him. Speed wasn't the only thing that was of the essence; time, too, was important, and she had none to waste. Besides, weariness was settling on her bones like a shawl, depleting her of the strength to fight him. "How far did I go?" was all she asked him.

"Not very far at all," he replied, but then he looked up and smiled so disarmingly that Avis wondered if he had meant to be patronizing in the first place. "But that's what we're here for, isn't it? Don't you worry your pretty little head. Put yourself in my hands and we'll have you doing miles in a matter of months."

He hauled himself out of the water and walked over to the desk to get a towel. Avis watched his powerful back and legs dripping and glistening with water. She found it impossible not to appreciate his strength and grace, despite the fact that his manner set her teeth on edge. Something about him reminded her of Laurence, although physically the two men could not have had less in common. Maybe it was his supreme self-confidence that grated on her so. . . .

At any rate, he was very much mistaken if he thought she had become his charge. Miles in months, was it? Well, he was in for a surprise if he thought she was going to stick around for any distance training once she got back on her feet. She was here to heal and that was all. He could find someone else to impress, someone else to turn into a long-distance fish. Who did he think he was, taking over her life after a half-hour swim? And she had swum pretty far, no matter what Keith Harding said; her own muscles told her that much.

But she had to keep sight of her immediate goals, even if Keith did not. Endurance—that was the name of the game. Hadn't she said as much in her own journal? And if Keith said she still had a lot of work to do, then she would do it, as long as it would help her get stronger. After all, they were essentially talking about the same thing—getting back on stage was one thing, staying there was another. Besides, she had to admit, something about him appealed to her, if only because he was such a fine physical specimen. She had an eye trained to admire beautiful bodies, male or female.

"Where did you come from?" she asked, to change the subject.

He turned around and tossed her a towel with a swift underhand. "Do you mean, was I born on this planet?"

Avis grinned through chattering teeth. "Ah, so you are human after all." She had to appreciate the fact that he had perceived the nature of her curiosity and her humor. "What I meant was, where did you work before this?"

Keith came back to the side of the pool and sat down beside Avis. "You mean, where did I work as a swimming coach? I didn't." He reached over and pulled the towel tighter across Avis's shoulders, but would offer no further answer.

Avis realized that he wasn't about to explain himself anymore, so she took another tack. "How do you know Tom, then?"

"Tom? God, Tom and I go back a hundred years." Leaving that intriguing statement dangling between them, he peered closer at her blue lips and chattering teeth and changed the subject. "Hey, you're getting chilled. That's no good for those muscles you just worked so hard to build up. Come over here."

He pulled her gently to her feet and led her over to the narrow massage table that stood behind Tom's desk. Tom had never used it; he said he had no use for massage, although Avis had suspected that he was simply awkward about the prospect of handling her young, female limbs.

Keith seemed to have no such compunctions. "Up you go," he said, lifting her onto the table with no apparent effort. "Lie on your stomach, and we'll see if we can rub those muscles up a bit."

Avis stretched out obediently. Whatever defiance she felt about his assuming command over her life disappeared as soon as his hands touched her body. She had been massaged so many times before that she felt no uneasiness at his ministrations. She understood the necessity for massage; if her muscles contracted after so much activity, they would very likely go into a painful spasm. Even worse, they could knot up in spasm, setting Avis's training program back immeasurably, perhaps fatally, for her dance career.

But she also knew, as soon as he laid his hands on her back, that she was being manipulated by an expert. His hands were huge, but not heavy, and they seemed to move along every muscle group and unravel the tightened cords with quick confidence. Avis felt the familiar warmth stealing along her skeleton, beginning at the nape of her neck and traveling down her spine to the base.

Keith spent more time on her legs than he did on her back, and as he worked, Avis was aware that her legs had been dangerously overtaxed by the swim. She must have gone a lot farther than she thought, despite his cavalier statement that she hadn't gone very far at all.

Arms spread akimbo so that she could rest her head on her elbows, she turned and looked back at Keith. "Come on," she cajoled. "Tell me the truth. I did pretty well, didn't I?"

He paused with his hands laid lightly across the backs of her thighs. She felt the warmth of his fingers spreading upward to meet the warmth he had created along her back. Her fatigue had turned into a drowsy lassitude.

"That depends." He looked at her half-closed eyes with a small, private smile. "You did pretty well, all right. For a dancer. For a swimmer . . ." He wrinkled his nose slightly.

"How far?" she persisted.

Keith gave her hamstring a playful pinch, and she jumped. "You're really big on measurements, aren't you?"

"Tell me."

He shrugged and started to work again on her thighs. "I don't know. A mile, a mile and a half—about sixty laps, I'd say."

"Sixty!" She would have jumped off the table, but Keith held her down, laughing.

"Yeah, sixty." His fingers worked to calm her down, but he was laughing at her excitement. "Sixty's not bad, for a dancer, as I said. But for a swimmer . . ." He shrugged again, this time with a grin. "For a swimmer, it's pretty decent too."

"Well, thank you for that, Coach." Avis turned so that her chin was between her palms. His compliment had pleased her out of all proportion to its degree. "But I'd appreciate it if you'd remember that I am a dancer and not a swimmer."

She spoke casually and half in jest. But from the way Keith's hands stopped moving abruptly on her leg, she knew he had taken her very seriously.

"Not a swimmer?" He spoke slowly and deliberately. "If you don't consider yourself a swimmer, Avis, then you have no business being here. No business at all."

He stepped back from the table as if he expected her to get right up and leave. There was no anger in his face, but his eyes were hooded and closed, and Avis knew he was disappointed by her statement. Despite her earlier irritation, she was upset by this prospect; somehow she did not want to risk his disfavor. His opinion was important to her. She wanted to erase that dead expression from his eyes and see him smile.

She sat up and dangled her legs over the side of the table. "Look," she said placatingly. "I didn't mean that it was no good to be a swimmer, or that being a dancer is better. I just meant . . ." She broke off, annoyed at her apology. Why did she need to apologize to him? They both knew that that was exactly what she had meant. She bit her lip and snorted softly under her breath. She was acting just like she had when she was a young dancer, eager to impress the coach.

"Relax. I know what you meant." Keith gently pushed her back to a prone position. "But I meant something quite different. I meant that while you're in this pool you are a swimmer. You must think of yourself as a swimmer, act like a swimmer, and breathe like a swimmer. Otherwise, you'll do yourself no good at all, even if your goal is nothing more than to get out of here and back on stage."

She couldn't see his face, but she could tell by his hands that he was intensely serious. And Avis had to agree. If she was going to commit herself, she had to commit her mind as well as her body. Wasn't that the way she danced? And didn't her life as a dancer depend on her success as a swimmer?

It was her road back, and, right now, it was the most important thing in the world. She recalled her journal entry, and bit her lip meditatively. Keith was telling her exactly what she had been trying to tell herself, that she had to dedicate all of her prodigious energy to swimming if she ever hoped to be able to dedicate herself to dance again. Her injury was not crippling, but it would be if she went back before she was ready. And, after all, she was twenty-eight and not eighteen.

Wracked by a sudden spasm of impatience, Avis sat up again, this time so suddenly that Keith took a quick step back to avoid being hit. "I want to swim again," she said.

"Are you kidding?"

"I never kid about things like this," she told him, her almond-brown eyes gazing at his steadily.

He watched her for a moment, then shook his head. "Nope. No go. You're exhausted. Your muscles are quivering from overwork as it is, and I haven't even begun to work on your foot yet."

"I have a physical therapist to massage my feet. You're here to help me swim. And I want to swim."

Avis was aware that she was taking a risk in talking to Keith that way. He fixed his gaze on her, and she had to force herself not to look away. But it was too important for her to take pains with politeness. She had to be better in two weeks, and if working harder would accelerate the healing process, then she was going to work harder than Keith Harding had thought possible.

She wondered if he thought her spoiled, or perhaps a bit crazy, demanding to go back in the water after the grueling workout she had just finished. But if he thought she was just another recuperating jock, he hadn't figured on the kind of dedication for which dancers were famous. Nureyev had danced the last scene of *Le Corsaire* with a broken ankle once. If this guy—this substitute coach—thought he was going to keep Avis Considine out of the water, he had sadly misjudged his customer!

Avis's narrow, heart-shaped jaw was set in a firm line. So far, Keith hadn't responded. As a matter of fact, he seemed to be staring off into space at a spot somewhere over Avis's left shoulder, completely unaware of the big dark eyes blazing up at him with silent challenge. His silence was unnerving. "You said sixty laps wasn't great for a swimmer," she prompted, "Well, I'm ready to give it another try."

There was still no reply, and Avis fidgeted uncomfortably on the table. "If I was in a dance studio," she went on, "I'd give it another try. No matter how tired I was, I would try again."

When Keith finally shifted his gaze back to her face, there was a faint glimmer of a smile playing around his generous mouth, and a hint of new interest as he watched the defiant figure sitting so straight on the massage table in front of him. "You want to try for another round, eh?"

"That's what I said." She thought she detected a note of condescension in his voice, and she bristled. "I don't say things unless I mean them."

He nodded. "I believe that," he murmured. "That's how you got into trouble with that foot in the first place, isn't it?"

Avis opened her mouth and shut it again without uttering the oath that came to her lips. He was so condescending to her. If he thought that spending eight hours a day in the studio was easy, she'd like to see Keith Harding try a triple pirouette. In pointe shoes! As if he would even know what a pirouette was! "Can I swim or can't I, coach?" She controlled the anger in her voice, but put an especially heavy emphasis on the word "coach."

The glimmer of a smile grew. "How many laps do you want to do? Twenty? Forty? Another sixty?"

Avis smiled. "I thought before that measurements didn't count? Who's counting now?" Her light eyes darkened dramatically when she was angry or excited, as she was right now.

Keith lifted his eyebrows, and Avis found sudden glints of blue in the green-gray seascape of his eyes. "I never said that," he replied levelly. "Measurements are important. You have to set goals for yourself."

Avis nodded. "I know. I do it in the studio all the time. The level of my extension, the degree of my turnout, the number of pirouettes, or fouettes . . . If I don't set a goal, I'll have nothing to work for, right?"

Keith nodded. A glimmer of excitement lit his face, but he was very adept at controlling it. "That's right. But there are unmeasurables, too. You have those when you dance, don't you?" He seemed to have forgotten the tension between them. For the moment, so had Avis.

"Of course. Style, interpretation, musicality." Avis broke off. Those were her strong points as a dancer, really. Oh, she had all the technicalities, the "measurables." But it was her ability to breathe life into those skills, to make the steps greater than the sum of their parts, that had raised her to the status of prima ballerina. And that, she knew, had come with age. Now she was considered a "mature" dancer. The thought made her shudder slightly.

If he saw the shudder, Keith did not guess at the thought that had provoked it. The glimmer was growing, and Avis felt like a reluctant scholar who has finally shown the teacher a glimmer of intelligence.

"But there's something else, isn't there? Something unmeasurable." Keith prodded her.

She was perplexed, as much over the answer to his question as she was over the fact that she should be having such a conversation with Keith in the first place. It was unusual, to say the least, to be discussing aesthetics with a swim coach. But, for some reason, it was important to Avis that she pass his little pop quiz. "Another unmeasurable . . ." she began, but Keith, who was by now smiling broadly, finished the sentence for her.

"It's energy. Dedication. Commitment. And you, Miss Avis Considine, have got it in spades." He put his hands under her arms and swung her down from the table. "OK, kid. You want more laps, you got 'em."

They were both grinning at each other now. Whatever fatigue Avis had felt had totally vanished.

"How many, coach?" This time the "coach," instead of being sarcastic, sounded friendly, almost a term of affection. Avis realized that she had never used the term when addressing Tom, but somehow it really seemed to suit Keith.

"Only twenty," he said. "It would be stupid to do any more today. I won't get anything out of you tomorrow." He laughed, and Avis wondered how she had ever thought his face severe. It was an intelligent face, capable of great warmth. He was actually handsome, she decided, but just not her type. "And I want you to keep that slow pace I showed you. It may seem sluggish to you at first, but you'll be surprised how much energy you can save. This," he added, turning her by the shoulders and propelling her toward the pool, "is not a test of speed or agility. We're going for stamina here. For brute endurance."

Endurance. That was the name of the game. Avis reached the edge of the pool and, turning, gave Keith a smart salute. Then she carefully lowered herself into the water and began to swim.

Chapter Three

*W*ednesday, May 14

Swimming really is a graceful sport. At first, I didn't think so, but I'm beginning to understand its music. That's what Laurence always used to say: the difference between walking and dancing is the music. The music in swimming is all very quiet, very subdued. But it's there, all the same.

I wonder why I never noticed it before today. And I wonder if Keith Harding has anything to do with it. I mean, he's everything I never wanted, in a man or in a teacher—he's too much like Larry for my tastes. Still, he does make me work, and work right. And there is something about him . . . something in the way he moves, and in his eyes . . ."

Avis put down her pen and dreamily let her journal fall back on her chest. She was lying down on the couch in her studio apartment later that night, making her entry in the journal as she always did at the end of the day. But tonight, for the first time in many nights, she was too tired to write. The muscles in her hand seemed incapable of holding the pen upright. Her legs, which were bent at the knee to prop up the cloth-covered journal notebook, threatened to collapse from the strain.

Yet she had not felt this good in many nights. If her body was unwilling to make the effort to write, her mind certainly had no problem wandering back over the events of the day. She felt that she had accomplished a lot, in both her physical and her emotional progress, and she had not felt so totally satisfied with her day's work since before she injured her foot.

It was because she had decided to do it full out that she had been able to swim so far. And the decision to commit herself to her therapy made her feel better about herself, too. Avis thrived on dedication, and one of the reasons her injury had hurt so much was the fear that she would lose that focus in her life.

Not that she would ever neglect her true love— dancing. Just looking around her studio apartment from the old red velvet couch on which she lay was evidence of her real dedication. The apartment was on the fourth floor of a big old building on New York's Upper West Side, home to many other dancers like herself. The walls were decorated with posters proclaiming past seasons of the National Ballet. On one wall, running between two windows, was a smooth, well-worn oak barre. The doors to the large walk-in closet were open, exposing the pointe shoes, hung by their pink satin ribbons like medals of past glories.

Even the kitchen was a testament to her chosen vocation. Old-fashioned Mason jars held grains and powders that spoke of past and present health-food diets, a subject on which Avis, like every other dancer she knew, was an expert. The refrigerator contained yogurt, juice, a staggering array of fresh fruits and vegetables, and nothing else.

Anyone walking into the room would know at once who lived there. They would also know that dance was everything to the inhabitant. Pasted to the door of the refrigerator, where Avis could easily see it from her vantage point on the couch, was a picture of herself. Surprisingly, it was one of the only ones in the room. She was wearing a short white tutu with a satin bodice, strung with an abundance of seed pearls. On her head was a narrow feather headdress. It was a picture of Avis in her role as Odette, the Swan Queen of *Swan Lake*, which was one of her favorite roles. She stood on pointe on one foot, the other leg extended up into space somewhere near her ear. Despite the elevation of her leg, she was wearing an expression of quiet joy, and her long arms were extended out in front of her as if enticing the audience to come and join her in her effortless fun.

Behind her, and just visible over her left shoulder, stood Laurence Lessine, wearing blue-gray tights and a flowing white shirt. He held her around her narrow waist, and he seemed to be staring at her with an expression of unequivocal worship.

Avis smiled at the picture. It was not sheer vanity which drew her to the shot. She had pasted it on the door to remind herself that looks—diets, bodies, types —were not everything. After all, even Laurence himself had told her that she wasn't the type to be dancing the classics. Yet there she was, a triumph of will over destiny. If she did not have the height to be a classical dancer, at least she had the elevation. If she did not have the classical proportions—small head, long waist, no hips, and endless limbs—at least she had the technique to overcome them. And if her shoulders were too wide, at least she had the expressive capabilities to turn that supposed liability into an asset.

Fortunately, she had never had a weight problem, and her obsession with health food was just that—a healthy obsession. Right now, hunger stole over her, but it had not yet overcome the lassitude, so she remained where she was on the couch, thinking about nothing in particular until the sound of the buzzer from the front door of the apartment house roused her.

Beth Keane's voice sounded scratchy over the old intercom and Avis buzzed her up, feeling more energetic just knowing she would soon see her old friend. Since embarking on her therapy regime, Avis had seen little of her company friends, and she was suddenly hungry for all the news about the studio.

While she was waiting for Beth to arrive on the interminably slow elevator, Avis went into the kitchen to prepare some food. She knew Beth would be willing to eat some fresh fruit and yogurt; Avis herself was always starving after a day of dancing, and she had never known Beth to turn down a healthy meal either. As she opened the door to the refrigerator, she smiled one last time at the photo. "Things haven't really changed, Larry, have they?" She still had something to overcome.

"What did you say?" Beth came in on the tail end of her question, and plopped herself down without ceremony on the couch Avis had just vacated. "God, I'm so exhausted I could expire! Do you know what he had us do today? Not only did we have class and rehearsal, but, since there's no performance, he had us stay until after eight o'clock strutting around on that outdoor stage in the park. He said he wanted to play around with a few staging ideas for his new piece. Play around —for four hours!"

Avis glanced up sharply from the bowl of fruit salad she was preparing, but Beth's eyes were closed, so she couldn't have seen the look of alarm that crossed Avis's face. She knew Beth was referring to Laurence, who was now the company's resident choreographer. And she knew that the "playing around" he had been doing concerned the new piece he was choreographing—the one that featured her solo.

"Laurence always plays around before he gets his staging straight," she said evenly. She wanted to get more information from Beth about any changes in casting Laurence might be considering. But she knew the only way to get it was carefully. "He changes details a million times before he gets it the way he wants."

"I know. But he could have had us work on the studio stage. Instead, he said he wanted to get a feel for the outdoor space." Beth rolled her eyes dramatically as she said this, and Avis smiled, having a perfectly clear picture of how Laurence looked when he said things like that.

"Well," she said, slicing cantaloupe into the now filled glass bowl, "that makes sense, doesn't it?"

Beth sat up and looked at Avis for the first time. "Not if the mosquitos are just coming out for spring training it doesn't," she declared. "And not if you have to parade around in front of three hundred hooting school kids, either. They kept yelling, 'Hey, are you gonna dance, or are you just gonna stand around up there like statues?' I swear, I felt dumb!"

Avis shook her head. She couldn't imagine the stately Beth looking or feeling dumb. Beth was the quintessential ballerina. She was blond, willowy and fragile, and had established her career on the classics, much as Avis had on the neoclassics. But both dancers had been willing and able to bridge the gap, and neither resented the intrusion on their respective territories.

Now, however, at thirty-five, Beth's fragility was beginning to turn to brittleness, and her delicately turned-out legs were beginning to give her a lot of trouble if she overtaxed them. But Beth seemed more than willing to relax into the character roles that seemed to be her future lot as a dancer. She had plans to start her own ballet school, and was engaged to a well-off businessman who seemed eager to set her up whenever she gave the word.

Still, Beth had not retired yet, and her identity as a dancer had not changed in her fifteen-year career. Avis knew exactly what she meant when she said she felt dumb standing on stage doing nothing. Stages were for dancing, and even decades of standing around during "blocking rehearsals" did not cure a ballerina of the urge to dance whenever the stage was beneath her feet.

"What are you doing in this new piece?" Avis asked cautiously.

Beth snorted. "Doing? I'm not doing anything yet. It's one of Laurence's abstracts, so I guess I won't be doing much. He said something about birds of paradise." Beth giggled. "It looked more like birds of prey, to me."

Avis winced. *Bird of Paradise.* That was the piece he had been choreographing for her when she injured her foot. Had he finished her solo for someone else? She did not dare ask outright; her pride wouldn't permit it. Instead, she picked up the bowl of fruit, and another of yogurt, and brought them over to the low trunk which served as her coffee table.

"Food!" Beth sat up eagerly. "I'm starved! How did you know?"

Avis grinned. "When aren't you starved?"

"When aren't you?"

"Never."

The two women grinned at each other and dug in to the meal.

"So," Avis said as they ate, "tell me what else is going on over at the funhouse." She knew that Beth would give out the information she was seeking one way or another.

Beth shrugged. "Not much. Danny and Denise broke up."

"Again?"

"You know how they are. Every time Danny gets assigned another partner, Denise gets jealous and accuses him of all sorts of shenanigans."

Avis shook her head. "Who is it this time?"

"Cheryl Cattier. Do you know her? She just joined the corps last season. I had never noticed her myself, until Laurence cast her in the new piece."

"Cheryl? Of course I know who she is. She's a lovely dancer." Avis remembered the young girl perfectly, mostly because she had reminded Avis of herself at eighteen. Cheryl was small, but perfectly proportioned, and she threw herself into every movement with a dedication born of determination and sheer exuberance. Avis knew exactly who she was; she would have been a fool not to recognize the future competition.

Although she had never harbored anything but goodwill toward the new dancer, a sudden stab of jealousy pierced her now. Of course Cheryl was the logical person to take her place in the Bird of Paradise solo! She felt her jaw tensing up, but she forced her voice to remain casual.

"What role did Laurence give her to dance with Danny?" Avis inquired, careful to keep her eyes on the plate of fruit before her.

"I don't know. Some demi-solo role. Ingenue lead, I guess you'd call it, if there is such a role in Laurence's no-story ballets."

Avis let her breath out in a sigh of relief. He hadn't given her part away yet after all! She felt a surge of warmth toward Laurence, her old friend and mentor, toward Beth, and toward Cheryl, because now she wouldn't have to hide any feelings of jealousy. "Beth," she said fondly, "I wish you weren't such a stick-in-the-mud! Hardly anybody does story ballets anymore. Ingenue lead, my foot!" She leaned forward and flicked the last bit of yogurt out of the bowl with her finger.

"Well, more's the pity," Beth said staunchly. "Anyway, I suppose the entire situation is going to change, because that poor kid hurt her knee today during rehearsal. I suppose Danny was so nervous about Denise that he caught Cheryl wrong during a lift." Beth shuddered. "Poor kid. By the way, that brings me to one of the reasons for this visit."

"Besides the food?"

"Besides the food, smartie. Laurence wants to see you."

"He does?" Avis felt her pulse quicken. "What for?"

"I'm not sure. I think it might have something to do with Cheryl, because he came over to me right after it happened and asked me to tell you to come by tomorrow."

Avis was silent. From long experience she knew that Laurence's motives were impossible to fathom. Perhaps he wanted to see her to discuss her role. Maybe he wanted to tell her that the role would not be waiting for her when she returned. Perhaps the sight of Cheryl's injury had merely reminded him of Avis's existence. It was not beyond Laurence to have forgotten about her altogether.

"Why didn't he just call me?" she wondered aloud.

"He said he had tried—several times. He said you were never around." Beth's clear gray eyes widened innocently. "I've been trying to call too, Ave. Where have you been?"

Avis shrugged. "Oh, nowhere special. At the gym . . . in the pool. You know. Just around." She didn't know which felt further away from her reality at the moment—the dance studio with all its complicated machinations, or the pool with Keith Harding. Taking a deep breath to clear her mind of his image, she smiled at her friend. "OK," she said brightly, changing the subject. "What'll it be for dessert?"

Avis went to see Laurence the next morning before going to the Sportscape Club for her daily workout. Laurence was much more likely to be in a good mood before the stresses of the day's rehearsal got to him, and Avis did not want to engage in any altercation with him today. She was far too eager to get into the pool and get on with her training.

Laurence Lessine had been Avis's first lover. That had been many years ago, when she was still a young and promising dancer and he was still dancing full-time. He had not yet begun to choreograph seriously, but everyone in the National Ballet knew that Laurence was going to be a luminary in their ranks someday. He acted the part.

When they were lovers, Avis had been dazzled by Laurence's hauteur onstage and his commanding presence off-stage. She had basked in the keen glow of his approval, both as a dancer and a lover, and she had been his ardent student in both areas.

But, after a year or so, the glow had begun to tarnish. Laurence, she had decided, was incapable of any deep emotions. He bound her to him, not because he adored her, but because he needed her pliable body as a laboratory for his emerging talents. Realizing this, Avis had also seen that she was not in love with Laurence. Their love affair had ended amicably enough; Laurence hated scenes. But Avis had been unable to avoid a feeling of bitterness, and a sense that she had been used by Laurence to satisfy his own needs. He had wanted to play Pygmalion, and Avis had been the best possible subject. But she had been young and impressionable, and despite the fact that she knew she was not in love with him, the cavalier ease with which he had cast her off and gone on to the next girl had rankled.

Now, more than five years later, Avis had finally forgiven Laurence and was even able, at times, to look upon his foibles with a certain exasperated fondness. He was high-handed, and he could be petty, but he was a talented choreographer. He had taught her more about the art of being a prima ballerina than she could have learned in years of practice.

With that fondness came the ability to be hurt by him still, and Avis, passing the National's three main studios, approached his office at the end of the narrow hallway with slight trepidation. Laurence would not hesitate to pull her from the Bird of Paradise solo if it suited him to do so. Emotionally, he could be brutal, and Avis knew she had to be on her guard.

"Morning, Larry." Avis slipped into the tiny cubicle without knocking. That privilege, and the privilege of calling him Larry, were the only leftovers from her years as his favorite.

Laurence Lessine was sitting in a swivel chair with his back to Avis, looking out a square of one-way glass at the studio beyond his office. Without turning around to welcome her, he lifted one elegant hand and motioned her to come stand beside him. "Sit here, Avis, dear. I want you to see something."

Avis perched on the arm of his chair. She was slightly miffed that he had not bothered to ask after her foot, or even to greet her with a smile. How quickly they forget, she thought dryly. But as soon as she sat down, Laurence's hand circled around her waist. "I've missed you, Hummingbird," he said, using an old nickname. "How is your injured wing?"

Avis smiled, more at Laurence's uncanny ability to

sense her annoyance at his thoughtlessness than at the term of endearment. "Healing nicely, thank you," she replied. She resisted the urge to rumple his hair, something she knew he would not have appreciated.

Laurence was something of a dandy. He always dressed impeccably, even in the studio where all the other dancers seemed to be vying for baglady- or bagman-of-the-year awards by the looks of their assorted clothing. He conducted rehearsals in trim dance pants made of soft chamois, and deep-scoop-necked tops that showed off his lean musculature to elegant advantage. When dressed in street clothes, as he was this morning, he favored Italian-cut slacks and soft cotton shirts that he wore with the same flair as he wore the poet's shirt in *Swan Lake*. One never knew if Laurence was dressing for real life or for theater.

Despite his impeccable taste in clothes, Laurence had a certain rakish quality. His face was handsome but gaunt, as if high living had taken its toll at a young age. Actually, he was forty, and lived the life of a dedicated purist in all his tastes. He had bright blue eyes with long dark lashes, and his brown hair always fell across his forehead, giving him ample opportunity to brush it back with a flourish.

Now his eyes were intent on someone in the studio, and Avis strained over his shoulder to see who it was. There was a class in progress, and the company members were in uneven rows of eight as they faced the teacher in the front of the room, directly below the mirrored-glass partition through which Avis was looking. Madame Arlenska, a middle-aged woman with auburn hair pulled back in a severe bun, was demonstrating a combination of steps, and no one in the class was standing still. Some used their feet to copy the movement of their teacher's feet as they moved with astonishing rapidity in the petite allegro combination.

Others mimicked her movement using only their hands, twisting and turning their wrists to approximate the pattern of steps. Everyone was absorbing the pattern in some way.

"OK, OK, let's get to it," Laurence murmured impatiently. "She managed all right on the barre work; now let's see how she's doing in the center."

"Who? Who are you talking about?" But Avis already knew the answer. Standing at the end of the second row, wearing an ace bandage around her left knee, was Cheryl Cattier. It was Cheryl whom Laurence was so intent on, and Cheryl whom he wanted Avis to watch as well.

"I thought she hurt herself yesterday," Avis murmured, watching the first row of dancers perform Madame's steps to the music.

"She did, she did." Laurence still did not take his eyes off the glass. "But she says she's all right. She showed up for class today and damned if she didn't make it through the barre without a hitch. But let's see how she manages without something to hold on to."

Avis looked at Laurence's rapt expression. She had seen that expression before; it meant that Laurence had found a new protégé. Well, she thought, she shouldn't be surprised. He had had many since Avis, although he still favored her as his "special ballerina." If she were to pick any young dancer in the company to be her successor, Avis would certainly have chosen Cheryl. She wondered idly if Laurence's interest was more than professional, and then decided that she didn't care enough to wonder.

But what she did wonder about was his reason for notifying Avis of his interest. Why did he want her to watch Cheryl Cattier, unless it was to tell Avis of her imminent replacement in the Bird of Paradise solo? Now *that* she minded very much.

"Well, what do you think?" Laurence turned and fixed his glittering eyes on her. "She's good, no?"

Laurence often affected a foreign mannerism in his speech. But today it irritated Avis. "She's good, yes," Avis said crisply. And she was. When it came time for Cheryl's row of dancers to perform the petite allegro, she executed the difficult and rapid combination of steps and jumps without a hitch, something few of the new corps members and not many of the soloists were able to do. What's more, she did not just execute the steps, she danced them with a stylish crisp energy that made her stand out even in the roomful of professionals. She had the uncanny knack of appearing to be in two places at once.

Avis watched Laurence's face, and her intuition was confirmed. Yes, this was his new obsession, this young brilliant dancer who cried out for the kind of polish in which Larry specialized. Avis looked back at Cheryl. Would it be possible not to be jealous of the girl? Not because of her past with Laurence, but because of her future with the company.

As she watched, though, something happened. Turning off of her left leg, Cheryl suddenly winced and crumpled, grasping the bandaged knee. She stopped dancing immediately and limped from the center floor. No one else stopped dancing, but there were many sympathetic looks following her as she left the room, her face pale and taut with misery.

Laurence spun irritably around in his chair. "Damn! I should have known. She's really hurt herself badly."

Avis lifted her eyebrows. "Didn't you know that yesterday?"

He shook his head. "She didn't want to see Dr. Grey, said it wasn't that severe."

"And you believed her?"

"I should never have let her take class this morning."

He was angry, but not sympathetic. Then he looked up at her. "Well, what do you think?"

"About what? She's terrific—and she's hurt." Avis knew he had not asked her to come in simply for her opinion of Cheryl Cattier.

"What do you think about therapy for her? Do you think your swim therapy will work on her too?"

Avis had expected many possibilities from Laurence, but not this one. "Are you kidding? How would I know? Ask Dr. Grey!"

"Of course I'll ask Dr. Grey. But I'm asking you first. You know how well you're doing with the swim therapy. How soon can I get her back?"

He didn't ask how soon he could get Avis back, and she could feel her heart beating faster. She felt a rush of pure hatred for Laurence, sitting there writing her death warrant.

But she would not let him know how she felt. The most she could allow was a show of uninterest. "I have no idea, Larry," she said, turning her eyes back on the classroom so he would not see them burning with anger. "I really don't think I'm qualified to answer that."

Laurence lifted her chin and forced her gaze back in his direction. "Uh-uh, Avis, my love. Not true, not true. You are qualified, but you won't." His clever eyes narrowed and he smiled. "You're afraid I'll give Cheryl the Bird of Paradise solo."

Avis was stung into confession. "You're right. She's obviously good enough for it, and I don't notice you asking how soon I'll be back on my feet." She could not keep the bitterness out of her voice.

"Avis. You're wrong." His voice could be like honey when he wanted it to be. "I'm devastated by your foot, that glorious arch. What will we do? But you know your injury is more serious than hers—you can tell just by looking at her. She walked out of that studio, Avis, she didn't have to be carried." He reached out for her hand, but Avis pulled it away.

"And I have no intention of willingly giving up your solo to anyone, not even Cheryl. After all, I put it on you, dear, and no one could dance it like you."

"Not even Cheryl?" she asked dryly.

He smiled brilliantly. "Not even Cheryl. As a matter of fact, I've decided to postpone the piece until the fall season, expressly so that you will have time to heal."

Avis felt better immediately; a great weight had been taken from her shoulders. But she knew Laurence better than to trust him with the simple largesse of his remark. "Then why are you so concerned that she heal quickly?" she asked.

"I need her for the summer concert," he said simply. "We're doing the second act pas de deux from *Swan Lake*. I need her to dance Odette."

Odette. Avis's favorite role. Avis's mood darkened again, but not much. After all, Cheryl should have her chance with Odette, too. Still, she was not about to be let out to pasture so easily.

"Larry," she said, taking up the hand he had just offered her. "What if I were to tell you that *I* could dance Odette in two weeks?"

He looked genuinely surprised. "I'd fall off my chair," he said.

"Would you let me dance it? It may be one of the last times, you know. Cheryl is an exquisite dancer, and she should have a crack at it. But . . ."

Laurence nodded. "I know. You're not quite ready to let it go yet, are you?" He shook his head. "I'm not taking it away from you forever, you know, Avis. God, you're not exactly over the hill, yet. But your foot . . ." He left the sentence hanging in the air.

"My foot will be better by then. And so will Cheryl's

knee, if she starts swim therapy with me. I know she will want to—it's a great program." Avis knew she was fighting for something much more than a chance to dance Odette again. Larry was right; of course she would dance it again. It was a role that one could dance for years, since it called on all a dancer's expressive powers, and not on her youth.

It wasn't the role of Odette that worried Avis, it was dancing again. Avis felt that if she couldn't get back into shape in time for the summer concert, she would have missed a great watershed in her career. She needed the pressure of a deadline. The summer concert was Avis's private apocalypse.

"Double-cast us," she said suddenly. "Let us both do the role on alternating nights. It's only a six-show season—we'll each do three. That'll give Cheryl a good chance to try out the role, and give me a chance to try out my leg."

Laurence looked dubious. "Are you sure you'll be ready? It's not that important a concert, no critics or anything, so your idea might work. But, if your foot gets reinjured . . ."

He shook his head, and Avis knew what he meant. If her foot was reinjured, it might be for good. But now that she had made a commitment, she could not go back on it.

"Give me Cheryl for two weeks. I'll have her ready for the role by opening night."

Larry smiled and Avis wondered whether he hadn't just gotten what he had wanted all along. "Opening night," he said with a courtly little nod, "is for you."

Avis couldn't wait to get to the pool. As soon as she left Laurence's office, she was seized by the desire to escape from the studio before it engulfed her. She was upset at not being down in the studio with all the other dancers. Her state of mind was still too fragile to resist being affected by the sight of all those healthy bodies doing what she wanted to be doing.

But part of it was the sense of helplessness which had affected her before when dealing with Laurence and other authority figures in the dance world. Dancers were not expected to argue with company authority. It was taken for granted that there were certain decisions that dancers simply were not trained to make. Avis felt that Laurence had simply taken it for granted that she would comply with his plan, and he was obviously confident that Cheryl would do the same. At intermittent points in her career—this was one of them—Avis found herself resenting the control which the company had over her life.

There was something else, too. Something about Laurence's manipulation made her feel irritated and stifled. She wanted to get into the pool, where she would be unencumbered by such machinations. It would be hard enough to have to teach Cheryl Cattier the role that Avis still felt belonged so intimately to her. Not only would she have to train Cheryl, but she would have to share her swimming with her as well. Avis felt there was only one thing she could do at that moment to reaffirm her control over herself and her destiny. She had to get in that pool and swim, and enjoy the solitude and freedom while she still had it to enjoy. It was also her only road back to the studio.

Because of her interview with Laurence, Avis was over an hour late at the Sportscape Club. She changed quickly into her teal-and-white-striped tank suit and, standing in front of the mirror, pulled her hair into its customary knot. She inspected her narrow chin, her longish nose, and the wide, childish mouth, all dominated by the luminous brown eyes which now gazed back at her with determination. "OK, Avis," she told herself with a grim little smile, "get out there and show us what you can do!"

As she entered the pool area, she saw Keith standing on the other side of the pool talking earnestly to a young man who had just come out of the water. Even from that distance, his bulk impressed her. His body made a strong expanding V shape from his shoulders down to his trunks, a shape that was amplified by the mass of russet hair across his broad chest. His trunk was trim but powerful, and his thighs burst out of the narrow suit in long arches of muscle. His calves were hard and rounded, and his feet stood firmly apart on the deck of the pool. He was by no means overdeveloped, but his musculature conveyed a sense of intelligent strength, of power put to wise use.

Then he turned and saw Avis and smiled suddenly. *Well,* thought Avis with relief, *at least he's not annoyed that I'm late.* After spending time with Laurence, she wondered how she could have thought Keith like him. Keith was a strong personality, but he was not manipulative, and they had no personal history with which to entangle one another. Her relationship with Keith was about swimming, and that was it. With depression still weighing on her mind, just seeing him was a relief.

Avis signalled that she would begin her stretches over by his desk, and he nodded and went back to talking with the other man. It was amazing, she thought, discarding her towel and preparing for her daily ritual, how she felt a proprietary sense about the pool already. She felt as if she belonged there, just as she belonged at the studio.

Keith approached the desk while she was stretching, but he made no move to disturb her. Avis had grown used to the gaping stares of other athletes at the Sportscape Club when they saw her amazingly agile body going through its paces. But Keith did not leer at her 130-degree extensions or her perfect splits. Nor did he ask her any of the questions she had come to expect of non-dancers when they saw her work. Even Tom had been unable to resist asking Avis if she was double-jointed, and if she could stand on the tips of her toes without her toe shoes.

Keith simply sat at his desk to complete some paperwork, leaving Avis to her own devices. She felt extremely comfortable in this atmosphere of professionalism and restraint; it was like being in the studio, but with none of the competitive tensions. Avis was not even aware that she hummed snatches of classical music to herself as she worked, or that Keith, hearing it, smiled quietly into his paperwork.

When she was done, she came around to the front of the desk. "I'm ready," she said.

He closed his file at once. "Then let's hit the water." He stood up and, reaching into the top drawer of his desk, pulled out two pairs of goggles. "Here. Put these on. It'll save your eyes."

Avis looked at the goggles. "I've never needed them before," she said.

He smiled. "You've never really gone swimming before," he replied. "Now come on, you dip them in the water to prevent fogging. They go on like this." Leading her to the poolside, he bent down and doused both pairs of goggles, then adjusted the tight straps over Avis's knot of dark hair. "That feel all right?" he inquired, peering through his goggles into hers.

Avis felt a sudden impulse to giggle. "You look more like a professor than a swimmer in those things," she told him.

He grinned, and his eyes twinkled a Mediterranean blue. "And you," he said, "look more like a swimmer than a dancer."

Avis bit her lip. That was not what she needed to

hear at the moment, not when she was beginning to doubt her identity herself. Keith must have noticed her reaction, because he added softly, "Of course, I'm not a professor, and you're not a swimmer, so it just goes to show that you can't trust appearances, can you?"

"I thought you said I was a swimmer," Avis retorted unwillingly. Again, she had the uneasy feeling that he thought of her only as a swimmer and not as a dancer, and even worse, that his image of her might rub off on herself. She *had* to maintain her identity, regardless of what he thought about her dance career! She could feel frustrated tears beating against her eyes, and she looked down to avoid Keith's face. The last thing she needed this morning was his solicitous pity. She just wanted to get into the water and swim her way back to health.

Keith reached out and lifted her up by the chin, guiding her slowly back to a standing position. "You," he said deliberately, "can be anything you want to be." His eyes flashed dark green for a moment, then paled suddenly. "I missed you this morning," he said, and then looked surprised that he had said it.

Avis was as surprised as he was, and unable to respond. It occurred to her, however, that she had been eager to see him, too, although she could not have said why. After all, he was just another jock, a temporary coach for a temporary training program. But something about him made her feel comfortable, just as the prospect of swimming laps in the big, steamy pool made her feel comfortable. For absolutely no reason that she could fathom, Keith Harding made her feel comfortable too. She felt that she knew him, even though he was constantly surprising her with his depth and sudden gentle perceptiveness. She was at home with Keith.

But she would not have admitted it to him for the world. After all, he had treated her high-handedly on occasion, and she had her pride. So, instead of replying, she merely stared at him. Luckily he did not seem to require a response. Instead, his eyes cleared to their usual color. "We'll concentrate on the breaststroke today," he said, walking over to the water and lowering himself in. "But I want you to go slowly, even slower than yesterday. The breaststroke is a beast of a stroke—you'll find yourself worn out in half the time you would feel from the crawl. But it's great for upper-arm strength and overall endurance, both of which you need." He looked up at Avis as she lowered herself into the pool beside him. "For your dancing, of course," he added with a twinkle.

Avis was surprised. The unexpected candor of his remark about having missed her seemed to have unsettled her far more than it did him. But his twinkle was reassuring, and she soon returned it. "Are you going to be swimming too?" she inquired. He hardly looked like he needed either upper-arm strength or endurance.

Keith laughed as if the question was absurd. "Try and stop me," he said, and he stretched out to begin his stroke.

Chapter Four

Thursday, May 15

I remember when I first started dancing in the corps at National Ballet. I was so scared and in such awe of the soloists and principals! I'll never forget that first class I took, that awful feeling that everyone in the world was watching me, and laughing at my gawky inexperience. I watched the prima ballerina dancing the adagio combination, and I nearly ran out of that studio in tears. I would never be that elegant, that graceful, that assured!

I was only 17 then—a year younger than Cheryl Cattier is now.

I wonder how old Keith was when he started to swim? It's hard to imagine him young and insecure. Was he ever unsure of himself? Will I ever be as sure of myself as he seems to be?

Oh, who cares about Keith Harding, anyway!

Keith was right. The breaststroke was definitely harder for Avis than the crawl had been. She didn't have nearly enough upper-body strength to carry it off, and by the twentieth lap, she felt as if she were sinking like a stone. But Keith would not let her switch to the easier stroke, and every time she lifted her weary head out of the water for a breath, he was right there beside her like a watchdog, his face serious but encouraging.

She had no choice but to go on. She did so, but without rhythm, without a sense of motion or grace such as she had felt the day before. She kept on swimming, because she did not know how she would have explained her failure to Keith.

Finally, just when she was getting up enough courage to tell him she couldn't take another stroke, he tapped her elbow and motioned her to stop. Avis struggled to find her footing on the bottom of the pool, but slipped, prompting Keith to pull her up and over to the ledge.

"Tough going, huh?" He did not look concerned.

Avis nodded and gasped—she could not speak. Keith, she noticed, was not even breathing hard.

"The breaststroke is a hard one to feel comfortable with," he said, noticing her forlorn expression. "It doesn't have the grace of the crawl."

"It's . . . it's impossible!" she managed to croak when she had partially recovered her breath.

Keith, taking the statement seriously, shrugged and considered. "Not impossible. But it doesn't work well for distances, because it does take more time. It's a good transitional stroke though, and you're going to have to work on it."

She thought about telling him that she had no intention of working on it, and then she remembered what he had said yesterday. He was right; if it was a challenge, she would rise to meet it. She didn't want him to think she was a quitter.

Keith must have seen the look on her face, because he laughed. "Now, wait a minute. I can just see you gearing yourself up for another thirty laps of breaststroke. Forget it. You did plenty for one day."

Avis grinned. "Was I that transparent?"

He grinned back. "Like glass. Now hop up there on the side of the pool and let me see your foot. Then we'll do some crawl for the fun of it."

He flashed her a brilliant smile of complicity before helping her up onto the ledge. Then, standing in the water at her knees, he took her injured foot in his hands. "You didn't wear the support bandage today— good. How does it feel?" His fingers, as sensitive as a surgeon's, probed her metatarsal.

"Tired," she admitted. "But not painful." She reflected, watching him press the once tender spots. "That's not what hurts." She reached up to rub her shoulder. *"This* hurts." Keith looked up from his work and raised his eyebrows slightly. "You weren't using your arms enough," he told her. "Too much shoulder, not enough arm."

Avis grimaced. "The story of my life. Too much shoulder, not enough arm."

Keith cocked his head. "You don't like your shoulders?"

"They're too broad for a dancer. They look all right on stage, from a distance. But up close, I feel like a chimpanzee sometimes." Avis never would have admitted this private awkwardness to someone she knew as slightly as she knew Keith. Even to her intimate dancer friends, she would not have acknowledged her weakness so frankly. But Keith invited such frankness; he almost required it. She remembered the look on his face when he had told her he missed her. It was as if he required it of himself as well.

Now he was looking right at her shoulders, as if trying to see them through her eyes. "Well," he said slowly, "it's what you see from the stage that matters, isn't it?"

Avis considered. She had never thought of it that way before. When she got ready to dance for an audience, she exaggerated everything about her—her makeup enlarged her features, the tutu exaggerated the smallness of her waist, even pointe shoes had been invented to accentuate and elongate the length of the human leg. Why not be content with broad shoulders if they served the same purpose on stage? After all, that was where it counted, not in front of a mirror in the studio.

"You know," she said, a slow smile spreading across her heart-shaped face, "I never thought about it quite that way before."

"I didn't think you had," Keith replied. "But that's what I'm here for—to make you think about your body in new ways." He looked at her torso and his eyes seemed to narrow slightly. He swallowed before continuing. "Ways you never even imagined before you met me."

At first, Avis's impulse was to scoff at this conceit. After all, he knew nothing about dance. Who was he to teach her about her body? But something about his eyes, that smoky glance of speculation beneath the deep-set lids, made her feel suddenly uneasy. She had a feeling he was thinking about neither dance nor swimming at that instant.

She herself was finding it hard to concentrate on a conversation that an instant before had been perfectly normal. "I . . . well, I . . . I guess that's a good thing." She was finding it hard to take her eyes off him, and she imagined she could see the pulse of his heartbeat sending blood coursing across his broad bare chest just inches away from her fingers. "I mean, about my shoulders . . ."

He wrenched his eyes back to her shoulders with difficulty. "Besides," he said a little hoarsely, "you've got terrific shoulders for a swimmer. As a matter of fact, they could even use a little building up." He took his hands and placed them both squarely over her shoulders. His touch was so warm and tingly that it made Avis jump. Her eyes flew wide open and met his, which seemed to be moving unaccountably closer to hers. His lips parted invitingly.

"Avis? Avis Considine?"

Keith and Avis both jumped at the sudden sound. They spun around and, squinting into the dim light, made out the figure of a tiny young woman standing uncertainly in the doorway.

"Avis? I . . . it's Cheryl. Cheryl Cattier. I came . . . Laurence said . . ." At a loss for words, Cheryl stepped farther into the room. She looked very young in her jeans and T-shirt, and her hair was caught up in a ponytail that accented her childish features. She looked scared and unsure of herself.

"Cheryl. It's OK, come on in." Avis scrambled to her feet and moved forward to meet Cheryl as she approached hesitantly. Avis noticed that Keith had made no move to greet the newcomer, which probably added to Cheryl's discomfort. She suspected his annoyance, but felt perfectly comfortable in greeting the young dancer in his place. After all, in a sense it was more her territory than his. He was the newcomer, even if he was nominally in charge. Still, he might have been more civil to a new "customer."

Cheryl's brown eyes shone with eagerness. "It's all right, isn't it? I mean, that I came right over? Laurence told me that you had offered to help me get on my feet again in time for the summer concert." She looked as if she didn't believe her good luck. "I really appreciate it, you know."

Avis could not help smiling. Good old Larry, rearranging the truth just enough so that it would be more appealing. How could Avis tell Cheryl that Larry had been lying, that Avis had not generously offered to aid her new rival in her recovery? It was all very convenient. "As long as Dr. Grey says it's all right, Cheryl, it's fine with me. The swimming instructors here will have you back in shape in no time. Dr. Grey did say it was all right, didn't he?" She would not put it past Laurence to underplay the seriousness of Cheryl's injury, either.

"I saw him just before I came over here. He took x-rays, but he thinks it's just a sprain and that swimming will help."

I'll bet Dr. Grey wouldn't dare disagree with Master Lessine, Avis thought dryly. She was feeling positively mutinous about Larry at the moment, but she knew it was not Cheryl's fault. "What kind of work did Dr. Grey tell you to do?" she asked kindly. "Did he give you a specific program—anything to avoid, like scissor-kicking, or anything?"

Cheryl's eyes widened. "I don't know. He said that the man in charge here would know what to do with me." She looked anxiously over Avis's shoulder. Avis suddenly remembered Keith. He was sitting on the side of the pool watching Avis, not Cheryl. Despite the fact that his face betrayed nothing at all, Avis could not meet his eyes. She knew only too well what Cheryl's sudden appearance had interrupted, and the very idea made her cringe.

"Keith, I'd like you to meet Cheryl Cattier. Cheryl is also with the National. She seems to have injured her knee, and—"

"I heard," he said quietly. "Dr. Grey has placed her in my hands. Or, more precisely, in Tom Miller's hands." He was looking at Avis as he spoke, then turned to Cheryl and smiled cordially. "Tom Miller is the head swim coach. I'm just here to fill in for him until he gets back from vacation."

Avis saw Cheryl's face fall at the thought of a delay

delay, and Keith must have seen it too because his smile grew warmer.

"Don't worry, I can get you started." He frowned. "Although I must say I don't think swimming is the best therapy for knees. Every other part of the body, but not knees."

Cheryl looked like she was going to cry. "Laurence said I had to get back in shape as soon as possible," she said, turning to Avis. "He said the swimming would be the fastest way. He needs me on stage in two weeks."

"He wants me on stage in two weeks too, you know," Avis could not refrain from pointing out. She wondered if perhaps Larry had neglected to tell Cheryl about the double-casting of Odette.

But Cheryl, suddenly shy, lowered her long lashes onto pale cheeks. "I know. Laurence said you and I would be alternating the Odette role—oh, Avis, I'm so excited!" The eyes she raised were burning with pleasure. "Are you sure you don't mind though . . . I mean, it is your role for the National." She blushed. "I've been watching you in that role since I first started coming to the National. I know every step. But I'll never be able to do it like you do . . . you're so beautiful!"

Avis smiled, and she wondered if Keith had heard her praises being sung. She was sure he had never seen her dance, and she wanted him to know that she, too, was an expert in her field. "Of course I don't mind. It'll be a pleasure to see you in the role." She genuinely meant it. "And since you've been watching me for so long, you won't need to be taught the steps. We'll be able to concentrate on polishing."

"I know it by heart," Cheryl declared, and then, more somberly, added, "but it won't do either of us any good if we don't get back on stage in two weeks."

"Don't worry about a thing," Avis said firmly. "We'll both be on our toes in two weeks' time. I can promise you that, and so can Keith. Right, Keith?" She turned to him with a silent entreaty that he seemed to read perfectly clearly. But she was sure he was capable of behaving rudely if he felt that he had been manipulated in any way. And Avis could not ignore the fact that Keith had been about to kiss her, in which case he was probably even more annoyed.

But Keith surprised her. "Avis is absolutely right," he said heartily. "Tell you what. Tom will be back tomorrow. For today, why don't you go into the sauna and take a good soak. That'll loosen your knee joints up pretty well without straining them. Then come on out and I'll work with you for a bit, get you doing a few easy laps this afternoon. That way you'll be more prepared to work with Tom when he comes in tomorrow. OK?"

Cheryl thanked him profusely and left, limping slightly in her eagerness to move fast. Avis watched her tiny shape recede down the hallway and then turned to Keith. "Thanks for that," she said briskly. "I was afraid she was going to burst into tears if she couldn't get started right away."

Keith cocked his head slightly to one side. "Is it that important to you that she recover quickly from her injury?" It was an innocent enough question, but Avis's guilty conscience, combined with the quizzical shrewdness in Keith's eyes, made it impossible to answer with a direct lie. Avis looked away before she spoke. "It's always important that a dancer get up on her feet as quickly as possible, for the dancer and for the company."

"I see." Keith's tone made it sound like he saw a lot more than he was letting on. "And how did this

Laurence fellow come to know so much about the
miracle swim therapy?" Avis could not tell from his
tone whether he was annoyed or merely interested.

"I told him about it this morning." But Avis knew
that this was not a satisfactory explanation. Besides,
why should she defend Laurence to Keith? "Actually,
Larry must have heard from Dr. Grey that I was doing
so well. Apparently, he's taken it into his head that
swimming is a miracle cure for any kind of injury." She
allowed herself a small, ironic smile. "Once Larry gets
a notion into his head, he doesn't really let go of it."

Keith's eyebrows went up. "Sounds like you two
have a lot in common," he mused too casually.

"Hah!" That was a laugh. It was Keith and Larry
who were so much alike. "And what exactly is that
supposed to mean?" His calm assurance made her want
to throttle the man.

Keith shrugged. "Not much. You've got this idea
that you'll be dancing again in no time, and I don't see
you as the adaptable type when it comes to ideas."

This assessment was more than Avis could bear.
"Well, that's just terrific, coming from you!" she
snapped. "You're here to help me meet my goals, not
throw a wrench in the works. Besides, it's really no
concern of yours. Tom and I set up a program, and all
you're being paid to do is see that I keep to it. You're
only temporary, don't forget."

He took a step closer to her that could only be
described as threatening. "Look here, Miss Prima
Ballerina," he said in a low voice that belied his
temper, "when you get into that swimsuit you're in *my*
territory, do you understand? I'm the one who makes
the rules, not you, or Tom, or some glitter-grabbing
dance master. And as for being temporary . . ." He
broke off and looked at her searchingly for a moment,
as if trying to read what was beyond her eyes. But Avis

was only concerned with maintaining her poise in the face of this sudden onslaught. Then Keith grinned genially, and his gruff tone melted away. "Well, we'll just have to see about that, won't we?" He actually wriggled his thick brows suggestively as he spoke.

Avis was taken aback. His intentions were almost as opaque as his actions. And who the hell did he think he was, referring to Larry as a glitter-greedy dance master? Actually, the more she thought of it, the funnier the description was, but she was not about to let Keith know that. Instead, she merely took a step away and said coldly, "I'm so sorry if I insulted you." Then, wondering if she had pushed him too far, she added, "I guess I should have checked. I didn't think that it might be an inconvenience for you." The apology sounded sullen, even to her.

Keith walked over to the desk and picked up two towels, one of which he draped over his shoulders before returning to Avis. "It's not that," he said, arranging the other towel across her back. "I was just hoping to be able to concentrate on you."

He held the two ends of the towel in his hands and looked right into her eyes as he said this. His unnerving candor took Avis totally by surprise, and she had no idea what to make of this remark. Did he want to concentrate on her because of her abilities, or because he wanted to see one project through at a time? Or was there another reason behind his curious statement?

Certainly she could get no clues from his expression. His eyes were fathomless, and although a pleasant half-smile played across his mouth, there was a somber note in their blue-green depths. Avis opened her mouth without having any idea how she was to respond, but Keith shook his head. "Never mind," he said amiably. "Why don't you have a seat and watch Cheryl take the plunge?" He released the towel and Avis took a sudden step back. "You never know," he added cryptically. "You might learn something."

His timing was perfect. Just as he turned away from Avis, Cheryl appeared, flushed and pink from the sauna. Keith walked up to her and led her over to the shallow end of the pool, his arm draped casually across her narrow shoulders, talking earnestly to her all the way.

Avis did a few desultory stretches, then settled herself in a chair to watch. Keith was demonstrating the overhand crawl stroke to Cheryl, who watched with the same rapt attention that she wore when in the rehearsal studio. Avis could not hear what they were saying, but she saw Cheryl imitate Keith's motion, then ask him a question, to which he responded with a nod and a grin.

Cheryl was a wonderful student. It would be easy to help her with the pas de deux, especially since she knew the steps already. Avis could see Keith warming up to her by the minute. He was smiling a lot now, and as he bent over Cheryl's shoulder to explain the side-breathing technique, Avis thought he got a little closer than was absolutely necessary.

"It doesn't look like he's so interested in concentrating on me anymore," she muttered, and then bit her lip when the meaning of her own words became apparent. Was she jealous of Cheryl and Keith? The idea appalled her, but she could not let it go. Of course, she would have been dishonest with herself if she had denied that she was jealous of Cheryl Cattier. After all, Cheryl had youth, she had talent on the rise, and she had Odette at eighteen, which was more than Avis could have said at the time. It was not Cheryl the person she envied, but Cheryl the dancer. It was Cheryl's future, which so clearly represented Avis's past. So if Avis was jealous of Cheryl, it was not because of Cheryl and Keith, but because of Cheryl and Odette.

Avis forced herself to abandon such thoughts. After all, her past was not dead and buried yet. She still had a lot more dance left in her body, not to mention in her soul. There was room for more than one Odette on the stage of the summer theater. She would just have to remember that, and remember that determination was what had propelled both Cheryl and herself into the positions they occupied today.

Still, sitting and watching made her impatient. Cheryl was in the water, cutting swift if rather splashing paths back and forth across the width of the pool. Keith stood on the edge, and reminded her not to scissor-kick, but to frog-kick, to protect her knee. Avis decided she could use a good soak in the sauna herself. It was clear that Keith was going to be concentrating on Cheryl for some time to come.

It wasn't until she lay prone on the slatted bench in the sauna, her eyes wrenched shut against the heat, that the picture rose up in her mind's eye. Keith had been standing on the edge of the pool; he had not gone into the water to swim with Cheryl.

Avis smiled and sighed with relief.

Tom returned on Friday, and everything seemed to straighten out and settle down with his appearance. He pronounced Cheryl's knee imminently curable by his own private method, and Cheryl seemed to listen to him with the same rapt wonder she did to all her other tutors. After having watched her with Keith, Avis felt a guilty rush of relief that things had worked out so well.

Tom Miller had once coached an Olympic swim team to a silver medal, and it had been the high point of his life. He was a classic athletic coach—rotund, graying, but solid as an oak door, and just as straightforward. His ministrations were laced with recollections of his past glories, and he undertook every training program as if it was a pre-Olympic tryout.

As he had with Avis, he took a special interest in Cheryl because he thought of dancers as a rare species of athlete, and because he enjoyed the idea of working against the clock. "I had a kid once," he said, standing over Cheryl as she lay on her side in the water, patiently doing slow-motion flutters to loosen her knee joint. "He had the same problem as you. He just pushed that knee and pushed it until it seized up on him. Too much hyperextension in his kicks, I told him. So I had him do just what you're doing now. For days, he lay there, fluttering away like a weak bird." Tom beamed down at his charge. "But we did it. Next round, he set a world record in the freestyle swim." Cheryl breathed a sigh of contentment and kept on kicking, gently, so that her knee would not overextend.

Avis had not yet done any swimming today; Cheryl's time slot had been scheduled to overlap only for a half-hour at the end of Cheryl's session. Avis had no idea whether Keith or Tom had arranged it that way, but she was pleased with the arrangement. She would be seeing enough of Cheryl when they started working on the pas de deux.

Now she lay on the rickety massage table while Keith worked on a spasm she had developed in her right calf. "You're overcompensating," he told her when she complained of the twinges. "Don't be afraid to work that right foot strongly now. It can stand it, believe me." Avis was encouraged by what he said, and she rested easily on the metal table while listening to Tom and enjoying the painful but pleasant sensations that Keith wrought on her sore muscle.

"You forgot to add that he created a new stroke in

the process," Keith said to Tom, winking at Avis. "The judges would have given the kid a gold, but they couldn't figure out what to call that funny footwork he used."

"Hah!" Tom chomped down on his ever present cigar, which he kept unlit "for the sake of the ladies." "What do you know about it, Harding? You were off in England at the time, as I recall."

Avis mused on the multiple messages conveyed by this offhand bit of information. It meant that Keith had known Tom for a long time and that Keith had been in England for some reason. She was conscious of the fact that Keith was a total stranger to her. Not that she minded—she had no reason to broaden their acquaintance beyond the pool. But what little she did know about him was intriguing and did not fit her image of a jock. Besides, she had the memory of that near kiss still haunting her, coloring all her perceptions of Keith, even to the way he touched her right now.

"What were you doing in England?" she asked him, deciding to concentrate on the facts in order to avoid dwelling on her mysterious attraction-aversion to the man.

"Not much. Going to school." Keith bent closer over her leg and spread some more oil on it to decrease the friction of his hand. Avis felt her calf heating up, but it was not uncomfortable.

"Not much!" Tom snorted. "Don't be ashamed, Harding. Tell the ladies." He raised his voice. "The kid was going to Oxford on a Rhodes scholarship."

Avis twisted her torso around to stare. "Oxford? On a Rhodes?" Her expression was incredulous.

Keith gave her a funny look. "Yes, as a matter of fact." He smiled, more from one side of his mouth than the other. "It's a nasty job, but somebody's got to do it."

Avis opened her mouth to reply, but something in his expression—a sullen challenge lurking behind his smile—made her shut it again. She got the distinct impression he didn't want to talk about it, talk about any part of his life. He certainly hadn't appreciated her disbelief. Well, she thought, turning around again, let him have his little secrets. It's not as if I care what he did or where he went to school, after all.

Cheryl was finally finished in the pool, and Tom set her up with a weight band around her ankle so she could do leg-lifts and strengthen the muscles on the sides of her knees. Keith kneaded her muscle for a few moments more and then moved his hands away. "OK, ballerina," he said, giving her bottom a swift tap. "Get on your goggles and let's do some swimming."

Avis got up, the casual slap on her bottom tingling more than her calf. Normally she wouldn't have minded such offhand familiarity; when one made her living by her body a certain amount of modesty had to be sacrificed. But she felt that Keith had deliberately done it to embarrass her. It wasn't like him to take an unprofessional liberty, and it wasn't like Avis to allow it. She stood by the table, glaring at him, and she could tell by the way he glared back that he was challenging her to say something to him about it while Tom and Cheryl were in hearing distance.

"I need to stretch out and warm up before I start," she told him. She had no idea why they were getting on each other's nerves today. Perhaps the presence of Tom and Cheryl was interfering. Certainly Avis didn't feel that unique sense of comfort and ease she had felt when they were alone together before Cheryl's appearance.

Keith shrugged. "Suit yourself," he said and, turning away from her, he walked over to the pool, dove in, and began to swim.

Avis stood watching him for a while. His stroke was clean and strong, and she was beginning to notice that he did some things differently than she did. She was so absorbed in staring at him that she jumped when she heard Tom's voice behind her.

"It's funny," Tom murmured. "I haven't seen Keith do this much swimming in years."

Avis turned, surprised. "Did you used to coach him?"

Tom nodded. "Yeah, but he was the same way when he was competing. I've never seen him swim unless he felt he absolutely had to."

Avis turned back to the figure in the pool. "Was he good, Tom? Was he a good, competitive swimmer?"

Tom was silent for so long that Avis had to look to see the smile on his face. "He hasn't told you about himself yet, has he?" Avis shook her head. "Then I'll have to let him tell you in his own time," he said. He walked away, shaking his head and smiling.

Avis turned back to the pool, where Keith was steadily traveling back and forth in the water, seemingly oblivious to the fact that she had not yet joined him. She watched him for a while, eagerly drinking in the sight of his graceful waterbound form. She could no longer pretend, even to herself, that she was not fascinated by Keith Harding. At first he had seemed to embody everything she did not want in a man—all Larry's faults with none of his saving sensibilities. But she had begun to suspect that Keith had a well of sensitivity to which she was not privy, and that piqued her interest as much as his physical attributes compelled her attention. She had no intention of pursuing him, of course. After all, he was elementally wrong for her, and besides, she had many more important goals to pursue. Still, she had to admit that he made her time at the Sportscape Club more interesting, although concentration was becoming a major problem when he was around.

But right now she wanted to swim. She slipped into the water while Keith was at the opposite end of the pool and began swimming. The water was cool as she pulled into the slow, measured crawl Keith had taught her to use. Light and sound in the pool room immediately became soft-focused, and the sensation of weightlessness soothed Avis's annoyance and dampened her curiosity. All her anxieties softened, just as the knots in her body melted away in the gentle pressure of the pool.

Her hands cut into the water in a neat sidewise slice from overhead. As soon as each hand struck the water, it rotated so that it formed an oar, pulling the water back strongly toward her thigh before lifting out again. Remembering Tom's comments to Cheryl, Avis relaxed her knees so that she kicked in small, quick flutters that left almost no wake.

She was beginning to improve her breathing technique, too, so that there was an economy of motion in the roll of her head and the expansion of her lungs. Her stroke was timed so that she got all the air out of her body just in time to lift her head up on every fourth stroke. After a while, Avis forgot about the mechanics of what she was doing and concentrated instead on the sheer relaxed rhythm. It took her a while to realize that Keith had come up beside her and matched his stroke to hers, so that once again they swam in tandem. They did not look at each other or in any way acknowledge one another's presence. But Avis could feel his body beside her, pushing away water as he cut cleanly along.

She was surprised that they could swim together so well. Avis had spent years learning the complicated art of partnering and the pas de deux, and she knew it took long months of practice to be able to perfect any kind of tandem work on stage. But in the water, with Keith next to her, it seemed to come naturally. Perhaps, she thought, the natural buoyancy of the water made it easier to connect. Or perhaps it had to do with Keith himself. Whatever differences they might have had, on some quiet level Avis had to admit that she and Keith were very much in tune. Once again, that sense of comfort and being at home with him pervaded, and she smiled to herself.

As she swam, Avis's mind wandered freely from past and present to future. She recalled the entry she had made in her journal a few nights ago. The difference between walking and dancing, as Laurence had taught her, was the music, the feeling with which a body moved through space. Swimming this way with Keith, she understood that there was swimming and there was *swimming*. The difference lay in the rhythm of the stroke and how the body felt as it moved through the water. Right now, as she swam beside his graceful and measured stroke, she felt pretty terrific.

She was just beginning to settle deeply into the pace of her laps when Keith stood up in the water and motioned for her to do the same. "Why'd you stop?" she asked, trying to focus on him as he stood before her, a watery, smiling image.

"Sixty laps," he said. "That's plenty, even for a water nymph like you." She could tell by the way he looked at her that there was no antagonism left between them. The water had washed it all away.

"That was sixty?" Avis's eyes widened in disbelief. "It didn't feel like sixty."

Keith chuckled. "Spoken like a true swimmer. But it was sixty nonetheless. Out of the pool, my girl."

Avis began to walk to the side ladder. "Keith," she said, "were you an Olympic competitor?"

Keith pulled himself out of the water and walked over to get a towel without looking at Avis. "I was an Olympic competitor," he said, "but I never made it to the Olympics. Here, wrap this around you and let me have a look at the calf muscle."

Avis obeyed, still thinking about what he said, or rather, what he did not say. "Is that because you went to Oxford?"

It was a purely intuitive question, and Keith looked up at her sharply. "I went to Oxford in spite of the fact that I was an Olympic competitor."

He seemed unwilling to clarify himself, and Avis decided it was not the right time to push him. She sat on the edge of the massage table with her legs dangling down, while Keith knelt at her feet to probe her calf.

"How does that feel?" he asked her.

"Much better. What made you decide you wanted to be an Olympic swimmer in the first place?" she asked without missing a beat. Other people's obsessions always fascinated her, and she knew one did not reach the Olympic level without being slightly obsessed, just as one did not reach some position in the National Ballet without being slightly obsessed.

Keith leaned back on his heels and looked at her quizzically. "What made you become a dancer? You had to, right?" He shrugged and stood up. "It was the same with me. I had no choice in the matter. There was nothing else I could do as well as I swam." He turned away from her and gazed into the still blue water with his hands on his hips.

Avis reflected on his comment. She had always known she was driven to dance, but she had never quite thought that there was nothing else she could do as well. It was a rather grim explanation for all those years of work and dedication. She got off the table and stood beside him. "I don't dance because there's nothing else

I can do," she said, musing more to herself than to him. "I dance because it's the only thing I want to do."

He turned and looked down at her. "It amounts to the same thing, doesn't it?" Then, before she could protest that it wasn't the same thing at all, he went on. "We do it because we have to, you and I . . . or at least, we did it because we had to."

She resented the change to the past tense. "I still have to dance," she said tightly. "That's what I'm here for, after all."

Keith nodded. "After all," he repeated, and Avis heard how defensive the words sounded.

"I mean, I enjoy the swimming, but . . ."

"But it's not the same as dancing, is it? It's not as gracious or as meaningful as dance, is that what you mean?"

Avis scowled. He had a disconcerting habit of twisting her words around so that they said something she did not want to say, however true she might privately believe it to be. "All I meant was that I'm a dancer and you're a swimmer. I couldn't expect you to go to a ballet and appreciate it the way I do . . . and you can't expect me to appreciate swimming the way you do." She did not bother to add that she was beginning to appreciate the grace and meaning of swimming quite well on her own.

Instead of arguing the point, Keith looked at her for a while in silence. "I'd like to see you dance," he said at last. "I think I could appreciate that."

"Oh, you'll see me dance, Keith," she said vehemently. "Never doubt that for a minute." She looked at him challengingly, as if she expected him to do just that, but he merely met her gaze steadily. "I have every intention of having you see me dance—you and the rest of the world."

If Keith had his doubts, he kept them to himself.

Instead, he threw back his head and laughed. "Spoken like a true fanatic," he said, and Avis could not help but smile at the delight in his voice. He may not agree, she thought, but at least he understood.

"Not many people appreciate a true fanatic," she said with a grin.

"I know, I know."

Avis held his laughing eyes for a long moment, and gradually the laugh left them and was replaced by something else—something so much more disconcerting that Avis swallowed and looked away toward the empty pool. "You know," she said, "I really don't feel tired at all, Keith. I actually feel relaxed."

The smile returned. "OK, ballerina. Another twenty, but no more, understand?" She nodded. "I don't want to tire you out for the Swan Queen's pas de deux."

With that he reached out and, sweeping her off her feet, threw her into the water with a wicked laugh.

Chapter Five

M onday, May 19

Only five days left until opening night. I'm not sure if I can stand the tension around the studio. It seems as if everybody senses how important it is for me to not only to teach Cheryl the part, but also to carry it off myself. I know, as the company stands around the edges of the studio and watches me rehearse with Vaughn, my partner, or put Cheryl through her paces, they're all thinking, "Can she make it? Can she stand up to the strain?"

Of course, they must all realize that I can make it, and that I will hold up. After all, I got this far, didn't I? And Larry has to see it most of all. I refuse to bow down to his . . . how did Keith describe it? His glitter-grabbing. He may want someone else in the spotlight when we do Bird of Paradise, but I'm not so easy to remove as he once thought.

All the same, I sometimes wish I was away from all this tension and back in the pool, with nothing to think about but my stroke and flutter-kick. And Keith. Despite all his difficulties, and the fact that I have no idea what he's about, it seems easier for me to be with him than it does for me to be in the studio. God! I never thought I would hear myself say that!

But it's true. As a matter of fact, I sometimes fantasize that I'd like to be anywhere but here, as long as it's with Keith.

No—never mind—cross that out. I didn't mean it.

Despite the constant tension, Avis threw herself back into life at the National as if she had never left. She took class in the morning, rehearsed all afternoon, and then gave Cheryl extra coaching lessons at night. The only thing she did not do was put on her pointe shoes. Instead, she worked in soft leather slippers so that she could save her newly healed metatarsal arch for when it really counted. Dancing on pointe was grueling enough for a healthy foot; to strain hers before she absolutely had to was something not even Laurence Lessine expected her to do.

But Larry expected her to take care of Cheryl, and Avis knew that he was watching her closely to see how she handled the delicate task. It was important that she impart the little secrets of the role to Cheryl, yet not obscure Cheryl's own interpretation of the Swan Queen. Avis remembered when Madame Arlenska had taught her the role seven years ago. Madame Arlenska had already been in her fifties by then—ancient for a dancer—but she had managed to impart the ethereal qualities of the Swan Queen by the slightest nod of her head or inclination of her shoulder.

Avis had a perfect pupil in Cheryl. She quickly realized that Cheryl had in fact learned the steps by heart, which left only the polishing to work on. And Avis understood that Cheryl would not be expected to interpret the role with the same grandeur that she herself had learned from Madame Arlenska. Avis's interpretation had been hailed for its elegance and daring, as if Odette had been driven slightly mad for love of Siegfried, her human paramour. Cheryl's interpretation would have to be a more demure, more vulnerable Odette.

It would work, and Avis was seized by the same excitement she always felt when something marvelous was developing in the studio. The magic was just as powerful, even though Cheryl was taking away half of Avis's glory. Avis saw that there would be more depth, more beauty in her own Odette from working with Cheryl. That was the miracle of ballet—the dance always became more beautiful with time.

But time was what she had the least of, and Avis worked feverishly to beat the clock. The one thing she would not give up was a daily swim. Her training was greatly curtailed because she was dancing so much, but she knew it would be deadly to forego the therapeutic qualities of her daily laps. Swimming was the only thing in her life at the moment that afforded a measure of relaxation, and Avis knew that being relaxed was as important as being in shape.

She dared to admit that she enjoyed seeing Keith, too. But the admission was made only to her journal. No one at the studio would understand the kind of pleasure she got merely from slicing through the water beside him, the kind of peace she found in his companionable silences. At the National, dancers were involved only with other dancers. Partly, this was because they had no time to meet the general public, but Avis knew from long experience that even if a dancer did meet someone outside the studio, it would have to be a special person to endure the total preoccupation with dance.

Avis had not yet determined that Keith was such a special person, but he did understand preoccupation.

That was why she looked forward to seeing him every afternoon, after rehearsal and before her session with Cheryl.

Still, as opening night grew nearer, her preoccupation with Odette grew stronger. As always happened before a performance, Avis found her waking life being consumed by thoughts of the character she was about to play, and she became more and more distracted. Usually this state of distraction was diminished if she had danced the role many times before. But this time she found she could not shake it. Too much depended on her having it right.

"Come on, Avis, we've done this a hundred times before." Vaughn Driscoll, her partner for the pas de deux, was beginning to get cranky after a four-hour rehearsal session with Avis on the afternoon before the dress rehearsal. Vaughn was a tall, lanky man of thirty with a Slavic physique and a shock of long black hair. He was a perfect Siegfried, conveying the image of passion and privilege with apparent ease onstage. Offstage, he was pleasant, but tended to be petulant. "I don't see the point in this," he went on, leaning wearily against the barre in the studio. "We know this adagio section by heart, and it's not going to get any better than it is now."

"Don't be a goose, Vaughn. Of course it can get better—it can always get better, or more exciting, or just different. That's what we're looking for, isn't it?"

Vaughn rolled his eyes. "I'm looking for my dinner break," he said. "Anyway, we can't do it full out because you're not on pointe. So there really is no point, is there?"

Avis was bending over the recorder, rewinding the tape to the beginning of the adagio. Then she straightened and turned to face Vaughn. "Hey. There's always a point, don't you see? We keep on rehearsing because we have to rehearse—because if we stopped, so would the magic. We have to keep on finding the magic in it for ourselves, or else how can we get the audience to believe it?"

Vaughn heaved himself off the bar with an exaggerated grimace, but Avis knew most of his reluctance was an act. "All right," he said lazily, "I'll do it again. But not for the magic." He reached out and tweaked Avis's flushed cheek. "I'll do it for you."

They smiled at each other and walked over the centerstage, assuming the entwined position that marked the beginning of the adagio section. Avis fitted herself perfectly into Vaughn's arms and waited for the music to begin. *This is what I've worked so hard for,* she said to herself as the bittersweet strains of the violin section sounded across the room. The studio was in half light, so it was just possible to imagine that she was in a foggy glen, dancing with her lover for the last time. She stretched herself across Vaughn's arms and dipped deep into an arabesque ponché, tipping her body forward and extending her arm down while her toe pointed eloquently toward the sky, the sense of yearning obvious in every inch of her quivering frame.

Then the strains of music increased and they began to dance. Avis knew that Vaughn was infected with the same magic as time seemed to stop and the room float around them like the mists off a lake. *This was what it was all about,* Avis thought, smiling as she spun into a deep swoon across Siegfried's back. *This is why I can do nothing but dance. The difference between dancing and walking is this—I'm only alive when I dance.*

Avis and Vaughn remained motionless for a moment after the music stopped. As soon as they slowly moved apart, they were both startled to hear the sound of clapping coming from the corner of the room.

"That was beautiful," said a familiar voice, and Keith Harding stepped out of the shadows.

"What are you doing here?" Avis said. She could not help staring at him; it was the first time she had seen him in street clothes. He was wearing tan corduroy pants and a pink sportshirt with an indistinguishable logo on the chest. Her first impression was how huge he seemed. He dwarfed Vaughn, and seemed to take up the space of two people in the low-ceilinged room.

"I was going to ask you the same thing," he said. "You were supposed to be at the pool two hours ago."

Avis looked at the clock on the wall, surprised. "It's six o'clock already? I had no idea!"

"I did," Vaughn said, grinning, "and I'm leaving this minute. Unless, of course, you want to rehearse that passage just one more time."

Avis was distracted. "No, that was pretty good. Thanks for staying so late, Vaughn. See you tomorrow."

"Pretty good?" As Vaughn passed by Keith, he gave him an appraising look and a wry grin. "She thought it was pretty good. Some people are never satisfied."

Keith waited until Vaughn had left. "He's right, you know. Some people never are satisfied." He smiled. "But that looked pretty good to me, too."

Avis was having trouble adjusting herself to Keith's presence in the studio. He seemed out of place. "It depends on what you have to compare it to," she said.

"Ah, right. And I have nothing."

She hadn't meant to disparage his lack of experience in ballet; it was just that she was caught off guard. "I didn't mean that," she said in some confusion. "I meant . . ."

"You meant, what am I doing here, right?" Keith went over to the tape recorder and shut it off. Avis realized that the tape had been flapping around on the reel for some time. "Actually, since you didn't show up for class, I decided to go out and get some errands done. And one of my errands was to stop by here and pick up two tickets for opening night. Of course, being a stranger to the National Ballet, by the time I found my way to the box office it was closed for dinner. So, I thought I'd mosey up here and see what kind of a place you live in."

"I don't live here." Avis thought she could detect sarcasm in his voice, and her reply was defensive. She could not think what to do with her body, which felt more naked in leotards, tights and a huge old T-shirt than it did in just a swimsuit at the pool. She shifted uncomfortably on her feet, unwilling to meet Keith's genial smile.

"I know, not really. But you do, when you're getting ready for a performance, don't you? Swimmers do the same thing before a competition. They move into the pool." He looked around the big room with its old windows full of failing light. "Not a bad place, I might add. Less damp than the pool, that's for sure."

His dogged good humor was irritating her. "How did you get in?" she asked. "The place is supposed to be locked when the front office is empty."

He raised his eyebrows. "It was wide open for me," he said, obviously unwilling to accept responsibility for the lax security. "Maybe Vaughn left it open so he could make a quick getaway."

Avis refused to smile, even though this was a wickedly accurate picture of Vaughn. "Well," she said, "now you've seen it."

"And I've seen you dance, too." He sat down on the wooden chair that Madame Arlenska often used to conduct rehearsals, and he looked completely at home.

"I'm impressed," he said, looking at Avis's figure standing uneasily in front of him. "You make it seem so easy."

"It's not." She wished she didn't sound so petulant, like a child who was being held against her will.

"I know it's not." His eyes traveled up and down her torso and limbs as if seeing them for the first time. Avis wondered if she would feel more comfortable sitting down. But there was no other chair in the room, and she did not want to sit at Keith's feet.

"Anyway, it was just a rehearsal."

Keith smiled broadly. "Oh, good. Then I'll be even more impressed when I see the real thing." He looked at her T-shirt. "Although I hope you'll be wearing something more romantic than that rag. Will you?" His eyebrows rose innocently.

"Of course I will," she snapped. Then feeling guilty, she added, "But it's not necessary for you to buy tickets. I can easily arrange for a pair of complimentary seats for you."

"Oh, you don't have to do that," Keith said, not sounding as if he meant it.

"Don't be silly." Avis was recovering her poise. "It's the least I can do for you. After all, I wouldn't be here if it weren't for you." She smiled genuinely at him.

He shook his head. "I doubt that, Avis," he said softly. "You would be here come hell or high water, and you know it."

Avis nodded, acknowledging the irrefutable truth of this comment. "But you did help. And I'm grateful for that."

Keith stood up. "You make it sound as if it's in the past. Are you planning to come to the pool again?" His head was briefly turned away from her, so she could not read the expression on his face as he spoke.

"I don't know," she said, looking around her at

the pale walls and floor of the studio. "I really should put in as many hours as I can manage here."

"As your coach," Keith said with a hint of irony in his voice, "I must disagree. You know perfectly well you're working with an unknown. That arch of yours is not as strong as it was before the injury—not yet—and more floor work is not going to help. You need to keep on swimming until it's healed, and that won't happen automatically this Friday just because of opening night."

"You're right." Somehow Keith's firm tone made it easier for Avis to agree with his advice. "It helps me relax, too." She smiled up at him. "I'll be there tomorrow."

"Good." He started for the door, and she fell into step beside him. "Besides," he said, "I don't want to lose you yet." She could not tell if he was joking or serious. "You're too good a swimmer to abandon me like that."

Avis felt it was a good moment to change the subject. "So you want two tickets for Friday night?" she asked as they left the studio and walked down the narrow hallway that led out of the building. She wasn't sure how she felt about the prospect of Keith's coming to see the ballet. Somehow, she was having trouble mixing her two worlds, and trouble was one thing she wanted to avoid on opening night. But then she decided her reaction was ridiculous, just a result of nerves. "I'll be glad to get them for you. You can pick them up at the Open Theater box office the night of the performance."

"I appreciate it," Keith said.

"Who are you bringing?" The question slipped out without warning, surprising Avis more than it seemed to surprise Keith. "I mean, not that I care, but . . ."

"Of course. Not that you care." Keith reached out and pulled open the heavy double doors that led from the studio area to the outer offices of the National. "As a matter of fact," he said, letting Avis pass under his arm. "I was planning to corral Tom into accompanying me."

"Tom! You're kidding!"

He shook his head as if taking her comment seriously. "No, I'm not. After all, he's as much in need of a dose of good culture as I am, don't you think? And I'm sure he'd appreciate it, especially if it's free."

Avis flushed in confusion. "I didn't mean that he wouldn't appreciate it . . ." She broke off, recalling that Keith had made several remarks to her that indicated that he knew more about ballet than he let on. "Besides," she said accusingly, "I doubt that you're a neophyte when it comes to ballet. I'm sure you can explain things to Tom."

He shrugged. "I've been to the ballet once or twice." He reached out one finger and chucked her lightly under the chin. "But that was before your time. And it wasn't the National." They were almost to the outer door of the building, and he turned and gazed out the glass entry doors. "Well, I'd better be going back to the pool. Tom will miss me."

Avis stood very still, aware of the spot where he had touched her so lightly under the chin. "What are you going to do now?" Keith asked her, one hand on the outer door.

"Oh, I don't know," she said, bemused. Keith had her at a disadvantage. She was so preoccupied with this information about him that she could barely pay attention to what he was saying. "I suppose I'll go home and get some rest."

"Perhaps," he said gravely, "you should think about putting on some decent clothes before you leave the building."

Avis looked down and realized that she was still in

her leotards and raggedy shirt. "Oh!" She turned and began to walk briskly back toward the studios, then remembered that Keith was standing there watching her. "Oh!" she said again, spinning around in confusion. Keith stood there with a half-smile on his face, waiting. "Thanks for dropping by," Avis said, hearing the inanity of her words even as she spoke them. "I'll . . . I'll see you around, I guess."

He shook his head. "Not around. Tomorrow. At the pool."

Then he left.

Avis was startled, more by her own reaction to Keith's unexpected visit than by the visit itself. After all, it was perfectly logical for him to want to see her dance, and Tom, too. Both of them had a professional stake in her recovery, as they did in Cheryl's. Maybe she would get them two sets of comps, so that they could see Cheryl dance Odette too. No, she didn't want a comparison. That was unworthy of her, and tremendously unfair to Cheryl. Two sets of tickets it was.

But why had she just acted like such a little fool around him? It wasn't the same as at the pool—Keith himself hadn't been the same as he was at the pool. At the pool he had seemed so quiet, so straightforward. This evening he had seemed more . . . complicated was the only description Avis could come up with. And her feelings about him were more complicated too. She wanted very much to impress Keith for some reason, but she had a suspicion that he was not a pushover. For one thing, he knew her too well. He had an uncannily accurate handle on what made Avis Considine tick; it was hard to fool someone who read you like a book. Avis felt she had no air of mystery where Keith was concerned, and mystery was something she had always been able to pull off. After all, her life was full of magical illusions—Odette, Camille, Coppelia. If she had no mystery in her real self, at least she could portray mysterious characters.

But Keith seemed to know exactly what was required to produce such illusions. He knew that she was a compulsive person when it came to her career.

She, on the other hand, knew very little about Keith Harding. He had been a competitive swimmer, probably under Tom's tutelage, but she did not know what kind of swimming he had done. He had not made it to the Olympics, but no one seemed to understand what had happened to prevent his competing. Even his stay at Oxford was clouded in mystery. For all his seeming straightforwardness, he was pretty good at illusion himself.

Avis decided that any attempt to unravel the mystery of Keith Harding would have to wait until after opening night. She had to devote all her energy to the Swan Queen's pas de deux. Nothing else, nothing at all, mattered.

When she set her mind to it, Avis was good at wiping out any distractions from her life. So for the next few days she did not think much about Keith Harding. She saw him at the pool, but she concentrated on swimming, not on him, and he seemed to find nothing wrong with her behavior. He took special care with her foot, and he allowed Avis to push herself further and further in the pool, although he did not let her do the rigorous breaststroke. He gave her her head, and she swam hundreds of laps of the crawl, feeling her body strengthen itself.

And always he swam beside her, silent, smooth, his stroke perfectly matched to hers, his very presence willing her to swim further. He seemed to understand her state of mind better than she did herself, and she found it very relaxing.

At the studio, however, events were building to a fever pitch. The technical rehearsal on Wednesday night was long and grueling, with the dancers forced to walk through their paces again and again while the lighting and sound crews "set" the program on the outdoor theater's lights and microphones. The tension of not being able to dance was even worse than that of having to dance, and by eleven o'clock that night the strain showed in drawn faces and sharp words. Avis went home and, for the first time since the very early stages of her injury, allowed herself a few moments to cry into her pillow.

The following night was dress rehearsal, and that went off without a hitch. The audience was full of dance and music students who paid a fraction of the regular ticket price. Their presence was as much a favor to the dancers, who thrived on their enthusiasm, as it was to the crowd itself. As was the common practice for solos and duets that were double-cast, the pas de deux was danced "double," both pairs of dancers working together on opposite halves of the stage. Avis put on her pointe shoes for the first time and, buoyed by the excitement of the crowd and her own adrenaline, danced the entire pas de deux.

It felt wonderful to be on stage again, and although her foot ached by the end of the piece, the warm grins of her fellow dancers and the roaring applause of the audience told Avis she had danced her Odette to perfection.

Cheryl, too, had done marvelously, and all four performers were surrounded by excited dancers as they went backstage after their final bow.

The first person to greet Avis was Cheryl. "We did it!

We did it!" she shrieked, wrapping her arms around Avis's neck. "I mean, you did it." Cheryl pulled back, and Avis saw that her eyes were full of tears. "You made me do it right, Avis," she said softly. "I'll never be able to show my gratitude to you for what you've done."

Avis smiled, moved by Cheryl's sincerity. "I didn't dance your part, Cheryl—you did. And you did a beautiful job."

Cheryl smiled shyly. "I think it was because I knew you were beside me on stage," she said. "I kept on pretending you were watching me, just as you did in the studio. I wanted to do it right for you."

Avis remembered feeling the same way about Madame Arlenska. "Keep that feeling, even when you're on stage alone," she said, giving Cheryl a brief squeeze. "Just pretend I'm right there watching you, and you'll be fine."

"That's great for me," Cheryl said, "but what will you do?"

Avis smiled. "Oh," she said, "I have my ways."

The day of a performance always seemed slightly unreal. There was class in the morning, and then a company warm-up at the theater before the performance. But for the rest of the day the dancers had nothing to do, and they were encouraged to relax as much as possible. For men and women whose days were so full of strenuous activity, the enforced rest felt odd, almost painful, and many young dancers made the mistake of spending the hours busily in some form of activity or another, unaware that they would pay the price when the curtain finally went up.

Avis was too seasoned to fall into that trap. She had even told Keith that she would not be at the pool that afternoon, and he seemed to agree. "I'll see you tonight, though," he said, and Avis felt a flutter of anxiety in the pit of her stomach. "That is," he went on, "if I can get Tom to come with me."

"*If* you can get . . ."

Keith shrugged. "Tom apparently feels that he won't get anything out of it." Keith allowed himself a small smile. "He feels that if you can't bet on the outcome, then there's no point."

Avis felt a rush of anger, which quickly turned to amusement. "Tell Tom he can bet on it, all right. He can bet on whether I stay on my feet or not."

As soon as she said it, Avis was appalled. She was not a superstitious person, but all performers had their private little idiosyncrasies, and Avis's was never to mention the possibility of failure aloud. She bit her lip as if to punish it for the offending comment.

Keith shook his head. "I wouldn't dream of even mentioning such a thing," he said gravely, as if she had offended him as well. "I'll just pretend you didn't say that."

Somehow, his determination to ignore the comment made it less dangerous. Nevertheless, Avis spent a long afternoon in her apartment, making a serious effort to control her nervousness. A little anxiety was good; it kept you sharp. Too much could be ruinous, leading to damning thoughts like the comment she had made to Keith.

Avis left for the theater early. Although she had been alone all afternoon, she relished the thought of those quiet moments in the theater before it began to fill up with excited dancers and busy technicians. The amphitheater in the park was a huge half-globe structure, the stage jutting out into an open courtyard and a broad lawn beyond. Behind and beneath the stage area, unseen and unimagined by the audience, was a warren of dressing rooms and prop rooms, all interlaced by a network of electrical cables and set frames. It looked like chaos to anyone who wasn't familiar with theaters, but to Avis it felt cozy and familiar.

She seemed to have been the first to arrive. Avis walked around on the bare stage, empty except for the sets for the first dance of the evening. The curtain had not yet been closed to accommodate the dancers' warm-up, and she could see out beyond the rows of bleached white wooden seating to the trees of the park beyond.

It seemed the perfect place to do the Odette pas de deux. The sun would not set for hours, which meant she would be dancing just at the moment when dusk turned to night, the magical moment when Odette was supposed to have appeared to Siegfried.

Avis stood for a moment on the small rectangle of reflecting tape that technicians had placed exactly centerstage. It was her "mark," the spot where she would be standing when the curtains parted for her duet. She could feel the mystery and romance of Odette swelling and filling her soul.

A sound from backstage reminded her that time was passing, and she wanted to get down to the dressing room and set up her things before the other dancers arrived. The principal dancers at the National had semiprivate dressing rooms in the theater where they usually danced, but the amphitheater had only two cavernous rooms marked "Male" and "Female," and she wanted to be sure she got a good spot in front of the long mirrors where the dancers made up for the performance.

The noise had been the stage manager, arriving to do a last-minute check of the technicals. Avis greeted him briefly and then went down the stairs to the dressing room. She had expected to be alone, but was surprised to see that Beth Keane was already there, sitting down at the far end of the long row of tables. The naked light bulbs framing the mirrors above her head were not yet on, and Avis could not see her clearly in the softer overhead light.

"Is that you, Beth?" Avis moved down the length of the room with a big smile. "I didn't know anybody else was here yet. What are you doing here so early? Same thing as me, I suspect. I like to get the feel of a place on performing nights, don't you?"

Avis had come halfway down the length of the room when it occurred to her that Beth was not answering her, and that she was watching Avis approach with an odd expression on her face. "Beth? Are you all right? What's the matter?"

Avis reflected quickly. Beth had very little to do in tonight's performance. It would not be unheard of for her to have a case of preperformance melancholy, to reflect sadly on the opening night excitement that was no longer hers to savor. Even for someone as sanguine about her future as Beth usually was, there were times when it hurt.

"You feeling low, Bethie?" Avis went and sat next to Beth, prepared to give her the kind of pep talk that Beth had given her not so many weeks ago. Avis reached up and switched on a string of lights. As soon as she saw Beth's face, she knew it was worse than that.

"Something's happened, hasn't it?" Avis's throat was dry.

Beth shook her head slowly. "Nothing's happened. But something's about to happen, I think." She bit her lip. "I know I shouldn't be telling you this, Avis—not now, not right before we open. God, I shouldn't be here at all! But I couldn't let it rest. It's not fair for you to go out there tonight without knowing."

"Knowing what?" The fear that constricted Avis's lungs was making it hard for her to breathe. Her voice sounded high and tight.

Beth appeared not to have heard the question. "I mean, we all know you're taking a big risk, dancing on that injured foot so soon. But it's not worth taking the risk when . . ." She looked at Avis guiltily and stopped.

"When what?" Avis leaned forward on her chair. "For God's sake, Beth, what are you talking about?"

Beth shook her head miserably. "It's something I overheard Laurence saying. He shouldn't have said it, and I shouldn't have been listening, but . . ." Beth leaned forward and took Avis's clammy hand in hers. "I know what it's like to be on the way out, Avis. It's worse than being out altogether."

Avis had to swallow several times before she could speak. "Beth. I'm already imagining the worst news possible. What is it? Has Larry decided to sack me? Am I going to get pulled out of the pas de deux tonight? Tell me what you heard!" Avis had a sudden and altogether unexpected image of Keith and Tom in the audience, and the look on their faces when they saw that it was Cheryl dancing instead of Avis. There would be pity on those faces, and Avis could not stand the thought. "Tell me now," she added urgently.

"Laurence was talking to Livia Chasen yesterday afternoon. You know her, she's one of the trustees of the company. She asked him why he had postponed the premiere of Bird of Paradise—she thought it was going to a preview at this concert, and she had told several other trustees to come tonight especially to see it." Beth paused and took a deep breath. "And I heard Laurence tell her that he was having difficulty with the casting, that he wanted to wait and see what happened with the *Swan Lake* pas de deux—with Odette."

Avis thought she had been thoroughly chilled and shaken by the mere prospect of Beth's bad news, but she was still unprepared for the shock of it. Her hands had gone from clammy to frozen. "With Odette?" she repeated dumbly.

Beth nodded miserably. "He said he wanted to see if Cheryl Cattier could handle herself in a lead role. That if she could handle Odette, he might be thinking of her for the lead in Bird of Paradise." Beth took one more deep, difficult breath. "He told her he didn't think you would be able to handle it."

Avis found that her voice was as cold and as brittle as her hands. "Did he say why?"

Beth shook her head. "If he did, I didn't catch it. They were coming my way, and I didn't want to be seen eavesdropping." She looked at Avis's stony face. "But I'm sure he only meant that he wasn't sure that your foot would be properly healed. The Bird of Paradise solo takes a lot of fancy pointe work, even more than Odette, Avis."

But Avis did not believe that any more than Beth did. "He wants a younger dancer for the part," she said, more to herself than to Beth. "That's why he's not complaining about my doing Odette so soon after my injury. He doesn't care if I hurt myself."

"But what about Cheryl? She was injured too, you know. Why would he risk both of you?"

Avis shook her head. "He knows she can do it—he doesn't want to know if I can. He wants me out, and this is the easiest way."

Avis could feel her heart beating inside her chest, and the sound of it seemed to fill the empty room. The horror of what she had just said left them both speechless. Was it really possible that Laurence would cold-bloodedly allow her to risk her entire career so that he would not be forced to choose between Avis and Cheryl? Avis tried to reason with herself, to tell herself that it was impossible. Not even Laurence, who had no scruples when it came to his own choreography, would risk a dancer's entire future for his own ends. He knew too well what it meant. Surely it would not be Avis whom he sacrificed so easily. Avis, whom he had known so long and once loved so well?

But he had not loved her well, she realized, and had never really known Avis as a person, only as a dancer. She had seen him ride over other dancers before; Beth, who sat before her white-faced, had had the rug pulled out from under her, too. After a few recurring injuries, she had suddenly stopped getting anything but character roles. Beth had borne the insult with her usual aplomb, and had ridden out the storm because she was able to shine in character parts. Her age and injuries had provided a graceful excuse, and her rich fiancé had provided a secure future.

But what would Avis do if she could not dance?

She had no choice. She simply had to perform tonight, and perform so well that there was no question of her not getting the Bird of Paradise role. That role had suddenly become the most important one of her life, and that meant that tonight's Odette was the most important Odette she had ever danced.

Laurence wouldn't dare take away Bird of Paradise if her Odette brought down the house. He might double-cast her in the new ballet, but that Avis could endure.

Tonight was starting to look like the most important night of her entire career. She thought about the picture of herself as Odette and Laurence as Siegfried on her refrigerator door. She would have to make Laurence wish he was up there with her on that stage.

She stood up, startling Beth, who had lapsed into her own private gloom. "I've got to get ready," she said, surprised at the strength in her voice. "I've got to get ready early so I can get Vaughn to go through the adagio one more time."

"Avis? Are you sure?"

"Sure of what?" Avis knew perfectly well what Beth meant.

"Your foot. Is it ready? Can you do it?"

Avis followed Beth's gaze to her foot, slim and narrow in a scuffed white sneaker. Then she looked up at Beth. "Look. I've got enough time for a quick hot soak, don't I? There's some mineral salts in my dance bag, and I noticed a hot plate in the hall. We can get enough hot water for a good ten-minute soak, and that ought to help a lot.

"I'll get changed and try to corner Vaughn. We can go over the adagio before company warm-up, and do the variations afterward." Avis forced a smile at Beth's incredulous expression. "Come on, Beth, of course I can do it!" Her lips drew together in a tight line of determination. "I have no choice, do I?"

Beth stood up, smiling, and shook her head. "Nope. No choice at all. You get the mineral salts and I'll start the water." She hurried to the door, but turned around just as she reached it. "We'll show them, won't we, Avis?"

Avis nodded after she had gone. "I hope so," she whispered. "I certainly hope so."

Chapter Six

Friday, May 23

The buzz of a theater before a performance always has its own electricity. The audience, arriving and finding their seats, always feels a tiny thrill of apprehension at the prospect of what they are about to see. Will it be good? Will it be great? Will there be some disaster, small or large, which will have everyone gasping on the edge of their seats?

But the excitement of the audience is nothing compared to what goes on backstage. There is a chaotic rush of activity in every direction, and to the untutored eye it appears that the prop man is about to send a stage set crashing into the head of a ballerina who is running through her steps on stage.

It never happens. The chaos is controlled and almost subdued. Except for terse conversations on practical matters or the occasional joke, everyone keeps pretty much to themselves. Energy must be conserved for the real thing—the performance itself.

It was because of the chaos, and because everyone else backstage was concentrating on the performance, that Avis was able to keep her pain to herself during those interminable hours between her conversation with Beth and the time she was due to go on stage for the *Swan Lake* pas de deux. She was not appearing in any of the other pieces of the program, but she warmed up with the company and got Vaughn to go through the adagio and variations with her when there was room on the stage. Even Vaughn, who was usually fairly attuned to his partner's moods, failed to notice the tightness of Avis's jaw or the determined set of her mouth.

After the first intermission, Avis put the finishing touches on her heavy stage makeup and went up to wait in the wings. There were three pieces before the pas de deux, and she preferred watching them to sitting downstairs in the dressing room, where the music and intermittent applause filtered down to the waiting dancers with maddening slowness. At least up in the wings, pressing her body against the heavy felt curtains and dodging the scurrying stage manager with instinctive agility, she could lose herself in what was happening on stage. She could always lose herself in that.

The question was, would she be able to lose herself when it came her time to dance? Would she be able to become Odette, knowing what she knew about the jeopardy of her future as a dancer? Avis knew that that future depended on it. If ever her talent as an actress counted, it counted now.

"Ready?" She felt Vaughn's hand resting on her shoulder and turned to see him smiling tightly. "It's time to trot," he added as he always did.

"Then let's trot," she replied as usual, wondering what automatic system was making it possible for her to act and sound so normal. All she could think of was Odette. If she thought about anything else, there was a terrible ringing sound in her ears.

The stage was completely black as, grasping hands, Avis and Vaughn groped their way to the faintly glowing magnetic tape mark on centerstage. For a moment they stood close together, head to head, both hands clasped tightly. It was an old ritual they practiced before assuming their positions. In the dark, Avis could hear Vaughn whisper to the stage manager that they were ready.

In that first moment, as the curtain parted to reveal her standing on pointe, her head downcast and her body tilted slightly against Vaughn's, Avis felt her insides freeze. She couldn't do it, she simply couldn't move a muscle when so much was at stake. If she moved at all, it would be to run off stage, out of the theater, away from the terrible pressure she felt.

But then she heard the flood of expectant applause as she and Vaughn were recognized. The lights changed, and the music began, and everything was all right. She was Odette, and there was no question of her being anything but the White Swan, no question of her doing anything but drawing the toe of one elegant foot up to the other knee and then extending it out in a slow, sensuous elevation that trembled with beauty. Her body opened like a flower to the audience, and she no longer had to think about what she was doing.

Vaughn felt her exuberance right away; all those years of working together paid off at moments like these. Instead of promenading her in a small circle as soon as her leg reached its required height at the level of her earlobe, he held her suspended for a moment while Avis allowed her leg to flutter a fraction of an inch higher. The effect was so perfectly swanlike and so technically dazzling that the audience gasped. This was what they were paying to see. Vaughn and Avis were not dancing exactly to the music, they were hovering above it and making it do their bidding.

The music swelled and swung into the first allegretto section, the duet's "happy" moments. Avis and

Vaughn used the entire stage, separating and coming back together in a series of delicate runs, swoons and lifts that celebrated their doomed love. Avis felt herself flying above the music, felt her feet carrying her across the stage without really touching it. She no longer feared failure; there was no way to conceive of it at a moment like this.

The adagio section went perfectly too, with Avis letting herself slip deeper into the ponché arabesque than she ever had before. Her body was an arrow pointed toward the earth, and her leg tipped at a perfect 180-degree angle to the sky, quivering as if it longed to fly up to the stars that were just beginning to twinkle in the late spring sky.

The variations were upon them so fast that Avis wondered if she had forgotten something. Had they really been dancing for fifteen minutes already? It seemed like no time at all, but then, it seemed like forever. There were only the solo variations and the finale left to go. Avis could feel the audience holding its collective breath, breathing when she willed them to breathe, their eyes following her as if held by a magic spell. Even when she stood off to one side while Vaughn did his variation, she felt their minds on her, on Odette.

It was during her third variation—the last—that the unimaginable happened. Avis was circling the perimeter of the stage in a series of turns and jumps, eating up space in a frenzy of urgent grace. She was Odette, who could no longer stay alive in human form for her beloved Siegfried. The evil spell which turned her into a swan was beginning to overtake her, and she fought frantically against it.

So absorbed was she that she did not feel it at first: when landing from a grande jeté, she did not feel the special marly dance floor the company had laid over the concrete stage. Instead she felt hard, cold cement, cruel and unyielding. The foot she landed on—her left—did not spring back as it usually did. Avis completed her variation, not missing a step, and only Vaughn noticed the slightly confused expression on Avis's face.

She never understood how she completed the finale of the White Swan pas de deux that evening. There was no pain—not yet. What alarmed her most was the sensation in her foot, which, with every step, seemed to crumble. She tried to tell herself that it was temporary, that it would go away as soon as she stopped dancing, but she knew with a sickening certainty that it was not so. All she could do was finish the duet; she dared not think beyond that.

It seemed that no one else in the theater suspected that anything was wrong. As Avis sank into her last swooning lift in Vaughn's arms, there was a moment of complete silence in the open-air theater. Then applause began to rain across the park like a sudden storm, gathering force until it was a thunderous ovation.

Avis barely had time to whisper to Vaughn, "Help me walk." He gave her a quick, shocked stare and then, setting her gently on her feet, put his arm around her waist and led her forward to the foot of the stage. The footlights made it impossible to see the audience, but from the way the sound rose Avis could tell they were on their feet. She and Vaughn smiled and bowed and then made their way back between the curtains.

"Come on, let's go out again," Avis said, listening to the undiminished sound. She could even hear it from the wings. Odette had been a triumph.

"Are you kidding?" Vaughn hissed in her ear. "You can't even walk. You're hurt—badly!"

She flashed him a panicked glare. "Did I dance like I was hurt badly? Come on!" She started to move forward without him, but stumbled. He came up behind her and swept her back out in front of the crowd.

"You," he whispered through a clenched smile, "are insane!"

They took five more curtain calls, and then Vaughn refused to go out again. Motioning to the stage manager, who had come forward with a bouquet of white roses for Avis, he whispered in his ear. Immediately the stage manager gave the signal for the house lights to be brought up.

It wasn't a moment too soon. The pain had just hit Avis, and she fainted for the first time in her life.

The first thing she saw when she opened her eyes was a crowd of people. She knew from the faint sound of music that the performance was not yet over, but it seemed that the entire company, along with the technical crew, was standing anxiously over her. She was in a small room that had once been used as a dressing room, judging from the wall-to-wall mirror that lined the far wall. But it seemed to have been used more for the storage of electrical equipment lately, because all Avis could see, aside from the pale faces, was an alarming array of wires and switch boxes stacked along the walls.

For a moment she thought she was in a hospital operating room. "Why are all these people in here?" she whimpered, and almost at once the faces began to recede. A hand reached up and switched off the glaring overhead bulb, leaving only a small worklight on a table above Avis's head.

"Ah," said the voice attached to the hand. "You're back in the land of the living."

It was Dr. Grey, gruff and concerned, who now swam into Avis's line of vision.

"Am I?"

The thick steely bands of his eyebrows drew sharply

together. "You are, but no thanks to yourself. Whatever possessed you to go on dancing, young lady?"

Avis closed her eyes. She still did not clearly remember what had happened. All she could recall was the euphoric certainty that she was reaching new heights in her portrayal of Odette, and then a rather confusing sensation of hardness where she had expected yielding wood. "I don't know what you're . . . ouch!" She felt a sudden stab of sharp pain in the bottom of her left foot. "What's that?"

"That," said Dr. Grey, "is a cortisone injection."

"I don't even remember hurting my foot."

"You did. You landed off the dance floor, square on the cement. Apparently you either misjudged your jetés, or you were going so full guns that you went farther out than you ever have before. This stage is four feet shorter than the National Theater stage, you know."

"I should have known. But I didn't. I didn't even think to ask. I never expected to . . . go so far . . ."

"No one expected you to go so far, child." His normally gruff voice was gentle. "You did a spectacular job out there tonight. Everyone's buzzing about it." The brows drew together sternly again. "But you had no place continuing after you landed on that cement."

"What should I have done? Apologized to the audience and limped off in the middle of the piece?"

"Yes!" He seemed genuinely angry. "You dancers! You expect to be immune from the pitfalls of your own chosen careers. You have some twisted idea of heroics, that you must go on dancing, even if it means you'll never dance again. Do you think you are immortal?"

Avis did not reply. She had heard this tirade before, but now, four words stuck in her mind so that she could not even respond with her usual retort. "You'll never dance again. You'll never dance again . . ."

"I'm tired of pasting your body back together when you don't seem to care about it yourself. I can't heal you if you won't help, can I?" Dr. Grey continued with his familiar monologue while he bent down to examine her foot more closely. Avis could not feel what he was doing; the cortisone had numbed her to his touch. But there was a strange sensation in her metatarsal.

"Is it true?" She spoke in such a whisper that Dr. Grey didn't hear her. He was still muttering with his back to her, and he continued to mutter until he looked up at a figure who appeared in the doorway.

"No one comes in—" Dr. Grey started to bark, but then, obviously recognizing the person, he changed his mind. "Oh, it's you. Well, you can come in. See if you can talk some sense into this girl."

It was Laurence, his face pale and drawn. He ignored Dr. Grey and knelt down by Avis's head.

"Avis, my God, what have you done?"

"Nothing, it's nothing . . ." Avis was still in shock. Part of her mind was still trying to figure out what had happened to her on stage, and the other was still repeating the dreaded phrase. "You'll never dance again . . ."

"It's not nothing," Dr. Grey snapped. "It's very serious, and if you would stop pushing these kids, Laurence, perhaps it wouldn't have happened."

"Me?" Laurence looked genuinely surprised at this sudden attack from an unexpected quarter. "I never pushed Avis . . . and besides, she's not a kid. She's a grown woman and she knows herself better than anyone. She said she was better, and she was." He turned back to Avis and took her hands in his. "It was an accident," he went on, more soothingly. "You could never have foreseen that you would get so far on those jetés. You danced sublimely, darling."

Looking into his cool blue eyes, Avis knew that he

was being sincere. Larry never lied about a performance, no matter what kind of shape the performer
was in afterward. Avis, looking into his eyes, found
herself smiling, soothed by the high praise. Sublimely.
That was what it had felt like to dance Odette. She had
accomplished her goal, had performed so exquisitely
that no one could ever imagine the Bird of Paradise
solo being taken from her on the grounds that she could
not—

Then it hit her. All at once, she remembered that
Laurence had wanted her out of the way, had wanted
an excuse to cast Cheryl in that solo. If he had known
that Avis would never dance less than sublimely, then
he could have arranged for her to miss her mark on that
jeté series. It seemed impossible to believe, but Avis,
with Dr. Grey's hideous refrain still pounding in her
ears, could think of no other explanation.

"You did it." She pulled herself to a sitting position,
surprising both Laurence and Dr. Grey. "You wanted
me to fail tonight, didn't you?"

The venom in her deep eyes made them glow with
anger, and even the imperturbable Laurence took an
involuntary step back. "What are you talking about?"

"You know damned well what I'm talking about. You
wanted me out of the way. You told Livia Chasen that
you want Cheryl to dance the role. You knew I would
hurt myself if I danced Odette tonight. You wanted it
that way!"

Larry got to his feet slowly, his nostrils flaring. Dr.
Grey stopped his examination and looked at him.
"What's she talking about?" Dr. Grey asked.

"I haven't the faintest idea," Laurence said coldly.
Then he turned to Avis. "Wanting you out of the way
and arranging to have you out of the way are two quite
different accusations, my dear Avis. Which will it be?"

The chill in his tone left Avis speechless with fury.

He was admitting his guilt, at least to having wanted her out of the way. If she had been holding a sharp object at that moment, his life would have been in danger."

"Larry, what is she talking about?" Dr. Grey asked again, but again Larry ignored him.

"What's the prognosis on the arch, Stan?" he asked.

"Not good. She'll be out for the fall season, at least."

Avis, who was only half listening, heard the confirmation of her death sentence. The fall season—it might as well be forever.

"Get out," she said tightly.

"Avis." It was Dr. Grey who spoke. Laurence merely looked at her.

"I said, get out. Both of you. Now!"

At her rising hysteria, Dr. Grey moved forward as if to do something, but Laurence held his arm. "No. She's right. She needs time to be alone, to think about what she just said. Let her be."

"All right. Your foot is bandaged and anesthetized, Avis. You should be all right for the night. Get home and get into bed, and for God's sake, don't walk on it! I'll be by in the morning to get you to the hospital for more tests."

He picked up his bag and left the room, shaking his head, obviously disgusted by both Avis and Laurence. Laurence stayed a moment more, only long enough to stare penetratingly into Avis's eyes. "How dare you?" he whispered, and then he turned on his heel and left as well.

Several other people tried to get in to see Avis as she lay on the narrow couch in the tiny dressing room behind the Open-Air Theater stage that evening. The performance was over, and even through her medicated haze she could hear her name being buzzed about as people discussed the tragedy. Her first visitor was Vaughn, anxious and upset. He was angry when she sent him away, though not as angry as Larry had been. His conscience, Avis thought bitterly, was not as guilty.

Then Cheryl came by, tearful and nervous. She got frightened when Avis ordered her out of the room, but Avis put that down to youth more than to guilt. Beth came a little later, after the sounds in the theater had begun to die down, and Avis was lying in a half-slumbrous state, unwilling to make the effort to continue her life beyond the moment.

"Come on," said Beth briskly, "we've got to get you home. Frank ordered a car to pull right up outside the theater with a wheelchair." Frank was Beth's fiancé.

"Wheelchair?" The word made Avis want to weep. "I don't need a wheelchair."

"Don't be silly. You don't need it, but Frank arranged for it, so you might as well use it, don't you agree?" Her voice softened. "You know how he is—never does anything halfway."

Avis knew Beth's efficiency was only a ploy to hide her real feelings. She could tell from the brittle way Beth began rolling up Avis's clothes and stuffing them into the dance bag she had brought that Beth was upset. But the brittleness was irritating.

"No," she said angrily, "I don't know how he is—and I don't care. I will not go in a wheelchair!"

To prove her point, Avis sat up and prepared to stand on her foot. Dr. Grey was right; there was no pain because of the cortisone. But the mere sight of her bare foot, encased in thick bandages and yet looking so strangely weak and narrow, made Avis queasy. She let her head fall back heavily against the wall. Her faded future lay beneath that bandage. "You'll never dance again . . ."

"Come on, don't be an ass. Let's go. I'll help you out

to the hall, and you can just sit down in that chair and . . ."

"No!" It was a wail of fear, and it froze Beth in her tracks. She looked around helplessly, not sure of what to do. Just then a voice came from the doorway.

"That's all right, miss. I'll take care of her."

"Who are you?" Beth asked angrily.

A tall man stepped into the dressing room, immediately filling the tiny windowless space with his imposing bulk. "I'm a friend of Avis's. I'll get her home. Thanks anyway."

There was something in the authority with which he spoke that made Beth believe him at once. She also wanted out of the awkward situation. "Is he all right, Avis? Can I leave you with this guy?"

Avis had closed her eyes in sheer misery, and kept them closed during this conversation. But now, as soon as she looked up and saw Keith standing over her, all her emotions broke over her in a huge tidal wave of sorrow and need.

"Oh, Keith!" she cried, and flung herself into his waiting arms.

He gathered her against him and held her silently for a moment. Then he turned to Beth and, over Avis's small, dark head, he smiled. "I think it's all right, don't you?"

Beth, who had never set eyes on Keith before, was shocked at this unlikely display of intimacy. Avis had never mentioned anything about a man in her life, and yet here was this huge stranger waltzing up and taking complete control of the situation.

In any other circumstances, Beth would have made it her business to find out what was going on. But given the fact that she had not been particularly successful in getting Avis home, and the fact that she had no desire to force her, Beth decided to let relief temper her natural curiosity. She looked from Keith's calm, sea-green eyes down to Avis's shining sleek knot of black hair buried against his broad chest. "I guess it's all right with Avis," she said, returning Keith's smile uncertainly. Then, deciding he had an extremely likable face, she broadened her smile. "It looks like she's in very good hands."

"The best." He did not move from his position; he was practically holding Avis up as he stood there in the center of the tiny room. He made no attempt to elaborate.

"You'll see that she gets home without hurting her foot any more?"

A hint of wry amusement underlined Keith's smile. "I'll take full responsibility. There was no trace of impatience in his voice, but somehow he managed to communicate to Beth that the interview had come to a close.

Avis had been listening to this conversation with only half an ear. She was still in shock and unable to think about the repercussions of her injury. But she had reacted instinctively to Keith's arrival with an outpouring of emotion that almost frightened her in its intensity. She remained silent until Beth left, not only because she had no desire to talk to Beth or to see the pity in her eyes, but also because she wanted to luxuriate in the warmth and safety of Keith's body. She felt as if she had come home.

After Beth left, Keith waited until silence filled the little space. Several dancers poked their heads in to say good night, retreating awkwardly when they saw Avis so obviously being guarded by a total stranger. Dr. Grey reappeared, and Keith told him he would be responsible for getting Avis to the hospital in the morning. Dr. Grey looked at him consideringly, agreed, and left.

A few distant banging doors and calls of farewell marked the departure of the last of the technicians, and then they were alone in the theater except for the clean-up crew. The entire backstage area echoed desertedly. Keith and Avis remained silent for a long while after those last sounds died away, each savoring the experience for their own private reason. Avis only needed comfort, and it seemed that Keith was the only one capable of providing it.

She could not have said why this was so. Keith seemed content to just hold her, although if she could have seen his eyes she would have wondered at the storm of emotion which seemed to be brewing in their calm depths.

After a long moment he reached down and, putting one arm under her knees, lifted her into his arms. "Come on," he whispered softly, "let's get you out of those clothes and into something more comfortable."

Avis looked down and realized for the first time that she was still wearing her white camisole and pale pink tights. Only the tutu had been removed. She felt stiff and constrained in the costume, and was grateful for the suggestion. But when Keith put her down gently on the edge of the couch, she felt a rush of faintness and had to lie back against the bolster. Her legs were numb, and it scared her that she could not feel her foot at all.

He saw her panic and reached up to soothe her hair back from her pale face. "Don't worry," he said, reading her thoughts, "it's not permanent. The sensation will come back when the cortisone wears off."

"That's what I'm afraid of," she whispered dully.

He shook his head, looking into her eyes. "Don't you understand?" he said softly. "You don't have to be afraid of anything now. I'm here."

Avis let her eyes slowly drop shut on his steady gaze. Keith did not know—he could not have imagined—how incredible it was for her to hear that. No one had ever said that to Avis before. She had always had to take care of herself in that sense. Fear—fear of failure, of injury, of being alone in a cutthroat business—was something all dancers lived with. There was a limit to the kind of support you could get from other dancers.

But Keith's support was total and unquestioning. She could feel it in the way he tenderly began removing the elastic straps on her camisole. The material was heavy since the costume was made to endure long use and heavy wear; but he made it seem as if he were removing the lightest silk. He cradled her shoulders in one arm and slipped the stiff satin and velvet bodice down her hips.

Lying there with her eyes closed and her mind as numb as her foot, Avis felt no embarrassment at the fact that Keith was removing her clothing. It seemed a perfectly natural thing for him to be doing, given the circumstances and the fact that they had been so nearly intimate before. At the pool, he had massaged her body through material so thin it might as well have been flesh, and in the water they had shared another kind of closeness. She trusted him then as she trusted him now. The fact that she did not know him at all was not an issue.

She opened her eyes as he bent to peel down her tights. He was looking at her face, not at her body as it lay totally revealed to him on the couch. She lay perfectly still, her eyes mesmerized by his as he worked the damp material over her knees, only turning to his task when he had to concentrate on the delicate arch of her foot.

As soon as he had removed the tights, he reached down into her dance bag, which Beth had left behind, and pulled out the oversized T-shirt she had been wearing when he saw her at the studio. He held it up and allowed himself the smallest of smiles.

"You were right," he murmured as he bent and lifted her neck again, this time to slip on the shirt. "It didn't matter."

"What didn't matter?"

"What you wore." He pulled the shirt down so it just covered her hips and then stopped to look at Avis. "You are the most exquisite dancer I've ever seen," he said with sudden feeling. "And don't tell me that I haven't seen many, because that's beside the point. You make magic when you dance, Avis. Sheer magic."

Avis bit her lips, not so much at the fervent sincerity of his words as at the fact that his eyes seemed to partially fill with tears. She searched his face for some explanation of this sudden surge of emotion. That frightened her. If she had nothing to be afraid of when Keith was with her, why did the sight of his face make her heart beat so heavily inside her chest? He could not lose control—if he didn't keep control, then who would?

But his face was moving closer to hers, and she could not take her eyes off it, regardless of the naked emotions that his features revealed. She could only watch, paralyzed by her own conflicting and confounding emotions, as the face drew closer and the lips became more inviting.

She could never understand what made her want to kiss Keith at that moment, there in that little room behind the drafty stage of the Open-Air Theater. She didn't recall having the urge to kiss him before, at least not on her own initiative. She did remember wanting to respond to his impulse that day in the Sportscape Club pool, but this feeling was different and entirely inexplicable. Her future lay in shards at her feet, and yet all she could think of was the probable taste and feel and warmth of his mouth and of her uncontrollable desire to melt her tongue against those wide, warm lips, those hard, white teeth.

It was Avis who closed the final gap between them with a little moan of impatience, Avis who lifted her arms and wrapped them around Keith's neck with a vengeance. She pulled his face down to hers so that his eyes appeared as two pools of fiery emotion.

The first contact was hard, so hard that it nearly knocked the breath from her lungs. Avis was surprised at the power behind her mouth, which touched Keith's hungrily, eagerly seeking entrance. She wanted to kiss Keith, but she had not expected there to be pent-up desire waiting for that first touch. *Funny,* she thought irrelevantly, *I've been wanting to do this for a very long time.*

But his kiss was equally hard, equally fraught with passion. His lips were demanding and covered her entire mouth. His teeth were avidly pressing against hers, and his tongue probed the corners of her lips and beyond. She had expected his beard to be bristly and hard, but it was soft and wonderful.

And then, as if they were both shocked by the extent of their desire, they pulled back. Without ever losing contact, the quality of the kiss changed, became tender, hesitant, everything that a first kiss should be. That initial panic had been uncontrollable, but now, having given in to it momentarily, the time had come to rein passions under control. Keith's mouth softened and began to move in gentle, nibbling motions around the perimeter of Avis's lips, even moving over her face in a tender exploration of the virgin territory he encountered. Avis nipped at his ear and the broad plane of his cheek, waiting patiently for his lips to return to hers. She, too, understood the nature of control, but she also knew that he would have to come back. And tonight, since she had no future, she could wait.

Keith settled himself more comfortably on the couch above her and seemed prepared to take his time. His lips moved deliberately across her face and down her neck, rubbing against bare shoulder and breastbone where her oversized T-shirt left the skin exposed. His beard was gruff and warm against her flesh, like a clean, rough towel.

Avis felt herself melting into the hard little couch, which now seemed as accommodating as a double bed. She could not understand how she could feel so comfortable; Keith was so big he could barely fit beside her. But she felt as if she had all the time and space in the world.

His lips finally found their way back to hers, where they were met with a welcoming barrage of kisses and a hungry tongue. Once again, the rhythm of their embrace accelerated as Avis's mouth opened and Keith searched hungrily inside. She could taste the warm, slightly bittersweet inside of his mouth, feel the smoothness of his teeth and the rough underside of his tongue with her own. His mouth seemed to envelop hers, so that she felt she did not have to breathe on her own.

Then she felt his hand, large and tender, moving slowly up the smooth expanse of her thigh. She pressed her leg closer against him, and felt him gathering her warm body in his hands, massaging the flesh and sending little shivers of fire up into her groin. These were the same hands that had massaged her skin so efficiently many times before. But suddenly they were invested with a new power—the power to heal was now the power to arouse.

His fingers moved slowly, easily up beneath the long tail of her T-shirt. It wasn't until they encountered the bare, heated flesh of Avis's narrow hip that they abruptly stopped. He had recalled her nudity beneath the flimsy shirt, and he pulled his mouth away at once.

"Uh-uh," he said in a deep, grainy voice, but his head, as he shook it, seemed unsteady.

"Why?" she asked, but she had meant to ask "why not?" She bit her lip at the look on his face.

"Because of everything," he said, and stood up for a moment with his broad back to her. "Because I have to get you home," he added, turning around. In the space of those two sentences he had recovered his poise. He knelt down and, pulling a pair of sweatpants from Avis's dance bag, he began to put them on her.

"Keith." The name was whimpered because she could feel the difference in his touch. This was the touch of the masseur, of the coach, that pulled the sweatpants to her waist.

"Avis." He spoke warmly but with a touch of amusement.

She was angry at him for having recovered so fast. "It's not fair," she said, not sure what she was referring to. "Nothing's fair." She felt close to tears.

"Ah, that's not you talking," he told her, helping her to sit up. "That's the medication Dr. Grey gave you. Now come on, I'm taking you home."

"What medication?" Avis asked, but as soon as she asked, she felt seized by drowsiness. "Take me home," she whispered.

"I intend to," Keith said, gathering her up in his arms as if she weighed nothing. "Now, if you can just stay awake long enough to tell me where you live . . ."

Avis's eyelids were dropping. "I don't live at the studio anymore," she told him from somewhere in a drugged fog. "So I must . . . live at the pool. . . ."

Chapter Seven

Saturday, May 24

Everything is changed now. Everything is ruined. If I can't dance anymore, what can I do? How will I define my life, how will I survive?

I think if I didn't have Keith Harding right now, I would die.

Keith had to carry Avis out of the theater. The painkiller that Dr. Grey had given her along with the cortisone had rendered her mercifully numb in her mind as well as in her body. She might have told him about the wheelchair, but she had no intention of relinquishing the pleasure of his strong arms encircling her as he carried her to the sidewalk where he opened the door to the waiting taxicab.

The driver, normally imperturbable in all city situations, tried not to notice that his passenger was entering the cab with a semicomatose young woman draped around his arms. But he was taken aback when Keith, after settling Avis onto the seat, began rummaging through her dance bag searching for her wallet. Avis, who lay back against the seat with her eyes closed, heard the exchange but could not bring herself to enter into it.

"Whaddya think you're doing?" the driver demanded righteously.

Keith looked up serenely. "I've got to know where she lives, don't I? Oh, here. Take us to Columbus and West Eighty-first, please."

The cabbie scowled disapprovingly, but drove on, muttering about men who took advantage of drunken young women. Avis heard, but did not care to set him straight. She was in limbo, between pain and numbness, and did not want to shatter the delicate balance.

When they arrived at her apartment building, the doorman, who knew Avis well, was even more concerned. "What happened to her?" he inquired anxiously. "Is she going to be all right?"

"I'm afraid she's sustained an injury," Keith told him, turning sideways in order to fit Avis through the doors without disturbing her. "The doctor gave her some pain medication and some cortisone. She doesn't feel a thing."

"And who are you? I've never seen you around before." The elderly man sized Keith up warily. "You don't look like a dancer, and I know all the dancers around here."

Keith gave him his most engaging grin. "Actually," he said without breaking his stride toward the elevator, "I'm just a stagehand. You know how those dancers are, none of them wanted to risk an injury of their own by having to carry her."

Keith shrugged conspiratorially, and the doorman, with a sage nod of agreement, let him go on. In the elevator, Avis opened her eyes.

"I heard that," she muttered thickly. "You certainly do have a convincing way about you." She tried to open her eyes all the way to see his face, but her muscles would not obey. "I liked the way you handled yourself."

"I'm glad you liked it." He bent his head and dropped a kiss on her forehead. "You handled yourself pretty well too."

"No, no . . . I didn't mean that. I mean . . . I liked that too . . . I meant . . ."

Another kiss landed on her nose.

"Shut up," he said, "and tell me which floor you live on."

When they got to the door of her apartment, Keith reached down and fished her key out of the dance bag that dangled from his elbow, all without so much as shifting her weight in his arms. Avis felt light as well as light-headed, but by the time he had her settled on the couch, she realized that reality was beginning to return. The only thing she could see from where she lay was the photo pasted to her refrigerator door.

"Take that picture down," she instructed crossly, and Keith, without asking which photo she was referring to, complied.

"Anything else you need?" he asked, turning away from her closet with an armful of bedding.

Avis shook her head, and then started to nod. "No. Yes. I want you to stay."

He had already pulled up a sling-back chair by the side of her couch. "Of course I'll stay," he said easily. "I'll stay all night if you like."

She looked up at him and smiled weakly. "I like."

"Then I'm here." He reached out and smoothed her hair, stopping when his palm reached her brow. "God, you've still got all that makeup on! You must feel like a mummy!"

Avis had not been aware of the stage makeup she still wore, but the thought of what she must look like, with the heavy pancake and the exaggerated lines almost obscuring her real features, made her sit up at once. "Oh, no! And I'll bet it's all smeared, too!" Her hand went to her face and encountered the thick spiky false eyelashes. Keith had kissed her when she was like this! She was mortified. "I'm going to wash this muck off right now." She started to get up, but he pushed her back down.

"Oh, no you don't. You're not going anywhere." He reached out and flicked a bit of stray mascara from her cheek. "I took off your clothes," he said with a soft half-smile. "I can certainly take off your makeup."

Avis lay back with a sigh. She wasn't at all sure how to react to this man. She knew they had just recently come perilously close to making passionate love, but she wasn't sure whether her impulse to do so had come from true passion or just fear. And now Keith was treating her with the kind of gentle intimacy he used during therapy sessions. Only this time it was different.

Or was it just her confused perceptions that made it different? She had no idea what had motivated him to kiss her so longingly, and even less idea what had made him stop. She watched him now as he moved easily around her apartment, going into her bathroom and emerging with soap, towel, and Vaseline and then going to the kitchenette to fill a bowl with warm water. He looked like he belonged, and she recalled the sensation she had had when she buried herself in his arms at the theater. She had felt like she was coming home.

He returned with his hands full and sat down, setting the bowl on the coffee table beside him. "Why the sad expression?" he inquired, leaning over her and beginning to swab gently at her face with a Vaseline-covered cotton ball.

"Why not?" she replied glumly. She didn't tell him that she hadn't been thinking sad thoughts, but confused ones. "I just ruined my entire career in one fell swoop. One stupid, thoughtless error."

He heard the growing bitterness in her voice and paused for a moment in his ministrations. "It wasn't a stupid error. It was an honest mistake. Anyone could have tripped on that flooring."

She caught his hand and looked up at him. "You mean you saw it?"

"Of course I did. You got me the tickets, remember? Good seats—the best in the house."

"Was . . . did Tom come with you?"

Keith smiled. "Alas, no. He chickened out at the last minute. Afraid we would ask him for the deeper meaning of life if he went." He chuckled.

"The deeper meaning is that there is no meaning. Honest mistake or screwup, it all ended in one split second, so what does it matter?" Gloom was settling heavily on Avis now.

"It matters. Besides, why should it be all over?"

"That's what Dr. Grey said, wasn't it?"

"I didn't hear what he said, but I'm sure it wasn't that. He had no way of making a diagnosis. And I'm sure it's not terminal."

"It's terminal for the fall season, so it might as well be."

"You're not giving yourself the benefit of the doubt," Keith said, wiping off the goop on her face with swift strokes. "You did it before, you can do it again. Hey, don't push my arm like that!"

But Avis had thought of something, and she wanted to pursue the thought undeterred. "No, wait. You just said something. It matters. You said it matters."

"Of course it matters." He reached for the soapy sponge.

"No, I mean, it matters whether it was a thoughtless error or an honest mistake."

"That's what I said."

"What if it was something else?"

He stopped trying to continue with his work. "What?"

Avis pulled herself up to face him. "What if it was neither? What if someone made it happen on purpose?"

"Avis, what are you talking about?" He looked very concerned.

"I'm talking about sabotage," she said, her eyes burning. "Laurence Lessine didn't want me to get the solo lead in Bird of Paradise. Beth heard him say so to one of our trustees. I wouldn't put it past him to arrange for me to trip on that bit of flooring. He could have had a few slats removed, or even removed a piece himself, with no one the wiser."

Keith stood up. "Avis, you are making a very serious accusation. Do you realize what you're saying?"

"Of course I do!" When she had begun to speak, she had not really thought about it, but now Avis was beginning to wonder if she might not be right. "I rehearsed three times on that stage, Keith—four, if you count tonight's run-through. I've never overshot a mark like that. Never."

"You've never danced Odette like that, either," Keith said, walking away from her and staring out the window to the lighted street below. "I heard all the dancers saying so when I went backstage." He turned to face her. "Perhaps that's why you danced so hard, why you overshot your mark on those jumps. You had a lot at stake tonight."

Avis saw a familiar look on his face. It was the look of sympathy, and she could not bear the sight of it. "You don't believe me, do you? You think I'm just trying to come up with an excuse for my own failure, don't you?"

"Avis—"

"You're just like all the others." She lay back heavily on her pillow. Her face felt scrubbed and raw, and her heart felt the same way.

"That's a ridiculous accusation, and you know it." He came back and stood above her, and she saw the glint of anger in his eyes. "I am not like all the others. But if you believe that anyone deliberately set out to ruin your performance tonight, you'd better be prepared to prove it—in front of all the others, not just to me."

Avis opened her mouth with a bitter retort and then thought better of it. What did it matter, anyway, who believed her and who didn't? Keith was right—she would never be able to prove it. And even if she could, what good would it do her? Her career was over, ruined, and nothing in the world could change that fact. "Never mind," she said with a dismissive wave of her hand. "Let's just forget it. It happened, and it's over, and that's that, right?"

He looked at her for a moment before answering. "If that's the way you want it to be," he said deliberately, "then yes, that's that."

She laughed sourly. "What's that supposed to mean?"

Keith lifted his eyebrows. "Exactly what it sounds like. If you're willing to give up, then it is terminal. End of Avis Considine, dancer. Period. Not even an exclamation point."

The finality of his words made Avis draw in her breath with a sharp gasp of pain. "Look, I don't need you around here making me feel worse than I already do. I know how bad it is without your help."

"You know nothing." He spoke with sudden vehemence. "You know nothing, Avis, except that you've been done out of a chance to shine, to be the star, and you can't get over it. That's much easier to accept than to take responsibility yourself, isn't it, Avis? This way everybody can feel sorry for you, and that's what you want, isn't it?"

His words were stinging, his expression cold. "No," Avis said, shaking her head to rid it of the lethal imagery he had described, "that's not what I want at all. I never want anyone to feel sorry for me, ever!"

"Then why are you whining about being done to?" His gaze was remorseless, and Avis felt herself cracking beneath the pressure.

"I just . . . I don't . . ." She felt the tears spill onto her cheeks and shook her head helplessly. "Oh, never mind. You wouldn't understand."

He knelt down beside her and took her chin between his thumb and forefinger, turning her head so that their noses were just inches apart. "Oh, wouldn't I? Wouldn't I just? You don't have a corner on this sort of thing, Avis, believe me."

"Why? Did you ever lose something that was as important to you as living and breathing? Did you ever have your life end in one evening, one split second?" She looked at him, disbelieving, even before he could reply. He looked annoyingly indestructible, as if nothing could keep him down.

His jaw tightened. "Actually," he said dryly, "it happened in the afternoon. But yes, I've felt that way before."

"What happened?" Her curiosity momentarily overcame her bitterness.

"It's not important. What's important is that you recognize that you've lost perspective, and that you do something about it."

"Is that what you did? When you went to Oxford?" Intuition told her she was right.

"I told you, it's not important. The important thing

is, what are you going to do about it? Are you going to lie around moaning about your life being over or are you going to pick yourself up and go on?"

"Go on and do what?"

"Try getting well, for starters. You haven't even found out the extent of the damage, but I'm fairly experienced in this kind of muscle injury and I can venture an educated guess. You've further damaged that arch pretty badly, but there's no reason it can't heal again—in time for the fall season, too, if you like."

Avis shook her head dully. "That wouldn't help. Larry will have to start working on the Bird of Paradise piece right away. By the time my foot is better, Cheryl will have the part down cold, and it will be too late for me."

"Cheryl?"

"Oh, yes, didn't I tell you about that part? He wants Cheryl to have my solo. He's been planning on it for quite a while." Avis bit the words off angrily.

Keith looked at her keenly. "You're not planning on accusing Cheryl of any complicity in your little scheme, are you, Avis?"

Avis had to turn her head away from his gaze. "Oh, no. I wouldn't dream of accusing innocent little Cheryl —or innocent little Laurence, either, for that matter. Let's just face it—I've lost the thing I've been working for for years and it's nobody's fault but my own. Are you satisfied with that assessment?"

"Are you?"

"What choice do I have?" When she turned her face back to him, her eyes were full again. "I think you know me, Keith. You know I need something to work for, something to live for. I need a goal, something to define my life. Without my dancing, I have nothing."

"Then find something," he snapped.

Avis was taken aback by his tone of voice. "What?"

"You heard me. Find something else. Get out there and look around you. Avis, the world does not begin and end in the dance studio, contrary to what you may think. You have other options, assuming, of course, that your future as a dancer is as bleak as you seem to think it is."

"Like what?" she inquired sarcastically. "The swimming pool?"

He shot her a lethal glance and held her gaze until she was forced to lower her eyes.

"I'm sorry," she murmured. "I didn't mean to attack you, Keith." She opened her eyes to find that his expression had softened, and that he was looking at her oddly. "Really, I mean it," she said, unable to read his eyes. "It's just that . . . I'm sorry."

Her voice trailed off miserably. She really hadn't meant to attack Keith; it was simply that he was the only available outlet at the moment. There certainly weren't any dancers around, which said a lot for her peers and their devotion to a fellow dancer. She smiled bitterly; when push came to shove, so to speak, she really was on her own.

Except for Keith. He was there; which was strange, considering that she barely knew him. But she was glad that he was, and she reached out instinctively for his hand. "I really am sorry," she repeated.

He lifted her hand and examined the fingers closely. "You're right," he said after a moment's reflection. "Now is the wrong time to deliver any sermons on motivation. You're hurting, inside and out, and I'm here to see that you feel better." He sat down on the edge of the couch and smiled. "How can I do that?"

"Kiss me," she replied promptly, and he did. He reached out for her eagerly and placed his mouth against hers with a soft chuckle of desire and delight. She could feel the cool tangle of his beard along her lips and chin, and the weight of his mouth pressed her head back against his palm, which opened to pillow the nape of her neck in its caress. He reached up and undid the clasp that held the sheaf of her dark hair, and it spilled in silky cascades along his arms. He pressed her closer, and she could feel his heart beating against her chest.

This time Avis's senses were crystalline, and she knew exactly what she was doing. She responded to his touch with instant arousal and pressed her body back along his, wanting to inflame him as much as she was inflamed. The only thing that could bring her out of herself was this intense desire to make love to him, and she could feel the pulse at the base of her throat beating an insistent throb of urgency into her blood. She reached her hands into the soft cotton placket of his shirt and rummaged through the burly thicket of his chest. His heartbeat accelerated, and he shifted his weight on the couch so that he could lie more fully across her arching torso. This time, she would not let him get away.

"It's your fault I'm wearing all these clothes," she murmured raggedly.

Lifting his head from her neck, he gave her a sleepy, erotic smile. "Then it's my responsibility to see to it that they're removed," he said. This time, there was no attempt at clinical objectivity. As he slipped the T-shirt from her shoulders, he paused to kiss her small breasts, arousing first one, then the other into hard tips of desire. His tongue took those tips and cultivated them so that they grew hot and dark, and Avis, her neck arched back over the arm of the couch, could not help from crying out at the surfeit of sensation which coursed up and down her body.

Then he slipped the shirt off entirely and began to travel with his lips down the firm course of her flat stomach, causing the taut muscles of her abdomen to contract with icy pleasure. Occasionally he would lift his head to be able to see her body more clearly, and then Avis could look down and see the fine straight line of his nose, and the sea-green eyes blazing aquamarine with passion. Then he bent his head and dipped lower, pulling the cotton sweatpants away from his searing path until they were banded around her hips. His beard further stimulated the course of his lips and tongue, rolling across her body like a brush fire.

Avis arched her torso in an agony of expectation, and he lowered his mouth to her groin, sending arrows of heat across her hips and thighs. She felt totally abandoned to his touch, unable to see or think clearly, not because of the medication but because of desire. She moved to kick her pants off, and was surprised at the rush of pain from her foot.

"Wait." Keith pushed himself up, his voice low and thick. "I don't want to hurt your foot."

"You couldn't hurt me," she said without smiling. "You couldn't hurt me unless you stopped now."

He did not smile at her urgency, but stood and removed his clothes swiftly. Avis saw his body through a haze, only vaguely aware of his broad bulk, his strength, his size. Then he lifted her up and moved her gently onto the floor.

"We need room," he said, and then he was on her, and in her, and she felt no pain but the exquisite pain of consummation.

Afterward they lay still for a long time, watching reflections from streetlights on the pale rose-colored wall of the room. Avis's body was warm and damp with sweat. She felt as if she had danced all night long. There was the same drained feeling of exhaustion coupled with total exhilaration. She could not move a muscle, but she could have danced all night.

Beside her, Keith shifted, and she turned to meet his smile. "Didn't expect this, did you?" she asked him lightly.

He pursed his lips. "Actually," he said softly, "I've been expecting it since I first laid eyes on you." He reached out and traced a line down the contours of her belly. "I just didn't expect it to happen this way—not tonight."

"Why not? It was exactly what I needed." Avis hadn't expected those words to be so callous, but from the way his hand paused and stiffened, she could tell he took it that way. "I'm sorry, I didn't mean—"

"No, no. Don't bother." He removed his hand, but he didn't sound hurt. "It *was* what you needed. There's nothing wrong with that, is there?"

"I guess not," she said, but the admission sounded rather selfish and she was ashamed. It had been what she needed, but it had been more than that. It had been what she wanted, too. "Anyway," she went on, "it's nice to have you here."

He leaned up on one elbow and bent over her face. "Nice to be here." He smiled and kissed her tenderly. Avis was all for reaching up and pulling him down to her again, but Keith sat up. "Now, I think it's time we started making plans."

"Plans? What plans?"

"Plans to get you back on your feet, of course."

The mention of the word feet called to mind the persistent throbbing in Avis's left foot, which had been growing steadily more painful as the cortisone wore off. "I don't think this is the time for planning," she told him.

"Ah, but it is. Right now is the only time. You've got to start right away if you're going to get on any kind of training regimen. Otherwise, you'll just end up making excuses until it's too late."

It was probably too late already, Avis thought, but she did not feel like arguing the issue with Keith. "I really shouldn't do anything until I get the results of the hospital tests tomorrow, don't you think?"

"Of course you should wait. But you have to plan your options. And in any case, the therapy will probably be very much the same regardless of prognosis."

"And what therapy did you have in mind?"

"Swimming, of course. Lots of it. Build up that arch again, and do some muscular therapy work in the water to build up the area around the metatarsal." Keith sat with his legs folded, the thin blanket he had pulled over them just barely covering him. His torso rose like a marble column, solid and creamy in the dim light of the room. He thought with his hands, Avis noticed, gesticulating gracefully as he spoke. His face, seen in profile, looked chiseled and intent, and she thought that he looked very much like a Greek statue. Adonis, perhaps, or Apollo.

But she could not listen to what he said because she had already made up her mind that returning to the stage would be out of the question for her. It was not only a matter of healing her injury, which she knew would take a lot longer this time than it had the last time, and a lot longer than Keith imagined it would. It was also a matter of her pride. Laurence Lessine no longer wanted her for the solo part. Even if he should decide to cast her in other parts, Avis would not take them. He had betrayed her, whether in actuality or in intent, and she knew she could never again allow herself to fall under his authority. Keith could not possibly have known, but a part of her life had ended tonight, regardless of the outcome of her injury.

"Swimming, huh? You think that's a cure-all for everything, don't you?"

He turned and looked at her. "It's a cure for most

structural injuries," he said gravely. Then, shaking his head a little, he added, "Unfortunately, it can't do a thing for what ails you here." He reached out with two long fingers and pressed lightly on Avis's left breast. "It can't cure a curdled heart."

So he did know. He was looking, not at her, but into her, and Avis felt tears of self-betrayal well up in her eyes. "You say you understand," she said, turning her head away so that he would not see her cry. "But I think you can't possibly know what it means to me. If I can't dance, what can I do?"

He reached out and turned her head toward him. "You can swim."

"I know I can swim. But I mean, what can I do for my life? I need a goal, something to work for. Swimming is just a means to an end, Keith. What happens then?"

He smiled slightly. "You swim," he said softly. "You swim hard. You practice, and you get very, very good, and you swim. That's the goal. The swim is the goal."

She was not at all sure that she understood what he was saying, but Avis felt her heart beating faster just because of the way he was looking at her, hard, as if willing her to see what he saw. "I . . . I don't understand what you're talking about," she began.

"I think you do. You're like me, Avis. If you don't have a goal to work for, you fall apart—you get scared. I'm saying, if you can't think about dancing again as your goal—even for a while—you have to find somewhere else to direct your energies. And that something might as well be swimming."

"Keith—"

"A race. An amateur distance swim. You've got the stroke, you've got the strength, and God knows you've got the determination. All you need is a little work and a lot of stamina." He was talking very fast now, as if he didn't dare let her interrupt. "I've figured it all out. There's an amateur ten-mile swim in August down off Cape May. It's the biggest MasterSwim competition on the East Coast. Strictly amateur, and no big deal as far as real distance swimming is concerned, but . . ." He bent closer to her, and she saw his eyes glittering like the sea on a brilliant afternoon. "You can do it, Avis," he whispered, "I know you can do it."

She sat up, compelled and a bit frightened by his intensity. "Keith, you can't be serious. I'm . . . I'm a dancer, not a swimmer."

"That's not what you said a minute ago. A minute ago you were complaining that your life as a dancer was over. What'll it be, Avis? Over or not?" He gripped her shoulders with two strong hands. "You can't sit here feeling sorry for yourself forever, you know."

"No, I don't know. I don't know whether I'll dance again, and I'm not just feeling sorry for myself!" Her eyes blazed angrily at him. How dare he back her into a corner like this? "And it's none of your business what I do or how I feel, anyway."

He had not removed his hands from her shoulders, and his fingers were digging painfully into her arms. "Oh, yes it is," he hissed, his face only inches from hers. "We just made it my business. Now, I know you're feeling betrayed by the world you've known and loved so well. All I'm saying is, it won't hurt to have another goal for a while, especially if it might eventually get you back on stage. You're an obsessive person, Avis, and you won't be able to work unless you're working for something concrete. A performance, a race . . . what does it matter?"

"It matters!" Avis exclaimed, but she was already beginning to think about what he had said. He was right about her being compulsive, about her needing a goal. And, even if she was wrong about her foot and her pride, and she could eventually go back to dance, Avis knew that the road back would be extremely long. Could she motivate herself to go on for months, never knowing whether it would pay off in the end?

The idea of swimming intrigued her. She had grown to love the sport, to respect its rhythm and grace and even to look forward to her time in the water as she had once looked forward to her time in the studio. It would never replace dance in her heart; dance was the real reason for her existence, the only form of motion that had real meaning and beauty in her eyes. But if she couldn't dance for a long while, she would have to do something. She would have to show Laurence Lessine that he had not taken her life away, only her livelihood.

"I can't do it." Her own rationalization scared her, and she turned huge charcoal eyes to Keith. "It's an insane idea. I'd never be able to compete in a distance swim."

"You're right. You need a lot of help. You'll have to change your stroke a little, and your breathing a lot, and you've got no endurance at all. But I can change that. You'll need to build up your shoulders a bit, the trapezius and especially the deltoids. But your legs are nice and strong, and we have a whole three months."

"Three months? To compete in a MasterSwim? That sounds impossible."

"Actually, it's only two months. May is almost over and the swim is the third of August. But the competitors in MasterSwim are amateurs like yourself." He smiled wickedly. "They're just very, very good amateurs."

Avis's eyes widened. "You know what I think? I think you're crazy, Keith Harding. And I have no idea what made you come up with this crazy scheme."

Keith's smile disappeared. He reached out and pulled Avis across the blanket and set her on his bare lap. Circling her shoulders as he would a child's, he spoke very softly into her ear. "My reasons don't matter," he told her. "Yours do. And I'm banking on the fact that you're as crazy as I am, Avis Considine." He nuzzled his beard against her neck, and Avis reveled in the delightful sensation. "So, how about it. Are you nuts too?"

She pulled away and shook her head. "I don't know, Keith," she said honestly. "I really can't say anything tonight. It's just all been . . . too much."

He nodded and, planting one more tender bite of a kiss behind her ear, set her tenderly back down beside him on the blanket. "You're right, of course. You need one thing right now, and that's a good night's sleep." He stood up and, after pulling on his slacks, began straightening up the couch bed.

Avis watched him for a while, trying to figure him out. But her eyes were beginning to get heavy again, and she decided that he was right; all she wanted to think about was a good night's sleep. She started to get up by herself, but he would not allow it. Instead, he went to her closet, pulled out an old-fashioned cotton nightgown that hung there, and, holding her like a small rag doll, slipped it over her head before lifting her into bed.

She smiled sleepily at him. "This is getting to be a habit, your dressing me like this, isn't it?"

He nodded. "I like the undressing better." He covered her and reached for his shirt.

"You're staying, aren't you?"

He paused, his hands on the buttons of the shirt. "Of course I'm staying," he replied after a quick look around the apartment for a suitable space on which to sleep. He took off the shirt and, taking an extra blanket from the closet, settled himself in the reclining chair Avis had inherited from her parents.

"You sure you'll be comfortable there?" she asked dubiously. "There's room on the couch, if we take off the back pillows." She smiled shyly at him, but he shook his head.

"No, you need to get a good undisturbed night's rest. I couldn't guarantee that if I shared your bed." For a moment his eyes glittered with longing, and Avis was almost ready to lift her arms to welcome him in beside her. But he shook his head more definitely and shut his eyes on her small body reclining a few feet away.

"Don't worry," he murmured soothingly. "I'll be right here if you need me." He opened one eye mischievously. "After all, I do have a stake in your well-being, don't I?"

And then he was silent, leaving Avis to wonder whether he referred to his stake in her as a swimmer or as a lover. The question of what her stake in Keith Harding might be, or in what her own future held in store for her, she preferred to leave until the morning. At the earliest.

Chapter Eight

M onday, May 26

If anybody had told me a week ago that I would be a different person altogether in a few days' time, I wouldn't have believed it. But that's exactly what's happened: Inside of a few short days I've become unrecognizable to myself. I used to live to dance, to be mistress of my future because I was mistress of my body. That's no longer true. I seem to have abdicated some of that responsibility, although I don't even remember making the decision. And now, it seems, I shall be living to swim.

But what happened to the dancer in my soul? And who is holding my soul now that it is no longer mine?

Avis thought she might know the answer to that last question, but in the cold grey light of the morning following her àccident, she was in no mood to consider her romantic involvement with Keith Harding. The cortisone had worn off, and the pain was considerable. By the time Keith opened his eyes, she had been awake for an hour, and her features, pulled into a drawn mask of suffering, told him all he needed to know about her condition.

To his credit, Keith did not inundate her with sympathy, nor did he make any reference to their lovemaking. Avis, watching him move about the apartment with efficient grace, could not help but recall the passionate pleasure those broad limbs had evoked, even in her traumatized state. He seemed to have taken it for granted that their relationship was now different, and saw no need to remark on the fact. Instead he concentrated on helping Avis get up, dressed and fed, and to the hospital to meet with Dr. Grey for the laboratory tests.

It was all right being in her apartment with Keith. There, she felt comfortable sitting silently, adjusting to her private pain. But once they were on their way to the hospital, and inside the pallid green room where she had to wait for the doctor, Avis felt her reserves of silence being drained. She was perilously close to cracking, and only the sight of Keith, calm and patient beside her, kept her from falling apart on the spot.

The news was as bad as she expected. All morning she sat through a battery of tests and submitted to Dr. Grey's exhaustive probing and questioning, concentrating only on her foot as if, by sheer will, she could make it heal. But the results were exactly what Keith had predicted—she had torn the bruised metatarsal, this time badly, and it would take at least six months of rest and therapy to heal it. Six months at the inside, Dr. Grey warned her. She should consider the possibility that she would not be back on the stage for as much as a year, if she wanted to ensure that the same thing did not just happen again.

Avis responded dully to this verdict; she had already heard it in her mind. Besides, Dr. Grey could not possibly know that going back to the National was out of the question for her for other reasons. He merely took her silent acquiesence for chagrin, since she had not heeded his warnings the first time. He departed, leaving Avis in Keith's competent hands.

That was how it came about that she ended up, two days after her comeback performance as Odette, back in the pool at the Sportscape Club. Keith, with the unspoken foresight she had come to expect from him, had packed her dance bag with swimsuits and towels, and, when they got into a cab outside the emergency-room door and he gave the club's address, she did not even bother to protest. Avis a swimmer? She could not contemplate the thought.

At the club, they parted to go to their separate locker rooms without a word. But just as she got to the door of the women's locker room, Avis felt a strong hand on her arm. She turned around slowly, knowing it was Keith.

"Avis." He looked more worried than he had all morning at the hospital. "Are you sure you want to do it like this?"

"Like what?" she countered, knowing full well what he referred to.

But he did not push her. He merely watched her expression for a moment, reading what Avis had hoped to conceal. It was not that she did not want to make a decision one way or the other—she simply could not. He smiled. "All right. We'll do it your way." He reached around and patted her on the rump. "Meet you at the pool in five."

Then he turned to walk down the hall. Avis stood and watched him, wondering if she should call out to him, tell him how frightened she was of failure, and even of success. But he walked away from her so resolutely that she didn't feel capable of calling him back. And, after all, how would she explain what she herself did not understand?

Avis was numb, unable to analyze her own feelings,

afraid that if she faced them she would find only pain and sadness. After all, her life had totally fallen apart. Her non-decision would have to stand, until she could wake up and think for herself. Now she felt nothing.

So she was extremely surprised, as she walked into the pool room and saw Tom and Keith, that she felt the familiar sense of buoyancy and expectancy.

"Ah, it's Avis!" Tom said in a feeble attempt to act as if nothing out of the ordinary had happened since he last saw her. "How are you, Avis?" His voice boomed with forced geniality.

Avis had to smile. "Fine, Tom," she called back. Reaching down from instinct to test the water with her toe, she caught Keith's gaze, which was fixed in a kind of dismal horror on Tom. Obviously he had warned Tom of the news and had tried to get him to act "natural." The attempt had failed, but the goal was achieved. She felt better already.

"And how are you doing this morning?" she inquired brightly.

Now Keith turned to look at her, and seeing her grin, he broke into a laugh.

"It's OK, Tom." Keith chuckled. "You don't have to pretend quite that vigorously that nothing is wrong. Avis can take it."

"Good." Tom's brow creased with concern. "Avis, honey, I'm so sorry. How are you really feeling?"

This was better. "Not too bad. The doctor gave me some cortisone to take the swelling down. Thanks for asking." She smiled at him.

"Hey, that's what friends are for. And don't you worry—Keith here's gonna make you good as new again. If anybody can do it, he can. He'll get you back up on that stage before you can say . . . Odette, or whatever it was you were dancing."

Avis giggled. "Odette is right. Sorry you couldn't make it Friday night, Tom. Keith told me you had . . . other obligations."

Tom threw Keith a look of obvious relief. "That's right . . . other obligations. Exactly right. Anyway, I'll come the next time, you can be sure of that."

Keith walked over to Avis and, without saying a word to her, bent down and began unwrapping the bandage that Dr. Grey had wrapped around her foot. "There's not going to be a next time, Tom. Not for a while, anyway. Avis is going to concentrate on her swimming, aren't you, Avis?"

Her eyes glittered in sudden challenge. "That's what I'm here for, isn't it?" she threw back to him. "I've got to do something, right?" It was as close as she had come so far to an agreement with him.

Keith stood up. "How does that feel?" he asked softly, "without the bandage."

Avis stepped gingerly on the foot. The arch was sore and looked even flatter than it had the last time, but walking without the bandage was no different than walking with it on, and the cortisone reduced the stabbing pain to a dull ache. "It's all right," she decided.

"OK. But I don't want you to walk on it. Keep the bandage off in the water, where there's no gravity to add extra pressure. But on dry land, keep your weight off it as much as possible." As if to underline his advice, Keith picked her up and sat her on the edge of the desk while he rummaged in the drawers for two pairs of goggles.

"I have to do some stretching," she told him.

He shook his head. "Not for a few days. Let's take it real easy for a while. Just some easy laps. We'll be building up soon enough, believe me."

"What are you building for?" Tom inquired. "You

just going to put her through the same training regimen?"

"Nope." Keith busied himself with the goggles while he replied. "I'm thinking . . . that is, Avis and I are thinking . . . of going for the MasterSwim competition in August."

There was a moment of complete silence. "The MasterSwim? Avis in the MasterSwim?" Tom looked from one to the other in disbelief. "Good Lord, whatever for?"

Avis answered before Keith could. "Because it's there," she said simply, and the grateful smile Keith gave her made the statement seem less absurd.

Tom leaned forward and faced Avis, ignoring Keith. "You sure about this, girl?" he asked her. "That's a lot of work for someone with hardly any swimming experience. A lot of work."

"I can swim," Avis said, listening to the growing confidence in her voice. "You've always said I swim like a natural, Tom, haven't you? And I've got the essentials because of my dance training. I've been in training for years, when you think of it." She looked at Keith, who was standing behind Tom and watching her. "Besides, you said I've got the best coach I could possibly have."

Tom turned around to face Keith. "I didn't quite say that," he replied slowly. "I said Keith is the best there is. He's the best distance swimmer there is, that's for sure. And if anyone can work out a therapy program to cure what ails you, it'll be Keith Harding. But as far as being a coach . . ." He was talking to Keith and not to her. "It takes judgment to be a coach. Judgment, not recklessness, not daring. Are you sure you know what you're doing here, Keith?"

Keith nodded slowly, but deliberately. "She can do

it, Tom," he said to the older man. "She can do it if she sets her mind to it. You know she can."

"More important," said Avis to them both, *"I* know I can." They both turned to look at her as if they had forgotten her presence. "At least," she added sheepishly, "I know I have to try."

Both men were looking at her closely, each for their own reason. Avis hardly saw them, however; she was reflecting on the fact that the decision, almost unbeknownst to her, had been made. It had been made because there was no other choice. She had to try or risk falling permanently into that dangerous numbness she had been experiencing ever since her accident. She felt a little bit of fear, true, but mostly she felt alive. She needed the MasterSwim, or at least the idea of the MasterSwim, to keep herself alive until she could decide on the course of the rest of her life.

She smiled over Tom's head at Keith. "I'm ready whenever you are, coach," she said lightly. All three of them relaxed at the same moment, and Avis realized that Keith had actually been afraid she would back out.

Tom shook his head, but he too wore an indulgent grin. "OK," he said, walking back to his desk and popping an unlit cigar between his teeth. "If you two kids want to go ahead and swim upstream, that's your prerogative." He looked from Keith to Avis and, for the first time, seemed to realize that there was something new about their relationship. His grin spread at this revelation until it seemed he could no longer hold the cigar between his lips. "Why not?" he inquired jovially, looking extremely pleased with himself. "Anything you kids do is fine with me . . . just fine with me." Then he sat down, chuckling loudly at his good sense in having brought Avis and Keith together.

"I think we'd better get out of here and in the water," Keith said, lifting Avis off the desk and slipping one arm under her shoulder to support her as she walked to the pool's edge. "He looks like he's prepared to give the marriage vows at any minute."

Avis laughed. It was absurd to think of her and Keith as a couple. After all, they were together because they had a job to do. Last night had been . . . well, she had needed someone last night and Keith had been there. It had all been very nice, but he was her coach. And Avis had learned that mixing business and pleasure did not always work.

But Keith was all business. He did not swim with her that day, or the few days after that. Instead, he stood for hours in waist-deep water, catching her at the end of every lap and explaining to her what she had done right or wrong. Initially, she was just swimming to loosen up, and he was full of encouragement, stopping her only to give her tips on how to kick with the least amount of pressure on her foot. He did not want her to use the foot while the series of cortisone injections was on, since he feared that she might injure her metatarsal further without knowing it.

By the time the series of treatments was over and the foot had returned more or less to normal size, Keith began to find more wrong than right. He started to work intensively on her stroke, and to stop her at the end of every lap with some correction or other. It was clear that he was working on creating a Master-Swimmer and not on rehabilitating an injured dancer.

Avis could not have told when the changeover came for sure. At first she resented his constant badgering, his insistence that she stop after every lap and analyze the structure of her stroke. It was clear that she still felt herself an injured dancer, while he had begun to think of her in terms of the swimmer-in-training. He was patient, but persistent, and Avis, who had been enjoying the soothing rhythm of her daily swim, began to resent his constant interruptions.

But by the end of the next week, she realized that she was adjusting herself to Keith's perception of her. His attention was so constant and so complete that she could not fail to absorb his assessment of her situation. She had not yet seriously thought of herself as a swimmer in the technical sense, she had agreed with Keith because it had felt right to agree. But now she assumed his image of her as her own self-perception, and she paid close attention when he pointed out a minute adjustment in her stroke or in her breathing technique.

In all this time, Keith had not once made an attempt to get close to her physically or emotionally. He was pleasant, and intimate as a close friend, and he had his hands on her for hours at a time. But it was not the kind of intimacy they had shared on the night of her accident. He massaged her body from head to toe without ever once arousing the kind of immediate response he had elicited so easily that night. He held her in the water, his hands covering her small breasts, but her nipples did not respond and her heartbeat remained the same. He rubbed her with oil when the constant immersion in chlorine water made her skin itch, but there was no passion in his huge hands as they rolled up and down her bare flanks. He held her head between his hands as he showed her how to breathe properly, but he never brought her face to his lips or looked into her eyes as if he wanted to make love to her.

Avis wasn't sure how she felt about this. On the one hand, she told herself she should be relieved. After all, she was as serious about her training as he was. And she had certainly not looked for further emotional attachments after the one night. But at the end of the day, when he smiled and said good-bye, then walked off to some unknown destination of his own without so much as a backward glance, Avis could not help feeling bereft. Her nights were long and lonely, and she missed his hands and lips then, although she would never have admitted it, even to her journal.

It also made her think obsessively about him when he was not with her. She had yet to solve the mystery of Keith's past life, and Tom Miller was no help at all, despite a concerted effort on Avis's part to get him to talk. All he would say was what she already knew: that Keith had been an Olympic competitor, and that he had gone off—because of some sudden illness or injury, she supposed—to Oxford, where he had studied something for two years. She had no idea what he had done there, or what he had done when he returned to the States.

"He'll tell you," Tom said wisely, keeping his eyes on his cigar or the pool. "In his own good time, he'll tell you."

"But why doesn't he just tell me now?" Avis persisted, watching Keith working with a man in the shallow end. "Why is it supposed to be such a big mystery?"

Tom turned to her. "Keith's got his own way of working, Avis, in case you hadn't noticed. He lives life by his own timetable. You should know that from training with him. You either go by his schedule or you go alone." His gaze softened as he saw Avis's confusion. "He's a good man. He's just driven. But I think you're driven too, aren't you?" He grinned widely at her, and Avis, much to her surprise, blushed. "You two go well together," Tom added, satisfied with this observation.

"Yes, we work well together." Avis put a definite emphasis on the slightly changed sentence, and Tom was smart enough not to pursue the issue. But Avis herself could not let it drop. Somehow, she had become very much involved with Keith Harding the swimmer, the coach, and the man. The question was, who was he, really? She knew him intimately, yet not at all.

Still, the issue did not come up when she was at the pool. There she had no time to think of anything but swimming; Keith's intensity did not permit it. She could think of nothing but water, and how to get through it in the most efficient way possible. Avis was used to training hard, it was second nature. But she had never worked with such concentration for so long. In the studio, she went from class to rehearsals for a number of pieces, and she was always working on something different. In the pool, it was only swimming that concerned her. She worked on one stroke for as long as she could endure it before she quit.

So far, Keith would not let her vary the routine, even though he promised that she would soon be adding weight training and other exercises to her regimen. Avis, who had been glad to stay away from the other areas of the Sportscape Club, began to look forward to the prospect of doing something—anything—as long as she could get out of the endless blue world in which she remained submerged for hours and hours every day.

The one good thing about her training, aside from the fact that she could feel her body getting stronger and stronger, was that she had no time or energy to think about the studio or Laurence Lessine. She was simply too busy to dwell on the bitter possibilities of her future as a dancer, or on the even more bitter possibility that Larry may have orchestrated her loss. When she arrived home at the end of the day, she was too exhausted, and too waterlogged, to think about anything but sleep.

Which was why she was so startled to look up one

afternoon and see, out of a hazy blur of chlorine, Cheryl Cattier standing at the edge of the pool.

"Can I . . . I'd like to talk to you, Avis . . . if I can."

Cheryl spoke in her usual hesitant, soft voice, but Avis heard the urgency in it. She looked at Keith, who was standing beside her in the water, and they exchanged perplexed glances. Keith looked concerned, as if he were afraid that Cheryl's presence might precipitate a crisis in Avis's concentration.

"Hang on." Avis swam to the side of the pool and climbed up the ladder. For some reason, Cheryl looked very small to her as she stood there in her jeans and T-shirt. Avis had not thought about how she felt regarding Cheryl, who had, after all, usurped Avis's role both as Odette and the lead in the Bird of Paradise solo. But now she saw that Cheryl was only a child, and she realized she felt sorry for her. After all, Cheryl was as much a pawn in the game Larry played as Avis herself was.

"What's the matter, Cheryl?" she asked gently, since it was clear that something was wrong.

"Nothing's the matter," Cheryl replied unconvincingly. "I just . . . stopped by to see how you were getting along." This was so obviously untrue that Avis let it pass. But Cheryl was looking at her with admiration on her face. "You look terrific," she said in some surprise. "I mean . . . you always looked terrific, but I didn't expect that you'd . . ."

Avis smiled. "You thought I'd fall apart from not dancing, didn't you?" She grinned. "So did I. But you know that swimming keeps you in good shape, if nothing else."

Cheryl shook her head. "I didn't get that much out of my work here. But, of course, that was only two weeks. Keith must have you on some training routine."

Avis looked over her shoulder at Keith, who was

trying very hard not to look like he was listening. "Some regimen," she said with a private little smile. "That he does." She waited for him to return the smile, but Keith busied himself with one of the pool filters and did not look up.

"Anyway," Cheryl began again, "I just wanted to stop by and see how you were doing."

Although she doubted that Cheryl had just stopped by to visit, Avis was touched, for she knew that Cheryl, although she would not say so, was embarrassed about having won Avis's roles by default. "I'm doing fine," she told her. It wasn't necessarily the truth, but despite Cheryl's kindness, she was not about to unburden herself to the younger woman, and she knew Cheryl wouldn't want her to in any case. "And now, come sit down and tell me what's going on at National—I feel like I haven't been there for years." It was true that Avis felt very far away from the place and the people who had made up her life for so many years. The fact that Cheryl was the first person to visit her since the accident didn't help her sense of isolation, either.

They sat down at Tom's vacant desk, and Keith, who had stopped working on the pool filter, stretched out and began to do slow, leisurely laps across the pool. Avis settled back in Tom's chair, her eyes on Keith instead of Cheryl.

"Things are pretty much the same," Cheryl was saying. "Everybody's trying to stay in shape for the fall season. We have eight weeks without a performance, and you know what that's like." She took a quick look at Keith in the pool before turning back to Avis. "Of course, those of us in Bird of Paradise are slaving away as usual." Cheryl laughed in a high, girlish giggle. "You know what Larry's like—a positive slave driver when it comes to—" She broke off and put her hand to her mouth. "Oh, I'm sorry, I didn't mean . . ."

Avis, who had not been offended by Cheryl's chatter, pursed her lips. "Don't worry, Cheryl. I won't burst into tears or anything." She smiled dryly. "I've made my peace with Fate, believe me."

And curiously enough, Avis found that it was true. Somehow, by avoiding all thought of the solo, the events of that Friday night had lost their sting. She still could not bear to think of the future, but the past no longer held such bitterness for her. Avis reached out and squeezed Cheryl's shoulder encouragingly. "Well, come on, tell me more!" Talking about the Bird of Paradise solo would only be painful for both of them.

Cheryl gulped and forced an answering grin. "Well, you know Beth has left the company, don't you?"

This was real news. Beth had called Avis at home several times and Avis had left messages on Beth's phone, but she and Avis had not been able to connect. "Why did she leave? What happened?"

Cheryl shook her head. "I'm not sure. I think she was planning to leave anyway, and she mentioned something about getting married. Basically, I guess she felt she just wasn't getting any good roles."

This last statement was the only one to ring true to Avis; Beth would never have left before her planned retirement date unless she was pushed out. The fact that she had not gotten in touch with Avis to talk about it was further proof, regardless of how proudly she had walked out the door.

Avis felt a flash of new anger toward Laurence Lessine. The news reinforced her feeling that he would go to great lengths to ensure that everything at the National went his way. She thought about Beth with a stab of pity, but her thoughts were interrupted when she caught the drift of Cheryl's next statement.

". . . and that's where I thought you could be a big help to me, now that she's gone," Cheryl was saying.

"What?" Avis swung her head around in order to concentrate."

"I said, that was where I thought you could help me. With the solo, I mean. There's no one else around, now that Beth's gone, who has enough experience to tell me what Laurence wants. I really have to be sure I get it right." Cheryl lowered her long lashes shyly. "I know it might be hard for you, Avis, since you're no longer dancing with us."

Avis smiled tightly. "I'm not gone yet, Cheryl."

"Of course you're not! That's why I think it would be good for you too. You can keep your hand in things while you recuperate!" Cheryl's eyes shone. "It's so important to me, Avis, that I get this right for Laurence. You know how important it is."

She did indeed. She had been in exactly the same position as Cheryl once, long ago. And she understood the urgency in the younger woman's voice. But she doubted that she would have had the nerve to ask someone who was in her own position to do what Cheryl was asking her to do. Even at eighteen, Avis thought she would have understood that it was too much to ask.

But now the reason for Cheryl's visit had become clear. Of course it made sense, especially since they had worked together before. Cheryl must have simply assumed that they could continue their working relationship. Cheryl could not possibly guess how drastically things had changed since then. Still, the naiveté behind her request was appalling, Avis realized she was staring at Cheryl, who squirmed uncomfortably on the wooden folding chair.

"I don't expect you to answer me right away," Cheryl said. "I mean, I really just stopped by to say hello. But I thought, since you're not doing anything else, that you might be able to help me out."

"I'm sorry." The voice came from close by, but it was Keith's, not Avis's, and both women jumped at the sound. Keith was leaning up against the ledge of the pool, his burly arms crossed under his chin. His expression was amiable, but unmistakably authoritative. "I'm afraid Avis has a lot to do; otherwise, she might be able to take you up on your request. You see, she's about to enter a swim competition. A very important one, and she needs to concentrate on herself right now."

Cheryl's eyes widened. "A swim competition?" She looked from Keith to Avis. "But why?" she asked simply.

It was a good question, but before Avis could make an attempt to answer it, Keith jumped in again. "Because she's good. Very good, in fact, and I can't pass up this opportunity to let her show everybody what she can do. Keith looked over at Avis as if she were a particularly desirable cut of meat, and now it was Avis's turn to squirm uneasily. "I just can't let you have her until after August, Cheryl. I'm sorry."

"August! But that will be too late!"

Avis was surprised by the urgency in Cheryl's lament. "Too late for what? The Bird of Paradise isn't slated to go on the program until late September. If I were to work with you, we'd have plenty of time. What's the rush?" Avis was careful not to commit herself to saying she would help Cheryl. It was still inconceivable to her that she could bear to stand there in a studio at the National and teach her own role to someone else.

"I know, but . . ." Cheryl looked from Avis's perplexed expression to Keith's serene one, and bit her lower lip. "Oh, never mind," she pouted. "I knew it would be too much to ask." Her pretty features were unable to disguise her discontent. "Never mind, Avis. I can see you have better things to think about than dance. Take care of yourself." She threw one last, dark look at Keith and flounced out of the room without another word.

When she had gone, Avis and Keith exchanged stares. "What on earth was that all about?" Avis mused. "I mean, coming in here to visit and then hitting me with a request that I tutor her in my role! And then leaving in a huff because I said I couldn't do it right away!"

"You didn't say it—I did."

He was right. Avis wondered why he had decided to jump into the conversation. She should have resented it, but since he had made it possible for her to refuse the request, she decided to let it go. After all, she would have plenty of time to make her own decision on that sort of thing later. Besides, he wasn't really controlling her life, as Larry had done, he was merely making it easier for her to do what she wanted.

Still, it was odd that he had been so adamant. It was almost as if he wanted Cheryl to believe what Avis herself had not yet fully accepted. She was going to be a swimmer, if not for the rest of her life, then at least for the next few months. Perhaps, if that fantasy became reality in other people's eyes, it would become fact for Avis as well.

"That's true—you spoke for me, didn't you." Avis pursed her lips, but she could not bring herself to thank him for getting her out of an awkward situation. "What made you think I wasn't going to help her, though?"

"I didn't say you weren't—I said you couldn't." Keith hauled himself out of the pool, glistening with water. "Besides, I don't think it's such a good idea for you to be around the studio for a while."

Avis's temper flared. "Don't you think that's for me to decide?"

Keith shrugged. "I thought you had decided. After

all, if you suspect Larry Lessine of foul play where you're concerned, I would think you would want to stay away."

He was standing over her now, and Avis's eyes narrowed as she looked up at him. "I thought you didn't believe me about Larry," she challenged.

He shrugged again and reached behind Avis to pull a towel from the back of the chair. "Stranger things have happened, I'm sure. Not that it matters, now. What's done is done."

"Now what's that supposed to mean?" she demanded. Her temper was on a short fuse these days.

"Nothing. I just thought we agreed to forget about that place while you're working here, didn't we?"

"Hmmph!" Avis glared at him. "That's easy for you to say. You don't seem to understand. That's like saying . . . like saying that you should forget all about swimming."

Keith narrowed his eyes. "It's been done," he murmured. "Believe me, it's been done."

His obtuse answer only fueled Avis's irritation. "Oh, so big deal! The great Keith Harding can do whatever he sets his mind to do! Well, Avis Considine can't! And I resent your implication that my dance career is over and done with, just like . . ."

She broke off, appalled. She had meant to say, just like Keith's swimming career. But that was pure speculation, and unjust on her part. Keith would have been within his rights to be very angry at her outburst; surely she had seen him blow up for less.

But he surprised her once again. He came around to her side of the desk and sat beside her. "Avis, he said gently as she forced herself to look at his face and not his rippled torso, "that's beside the point. Look. Would you have agreed to help Cheryl if I hadn't spoken up? The truth now, would you?"

Avis immediately felt remorseful for having accused him of sabotaging her plans. He only wanted to help, after all. She tried to concentrate on the glistening water in his russet beard. "Of course I would. I mean . . . I should have helped her, shouldn't I? After all, it isn't her fault that I . . ." Avis stopped again, compelled into a chagrined silence by Keith's slowly shaking head. "You're right," she said after a pause. "Who am I kidding? If I had agreed to help Cheryl, it would only be because I felt too guilty to say no. As a matter of fact, I don't think I could stand being with her in the studio—not for a while, anyway." Her face relaxed into a grin. "Thanks for bailing me out," she said with relief.

Keith rubbed his hands together briskly, obviously satisfied with the way the dialogue had concluded. "Any time, kid," he said with mock gruffness. Then, more seriously he added, "I'm glad I guessed right about you."

"You guessed right." Avis wished she had been able to guess right about him more often. Too many times she underestimated him. It was a holdover from thinking he was like Larry, when actually he was the farthest thing in the world from that. Keith could be hard on her, but he really had her best interests at heart. She squinted up at his silhouette against the huge windows. He guessed right about her a lot, she reflected. It was uncanny, and not a little unsettling.

"How did you guess?" she inquired, curious.

He grinned and chucked her lightly under the chin, the first personal gesture he had made toward her in days. "The coach is always right, even when he's wrong. It's a cardinal rule in sports."

Avis did not laugh. "It's a cardinal rule in dance, too," she said glumly, thinking of Larry. "The director is always right."

"Even when he's wrong. Don't ever forget that part, Avis. "Keith stood up, rolling his towel into a tight ball. "But there's a difference between a coach and a choreographer."

"What's that?"

"The dancer takes the choreography out on stage with her; the choreographer is out there, too. But the athlete is all alone when she competes, all alone with the effort and the glory." The towel was now a little ball between his massive fists.

"She doesn't get to share the pain of failure, either, though, does she?" Avis asked. The analogy was making a lot of sense. It made her think about swimming in a whole new way.

"That's true," Keith agreed. "But there's another difference." He grinned slyly. "There's no way anyone can pull the floor out from under you when you're in the pool. So let's get to it, kid. You're safe in the water—safer than anywhere else on earth."

He threw the balled towel at her suddenly, and Avis reflexively caught it between her hands.

"Not bad," said Keith. "For a dancer."

Avis threw the towel back. "Not bad for a swimmer, either, I'd say." Then she jumped into the water before he could grab her.

Chapter Nine

M onday, June 16

I was doing my Nautilus circuit today and watching Keith work with two newcomers to the Sportscape Club. It's amazing to watch him handle people—he never reacts the way they expect him to. The man he was helping expected him to talk basketball, and made rude remarks about some women who were lifting free weights nearby. Keith acted like a college professor might with a randy freshman—superior and disapproving. With the woman, who was cute and giggly, he was cool and detached, like a medical technician.

I wonder where he gets all these characters, and how he can pick exactly the right one to neutralize the games people play with him? I wonder what his connection is to Tom Miller and the Sportscape Club, why he feels responsible for the walk-in customers when he's supposed to be concentrating on me?

I wonder what he feels about me? More to the point, what do I feel about him? My emotions are so tangled up right now, but they all seem to be tangled up in Keith. I shouldn't be letting this happen to me, not now, not when I have so much work to do.

But I don't seem to have much choice.

The Nautilus circuit was a whole new experience for Avis. She had never had to concentrate on her upper-body strength before. Her arms, as Laurence had so often told her, were to be like willow branches, soft and long and supple.

Keith had a different idea.

"I want you to be able to press fifty pounds," he said matter-of-factly to her when they had first begun to work with the weight machines.

"Fifty pounds? That's almost half my body weight!" Avis was appalled at the mere thought of pulling on the heavy metal plates which were attached to pulleys to create the greatest muscle resistance.

"Almost half? What do you weigh?" Keith looked down at her body, clad in thin cotton shorts and a sleeveless T-shirt, as if he was calculating her poundage to the ounce.

"A hundred and two," she told him. "Not bad for five foot four."

Keith let his lips curve into a tiny smile. "Make that fifty-four pounds you've got to press," he said, turning to readjust the weight plates. He was clearly not impressed with the figures she had given him. "Of course," he added, still busy with the machine, "when we get you up to racing weight, you'll be able to press more."

Avis swallowed. "And what, may I ask, is racing weight supposed to be?"

He turned around slightly, but she could not see the gleam of humor in his eyes as he spoke. "Oh, for you?" His gaze traveled appraisingly up and down her body.

Every time he did that, it made Avis wince. His appraisals were always so intimate, they were almost an invasion. Yet he gave no sign of any interest other than a purely functional one. It had been several weeks since they had made love on that single, fateful night, and sometimes Avis wondered whether Keith even remembered it. Perhaps it hadn't happened at all.

"For your build, I would say you'll have to be at least one hundred and ten, maybe a hundred and fifteen."

"No!" She shrieked so loud that everybody in the Nautilus room heard her. "Keith," she hissed, lowering her voice after an embarrassed look around the room. "There is no way I am going to pack on an extra ten pounds. Are you crazy?"

He shook his head. "I'm not sure," he replied as if he had given the question some serious thought. Then his voice got firm. "But the question of my sanity has nothing to do with the fact that you, Avis Considine, are going to weigh a good ten pounds more than you do now, if I have to force-feed you peanut butter malteds every day." His severe features broke into an impish grin. "Actually, that sounds like fun." He advanced on her as if he had every intention of doing exactly that.

"Keith . . ." She backed nervously away. "I eat a lot of food as it is. How do you expect me to put on weight when you work me like a slave all day long?"

"You will put it on when *I* start feeding you. And don't look so sick about it. You'll lose it all in the water, believe me."

His reassurance was only marginally successful. Avis nodded her agreement, mostly to get him off her back on the subject. But she privately swore that she would never let him achieve his goal.

During the morning they swam. In the afternoon they worked with the weights. Avis soon understood the efficiency of the Nautilus machines. She wasn't getting bulky muscles, but she could feel herself getting stronger. She knew enough about bodies to be able to appreciate the fact that strength and stamina could not do her any harm, psychologically as well as physically.

Up until that point, Avis had not really thought about the actual race she was going to enter. It was still just an amorphous event that would occur sometime in the future. It was something that Keith had dreamed up, and she was going along with it only because she had nothing better to do with her time. She had to admit that the physical activity was helping her injury heal quickly, and she had never been in better shape, despite the fact that she was not dancing. But even more important, she was able to immerse herself so completely in the training that she could virtually forget about her troubles with the National. She took her wait-and-see attitude very seriously and, even at night, when she was alone and most prone to disturbing thoughts, she forced herself to think about swimming.

She often thought about Keith. He had let little tidbits of information about himself slip out in their weeks of constant companionship, but the information had only served to whet Avis's appetite. Keith had been on the Olympic squad as a 200-meter freestyler and Tom had coached the relay team. It had been a sudden and unexpected shoulder injury that had made Keith decide to leave competitive athletics for good, even though he could have rehabilitated himself and gone back into competition. He had gone to Oxford because they agreed to honor an old scholarship that Keith had not taken advantage of when he had begun his swimming career right after college.

Keith's major area of study had been music, eighteenth-century music. He knew much about Mozart and Beethoven, but he seemed to be uncomfortable talking about it, and always managed to steer the subject back to swimming.

It was such an unlikely combination—the athlete and the music scholar. But Avis, who had thought from the start that Keith Harding was an unlikely swimming coach, was not surprised. She was only eager to know more. To her disappointment, as the days grew longer and summer began in the city, Keith began to get increasingly single-minded: The only important thing, he told her, was to swim.

In late June, they drove south to Cape May, New Jersey. They sped down the interstate through the verdant Jersey countryside to where the MasterSwim Five-Mile Freshwater Competition was going to take place.

Avis stared out the window, not paying close attention to Keith's description of the swimming facilities. "Is the pool there especially good for distance swimming, or what?"

She sensed rather than saw Keith turn to stare at her. "Pool? What pool?" he asked incredulously.

She turned to face him. "What do you mean, what pool?" she countered.

He pulled his eight-year-old BMW over from the passing lane to the slow lane, his mouth set in a firm line above his cropped beard. "Avis, you didn't really think you were going to swim five miles in a pool, did you? Pools are not fresh water, and that's what the name of the race is—the MasterSwim Five-Mile Freshwater Competition. Remember?"

She stared at him as if she had never heard the words before, and, in fact, it was the first time their meaning had really sunk in. "Do you mean," she inquired slowly, "that I'm going to be swimming in . . . real water? Like the ocean?"

Keith managed to hide a shiver of amusement that threatened his composure. "Avis, the Atlantic is not fresh water either. You'll be swimming in a river. A lake, really, but it's so long and narrow that they call it the Housefellow River Lake." He turned his attention back to the road, and the sporty little gray sedan picked up speed. "You'll like it. It's nice and clean, and not as cold as the Hudson is this time of year."

"Keith Harding." Avis faced him determinedly, her lips set in a firm line. "I have no intention of swimming the Hudson, or the Atlantic, or the Longfellow—"

"Housefellow. Named after Augustus Housefellow. A riverboat man." The amusement was beginning to show around the corners of his mouth and even more in his eyes, but Avis was too irate to notice it.

"I don't care what his damn name is. I'm not going to swim in his damn river!" She was looking at him as if he were a complete stranger. He was insane if he thought she was going to swim out in the open air—in a river, no less. "What about currents? What about undertow? What about fish?"

Keith could contain his mirth no longer. He broke out into huge gusts of laughter that were so infectious Avis had a hard time keeping a stern expression. It got even harder when he reached out one long arm and circled it around Avis's shoulder, pressing affectionately against her neck. "Oh, you are too much!" he declared when he had recovered. "You are really, really too much. Did you really think you would be swimming for five miles in a pool? Do you know how many laps that is? You'd get seasick from all the turns before you got worn out from the swimming! A pool!"

She tried to keep a firm grip on her indignation. "Well," she said, "you might have told me. You might have given me a little warning. I don't know the first thing about this competition."

He shook his head, his eyes still full of laughter. "Oh, I've told you before, all right. You just haven't been listening. Admit it, Avis. You haven't really given this race a moment's thought. It hasn't been real to you until now, has it?"

"It sure hasn't. And now that it is, I'm not at all sure I like what I hear." She sat far away from him in the car with her arms firmly folded across her chest, trying not to give in to the gentle caress of his hands on the nape of her neck.

They had reached the exit, and Keith pulled the car onto a small country road that wound through farmland on one side and woods on the other. "OK," he said patiently. "Listen up, because I'm only going to say this once more. The MasterSwim program is a nationwide network of amateur swimmers who swim regularly for the love of the sport. They sometimes sponsor competitions among themselves, although their rules insist that any qualifying swimmer can compete. This particular competition has been going on annually for the last eight years. It's a mixed race for men and women, a freestyle distance competition held in an ideal freshwater location. The Housefellow River Lake is eight miles long, but the five middle miles are perfect for freshwater swimming. As I said—nice sandy bottom, clean water, no sludge or sewage problems, and the water stays a nice even seventy-eight degrees from mid-July to mid-August." He gave her a quick look. "The wildlife is minimal. They haven't lost a swimmer yet to killer sharks."

"Very funny." Avis was lost in the view that filled her window, so her attempt at a sullen reply was weakened when she added. "Oh, look! Water!"

"That's the ocean." His eyes sparkled with mischief. "Want to stop for a few quick practice miles?"

This time she shot him a swift, withering look, and he

raised his hand to ward off her retort. She was glad he put it back on her shoulder when he was done. "We'll be at the lake in a few minutes," he told her. "Wait until you see that. You can see the ocean from the road on one side, and the riverbank on the other. It's a beautiful place, Avis. You'll like it."

Their eyes met, and she saw the question in them. Was she willing to swim or not? Now was the time to say no. If she had not realized the difficulty of this competition, she did now, and she had to admit that the thought of swimming for three hours in a lake frightened her to death. But Avis had committed herself to the race, whether consciously or by default, and she was not the type to let such commitments go lightly by the wayside. She was also not a quitter.

The Swim represented a challenge. All her life Avis had worked toward a specific goal, mastering a technical skill, getting into a company, perfecting a role for a performance. Her life was a series of plateaus, each one worthy of the struggle.

Without dancing, she realized that she had very little else that mattered in her life. She had her family, whom she saw intermittently since they were spread out all over the country. She had her friends, most of whom were dancers and could no more conceive of a life outside the company than she could have a few months ago. And she had swimming, which had started out as a way to return to dancing, and seemed to have become, through no effort of hers, an end in itself. She enjoyed the sport, and threw herself into the training with the total concentration that was the only way she knew how to work. But now it had become something else—the first challenge in her memory that she was not sure she could meet.

There was one other thing, though. She also had Keith Harding, if not as a lover, than as a companion in a singularly intimate and complex relationship. He was her coach, her mentor. He had pulled her away from a frightening situation and a depression she could not bear to contemplate. He was confident that she could swim fast and far enough to enter the MasterSwim competition as a serious contender. He had never said he was sure she could win, but she wasn't looking for that. As a dancer, she had not wanted the laurels, only to dance as perfectly as she could. It would be the same if she were a swimmer.

If she were a swimmer. The mere idea was enough to make Avis want to laugh out loud. Avis Considine, a distance swimmer? It was ridiculous!

The MasterSwim Five-Mile Freshwater Competition might not be as big a dream as dancing Odette in *Swan Lake*, but barring any *Swan Lake*s on her horizon, it would have to do.

Besides, she did have Keith. She had his faith, his confidence, his friendship. And she had once had his body, which was nice to think about too.

She turned and smiled at him, her small, expressive face lit with anticipation. "Well," she said, "let's get on with it. Take me to your water."

Swimmers, Avis soon found out, were a lot like dancers. They all practiced their sport with single-minded concentration, watched each other with ferocious interest, and when they were not in the water, thought of nothing but swimming.

The swimmers in this group were not professional swimmers. They were amateurs—seasoned amateurs, unlike Avis, but amateurs all the same. They did not make their living by their bodies. They did other things besides swim, although, to listen to them as they gathered at the Housefellow River Lake that summer afternoon, it would have been hard to guess what.

There was a housewife and mother of two, a doctor, a lawyer, and the owner of a hardware store. There were a few collegiate types, and some people who looked like they might have been professional athletes at one time or another. But, for the most part, they looked like regular people. It had been a long time since Avis had been in the company of so many nondancers, and she found the absence of talk about turnout, touring, and toe shoes curiously refreshing.

It was also refreshing not to be looked on as an oddity. These people took their training quite seriously, as Avis could tell as soon as the swimmers began warming up prior to going in for a trial swim. No one seemed to think it worthy of comment when Avis, after stripping down to the new thin lycra Speedo tank suit Keith had given her, began to do her incredible stretches on the grassy banks. Avis waited for someone to gasp at her 180-degree extension, but then she noticed a few other women who came pretty close to it themselves, and she decided that she could do her warm-up routine in peace.

The MasterSwim officials were there, not to time the swimmers, for this was not a compulsory trial swim, but to answer any questions. Avis felt their presence lent a reassuring air of authority to the event, especially since very few of the swimmers had coaches with them.

In all, it resembled more of a friendly company outing than a serious competition. Everyone seemed to know one another, and asked after families and friends as they might at a reunion.

Keith was a particular favorite. It appeared that he had not been "on the circuit" for quite a while, and there were many people who hadn't seen him for years.

"Did Keith used to compete in the MasterSwim races?" Avis asked a woman who apparently had been around the swimming scene for a long time.

"Keith Harding? God, no. He was always in another league altogether—he was Olympic material. None of us here are that good." The woman looked up from where she sat on the ground, stretching her hamstrings, to where Keith stood, surrounded by well-wishers. "But he used to come and judge MasterSwim races, and most all of the people on the swim circuit know each other anyway." She squinted and grinned. "He sure looks good, though. All those years away from the competition don't look like they've hurt a bit." Her gaze turned to Avis. "You a particular friend of his?" she inquired.

Avis thought about this for a moment. She thought she knew what the woman meant by "particular," but she had no intention of revealing any personal information to a stranger. "He's my coach," she said.

"Your coach?" The woman pursed her lips in surprise. "That's a new one for Keith. Where'd you get hooked up with him?"

"At the Sportscape Club. He's working there with Tom Miller."

"Hmmm." The woman looked at Avis with new interest. "He doing a lot of coaching there?"

"Not much. Just me, as a matter of fact." Avis couldn't keep the edge of pride out of her voice as she said it.

"Well, well, well. You must be quite a little swimmer!" The woman appraised Avis's body carefully. "He must have some big plans in store for you, then. The MasterSwim is just the beginning for someone like Keith Harding. He believes in going all the way to the top or not at all."

Avis would have loved to have gotten an explanation for this intriguing statement, but she was out of time. The officials gathered the swimmers together and explained that they would only be swimming one mile, and that only those who could not complete the mile would be disqualified from the actual five-mile race.

Avis was scared, even though she had swum a mile more than once in the pool. Something about the open space of the lake made her nervous. The boundaries weren't clear, and she didn't like the slight ripple that floated across the silver-blue surface. But Keith reassured her and, watching the eager faces of the other swimmers, she could not help but feel the excitement overcome the nervousness. She had not been on stage in front of thousands of people for years without learning how to get herself "up" for a performance.

As it turned out, the only shock was the first chill of the water as she jumped in to begin her swim. One mile went by very quickly, and Keith, who was timing her from the shore, was surprised at her speed.

"Thirty-one minutes eighteen seconds. Not bad," he said as he pulled her out of the water. About half the other swimmers had finished before her, but she was not concerned about that. The feeling of swimming in a group, of cutting through the water in clean, steady strokes, the rhythm of moving out in one direction seemingly without end, unhampered by the hard edge of a pool, was exhilarating. Avis knew then, for the first time since she had begun to swim, that she could swim very far.

"How do you feel?" Keith asked, kneeling down to towel her legs dry. She was shivering, but she didn't realize it, and she gave him a grin through chattering teeth.

"Starved," she said. "I could down ten peanut-butter malteds."

He laughed loud enough that several people nearby turned to stare, and he wrapped his arms around her hips, squeezing hard enough so that she was lifted clear off the ground. "Terrific!" He chuckled. "Ten p.b. malteds, coming up."

Instead they had steak at a little roadside inn halfway between Cape May and the city. Avis had changed into white slacks and an oversized striped shirt while hunkering down in the back of Keith's car as he sped along the highway. She also managed to put on a little makeup by resting her arm against the back of the seat and relying on years of practice at applying stage makeup. By the time they pulled into the restaurant, she was looking less like a tired swimmer and more like a good-looking woman out on a date with a good-looking man.

The efforts did not seem to be wasted on Keith. He was clearly delighted with her performance, but just as clearly delighted with her appearance. All through dinner he kept leaning over and looking into her eyes, as if he had never seen their deep shiny color before. Once again, Avis wondered if he wanted to repeat their night of lovemaking.

But it didn't matter. She had a wonderful time with him, and they never once referred to either her dancing or her swimming career. Instead they laughed and talked about nothing in particular, and when they talked about anyone, it was Keith.

"Why eighteenth-century music?" she asked him at one point, letting him add extra sour cream on her baked potato.

"Why not?" He held out the spoon, still covered with remains of sour cream and chives. "Here. Lick this."

"Keith. . . ."

"Lick it!" he said sternly, and Avis, giggling, complied. "I guess," he went on, returning to her original question, "people think it's unusual for an athlete—

particularly a swimmer—to have developed such a love for music. Swimming really is a silent and lonely sport. When I was younger, the two things were separate in my mind. But when I began swimming at the Olympic level, I realized I needed something to get me through the water. I needed a rhythm, and naturally I thought of music, which I had been listening to all my life. My mother was a concert pianist, you see, and we always had music in the house."

"That's why you knew so much about *Swan Lake*. That music is considered mandatory in any pianist's repertoire."

Keith nodded but offered no more information about his early life. "I began to memorize scores and sing them to myself underwater—certain kinds of music for certain kinds of swimming." He smiled. "Mozart is good for the 200-meter, but you can't beat Beethoven for the 400-meter freestyle."

Avis smiled at this novel application of the classics. "What about distance swimming?" she asked. "What's good for that?"

Keith raised his hand for the waiter. "Two desserts," he told her. "That's what's good for distance swimming." He grinned disarmingly, then suddenly got serious. "That, and the overwhelming desire to go the distance."

"Do you think I have the desire to go the distance?" Avis pointed to a sundae on the dessert menu without even looking at it. She was too involved in her discussion with Keith, and had no intention of finishing off a huge steak dinner with a big ice-cream dessert.

He stopped eating. "Avis, when you first came into the club, that was about all you had going for you. But that was enough for me. Watching you work to recuperate, I remembered what it was like to be on top and to have to struggle to stay there. You have an attitude of commitment in everything you do. It's still the most important thing you have going for you." He grinned. "Besides a great body and arms that are too long for a dancer—but great for swimming."

But Avis was suddenly in no mood for levity. It was very important to her that she understood why Keith had chosen her to compete in the MasterSwim competition, and what else he had in her mind for the future. She felt as if she were seeing a new aspect of her life unfold before her like an unfamiliar photograph of herself. Her eyes glowed like dark opals as she stared at Keith, trying to fathom his vision of her. "But is it enough? I want to know, Keith, is it enough to have that commitment?"

He understood her intensity, and became serious at once. This was the first evidence Keith had heard of Avis's competitive desire to swim, but he accepted it without question. "It is if you have the physical ability and the proper training." He paused and looked into his brandy snifter reflectively for a moment. "Was it enough for you as a dancer?" he asked.

Avis did not even have to consider this question. "When I was dancing," she said softly, "I felt that I was alive only when I danced. When I had to stop, it took me a while to realize that life might go on. But then, today, out there in the water . . ." She paused, surprised by what she was thinking. "Today in the water I felt sort of the way I used to feel when I learned a good role. I felt like, if I really wanted to do it, I mean really, really set my mind to the problem, then I could do whatever I wanted." She looked up, her eyes wide. "That's the way I felt about dancing."

Keith nodded. "I know exactly how you feel. I felt the same way about swimming, and then, when I started to study music history, about that. I felt, if I really put my mind to it, there was nothing I couldn't do."

"And now?" Avis felt as if the entire restaurant was hushed, listening to their conversation. "What are you doing now, Keith? What have you set your mind to now?"

A dark shadow passed over his sea-green eyes, like a sudden squall on a sunny day. He bent his head to the snifter again. "It's different now," he said quietly.

"Why? What's different?" If it was different for Keith now, what would it be like for Avis in ten years? "What's different now?" she asked again.

"Now," Keith said, "I have someone else to live for. So eat that sundae before I make you drink it."

On the way home, they were very quiet. Avis was musing on Keith's last words, and Keith was fiddling around on the radio until he found some Bach partitas, which seemed to suit his mood. He turned the radio up quite loud, and the elegant, mannered strains filled the car, floating out into the warm summer night through the open windows.

What had he meant, that he had someone else to live for? Her, obviously, but Avis wasn't sure whether she was reassured or frightened by the statement. She had been so passive about her life for the past few weeks, and suddenly she realized that Keith had basically taken it over. That was all right if he had only the MasterSwim competition and Avis's recuperation in mind, but what if he meant more than that? She remembered the woman at Cape May who had looked at her with a combination of envy and pity when she had said Keith was her coach. What future did he have in mind for them? Was this to be a replay of her relationship with Laurence?

It was an unsettling thought, but somehow, once they left the restaurant, it became less and less absorbing. The mood in the restaurant had been taut with hidden and unstated meanings. But now, with the resonance of Bach playing on the stereo and Keith's serene profile against the night sky, she began to relax. He had probably not meant anything sinister, she reassured herself. After all, he had been nothing but a help to her, and if she discovered a new aspect to her life through swimming, then so much the better. Even if she went back to dancing, she need never again feel that she was only alive when she danced. There were other things to live for. Swimming, good food, good music, and good friends.

The atmosphere in the car was warm and intimate, and at first Avis was not aware that it had become charged with anything other than camaraderie and the glow of a successful day. As they pulled into the city through the Lincoln Tunnel, she became aware of a new kind of tension in the car. Keith's arm, slung comfortably over the back of her seat, had moved forward, so that his fingers were able to filter idly through the thick dark hair at the nape of her neck. Suddenly, without warning, he undid the barrette that held her hair in a chignon at the back of her head and, as his hands plowed through the falling sheaf of dark brown strands, she heard him utter a shuddering sigh.

This was not a playful teasing motion on the back of her neck, nor was it the expert exploratory hands of the masseur. His fingers sent electric impulses of arousal up Avis's skull and down her spine. She felt herself leaning back into the palm of his hand, and had to force herself not to turn to him and destroy the magic of their tacit dance of arousal.

Instead she sat very still until, as they pulled up onto a quiet street outside Avis's apartment, Keith stopped the engine of the car. The sudden stillness was arresting, and for the moment neither of them moved. But Keith's fingers still made their magic way up and down her neck, and Avis could not resist a deep sigh.

Then Keith turned to her abruptly and gathered her against his chest with a deep, shuddering growl in the back of his throat. Avis struggled to free herself from the warmth of his cotton shirt and lifted her mouth up to be kissed. He looked down at her upturned chin and sighed.

"I shouldn't be doing this," he muttered, shaking his head. "This is all wrong for us. This isn't what I want for you."

"What do you want for me, Keith? And what about what *I* want?" Avis realized that, at the moment, she cared more about the second question than she did about the first. She also understood that she had been wanting this all along—to be back in Keith's arms and to have his broad, strong body covering hers.

"I thought I knew what you wanted," he said, covering her mouth with short, tiny kisses. "I thought I was taking care of business for you."

She shook her head, letting her loose hair flutter across his open throat. "You were wrong," she murmured against the beard on his neck. "I want this too."

He pulled one hand free and cupped her chin, nearly losing the delicate point of it in the depth of his palm. "You," he said, with a ragged little laugh. "You want it all, don't you? I can understand that. God, can I ever!" He bent to kiss her then, fierce and hungry, and his hand slipped inside the wide neckline of her shirt to caress her waiting breasts. She could feel his heartbeat accelerate, and then he pulled away.

"I have to take you upstairs now," he said gravely. "There's not enough room in this car to do what I want to do to you."

The frankness of his words and the fire in his eyes melted Avis's insides even more than the kiss and the caress. They slid out of the car, holding each other tightly around the waist, and made their way into her building.

It seemed an eternity before the rickety old elevator came to the ground floor, and even longer before it made its stately way up to Avis's apartment on the fourth. Finally they were outside her door, and exchanged one long, lingering kiss before Keith took the key from her hand and fumbled to put it in the lock.

He needn't have bothered. The door swung open of its own accord, and they were face to face with Laurence Lessine.

Chapter Ten

M idnight, June 18

I've wondered many times what it is that draws my life together with men like Larry and Keith. I know I was brought up, as a dancer, not to question the authority of the people who run my career, and therefore my life, but what is it about these two men that makes them take so much control? What do they share in common? Larry shaped and molded me as a dancer because it was important to his career as a choreographer. Keith is shaping me into a swimmer; is it important to his career as a coach? Larry was always able to convince me that what he did for me, he did for my own good, even when he left me. With Keith, nothing is that clear.

Have I gone out of the frying pan and into the fire? The only thing I am sure of about Larry is that he was—is—incapable of loyalty or love.

About Keith I am not so sure.

You're out late, aren't you?" Laurence folded his arms across his chest and leaned against the side of the door. His eyes took in everything: Avis's disheveled blouse, the flush on her face, and Keith's sudden suspicious look.

"What is he doing here?" Keith inquired tightly.

"I was about to ask him the same thing." Avis turned blazing eyes on Larry. She never remembered being so angry at anybody in her life. "What the hell is this all about?"

"I thought you might need some company," Larry said, moving aside with catlike agility to let them pass into the apartment. "It's been ages since we've seen you down at the studio, darling. We miss you." He glanced up at Keith with a faintly flattering stare. "I can see you haven't missed us, though."

Laurence had an uncanny way of disarming anger. He was so smooth, so controlled, that it seemed ungainly to throw a tantrum in his presence. "How did you get in?" Avis asked in a more precise voice. She did not dare to look at Keith, who was standing very still, filling the open doorway.

"Old Bill, down at the door. He remembers me well." Larry's dark eyebrows curved sardonically upward. "He doesn't forget me, Avis."

"Oh, Larry, cut it out." Avis was suddenly exhausted. "Tell me what you came for, and then please leave. Keith and I would like to be alone."

This was a tactical error, since it put Keith in the position of obvious lover rather than establishing his importance in Avis's life. She knew that Larry had picked up on the oversight. "I came to discuss the ballet with you, Avis," he said, oozing sincerity. "If it's not important to you, I can leave. You've got other business to attend to. But," he added as an afterthought, "I think it's pretty important to your career that we talk soon."

He made a gesture as if to leave, and Avis, without even thinking, said, "No!" He had been banking on her dance career to force her to respond. Avis bit her tongue. She hated herself for playing into Larry's charades, but she had no choice. She had not yet reached the point where she had any distance or objectivity about her dancing. If Larry wanted to talk about it, then she must comply.

For the first time, she looked at Keith, expecting to see him glowering at her from the door. But he did not look angry. Instead he was gazing pensively at Larry, as if trying to read a particularly difficult message. His gaze was so penetrating that even Laurence squirmed under it, and he shifted his gaze away from Keith's frank stare. This seemed to satisfy Keith, because he looked at Avis at last, still without any reproach in his expression.

"Right," he said briskly, and pulled away from the door.

"Keith!" Avis felt a moment's panic. She didn't want Keith to leave, not to leave her alone with Larry. She was not yet ready to face Larry alone. She went out in the hall after him. "Please don't go," she whispered, well aware of Larry's presence through the open door.

Keith turned and looked down at her with a patient smile. All traces of arousal seemed to have left him, while Avis's breathing had still not returned to normal. "Do you want him to go?"

Avis turned and looked back inside. She did not want Larry to stay, yet the thought of his leaving, possibly with an unmade offer for Avis to return to the fold, was something she was not prepared to risk. "He'll only be here a little while." She put both hands on the arms of his cotton sleeves. "Please stay," she begged.

He removed her hands gently and stepped into the open elevator, which seemed to have come in record time. "I'll be at home. I'm in the phone book if you need me." And he was gone. Avis turned back to the apartment, feeling slightly sick. She felt as if she had made a grave mistake, and she had not yet even begun to talk to Larry.

She walked back into the room angry. But if she expected Larry to be placating, she was wrong. "What's this I hear about your becoming a swimmer?" he demanded, and she could tell, from the hard sparkle in his blue eyes, that he was as angry as she was.

"I'm not becoming a swimmer," she snapped, moving to sit down on the couch without offering him a seat. "I happen to be swimming as part of my therapy program. It was your idea, if you will recall."

"It wasn't my idea for you to turn into a jock. This bruiser's your coach, huh? He's got you all hooked up into some ridiculous fantasy that you can become a swimmer, just like that, huh?"

If Larry hadn't hit all her private fears about her swimming right on the head, she would have thrown something at him, or certainly thrown him from the room. But he knew exactly what to say. Keith was nothing but a jock, and all he wanted was for her to become a jock. And the idea that she might actually be able to swim competitively was ludicrous as well as dangerous.

Instead of throwing a vase, she threw him a dirty look. "Sounds like you've got some spies working on me, Larry. I didn't realize I was that important to you. It certainly didn't seem like it at the Open-Air Theater a month ago."

Larry's eyes narrowed dangerously, and Avis wondered if that was a sign of guilt. "Not a spy. Just a scared little dancer coming to you to ask for help."

"Cheryl!" Avis had totally forgotten about the visit Cheryl had paid, and about her abortive request for tutoring. So that was what this was all about! Her anger renewed itself.

"She said you acted real high and mighty, like you didn't have any use for the National anymore." His lips curled into a thin smile. "But you and I know better, don't we, Avis?"

"Did you really expect me to agree to help her learn my role? After what you did to see to it that I didn't get the role?"

"Now what the hell do you mean by that?" Laurence seemed really surprised by this statement, but Avis was too angry to notice.

"And another thing. Who the hell do you think you are, forcing Beth to leave the company before she's good and ready? Why, she knew you when you were a struggling corps member just like she was. How dare you cast her off like some old shoe?"

The thin smile reappeared. "Are you sure we're talking about Beth here, Avis? Are you sure we're not talking about Avis Considine?"

Avis stood up. Her whole body was trembling, and she could not control it in a sitting position. "My career as a dancer will be over when I say so, Larry," she said through clenched teeth. "And until then, I'll do what I damn well please. I'll swim the damn English Channel if I want to, and I'll turn into a jock if I like. And I will not coach your little protégée! My life is my own, do you understand? My own!"

Larry straightened up from his position reclining against the wall. "Is it really?" he asked in a soft, insinuating voice. "Now, that's something I'd like to see!" He walked over to the door, and Avis could tell from the rigid way he held his normally supple back that he was very mad. At the door, he turned slowly with a deliberate grace calculated to make her remember that he was a dancer. "I'll tell you something, Avis. Your life can belong to whoever you want. If you care to fool yourself into believing that it belongs to you, that's your problem. But don't ever, ever, think that your dancing career is yours to call. Whether you ever dance again or not is my decision—and mine alone!"

This time she was ready to throw something, but Larry was gone. The pottery vase hit the door behind his head a moment too late.

Avis, blinking back tears, stared at the shards spread out on the rug in front of the door. The tears, she knew, would be dangerous, so she decided on action instead. Getting up from the couch, and ignoring the fact that she seemed to be rather shaky on her feet, Avis went to the kitchen closet for a broom and dustpan and proceeded to clean up the mess she had just made. She forced herself to concentrate on the pale melon-colored pieces, straightening up occasionally to try and fit some of them back together. Anything—anything was better than thinking about what had just happened.

But cleaning up the pieces was not enough, and, when she had them all spread out on a sheet of newspaper on the kitchen counter, she realized that she would never have the patience, or the self-control, to go about gluing them back together tonight. Although she had managed to keep the tears at bay, she could feel the anger building up inside her like a good head of steam. She was more convinced than ever that Larry had had something to do with her accident, and she felt that if she didn't talk to someone about it, she would scream.

She actually tried to call two other people before she remembered what Keith had said: "My number's in the book. Call if you need me." Of course. He was the only one who would understand. In a fever, she grabbed her phone directory and began riffling through the pages, missing the correct page again and again in her hurry.

There were two Keith Hardings and one K. Harding

in the book. Avis swore, and then scribbled all three addresses on a piece of paper. One was a Park Avenue address; she doubted that was her Keith. The other two were both on the East Side. Well, she thought, grabbing her bag and making sure to double-lock the door behind her, *the most that can happen is I'll be embarrassed.*

She took a cab, something she rarely did, even at night. But she was still feeling slightly unsteady, and the last thing she wanted was to have to keep her wits about her while walking the city streets late at night. The smallest deviation from the straight path she was traveling to Keith's door, and Avis felt she would fall apart.

Fortunately she found the right Keith on the first try. He lived in an old brick high-rise in a less than fashionable building on the Upper East Side. There was no doorman, and the smells of food were apparent in the hallway even at that late hour. Avis found his name on the directory and took the elevator, her heart pounding.

She rang the bell and then knocked impatiently. It seemed like an eternity before Keith came to the door, and when he did, it was clear that he had been asleep. He was wearing a long blue kimono with a Japanese print that made him look like a warrior of some sort. But Avis was so glad to see Keith and not some angry stranger that she barely noticed his nakedness beneath the robe.

As soon as he saw her, Keith reached out and pulled her into the room, catching her up in an embrace that was meant for comfort, not arousal.

"What happened?" Despite his sleepy eyes, he was instantly alert.

Now that she had arrived, Avis found herself unable to talk. She kept on shaking her head and muttering "I don't believe it—I really don't believe it," while Keith led her over to a beige Haitian wool couch and left her there to pour a drink from a side-table bar.

"Drink this," he ordered, and sat down beside her to hold the brandy snifter up to her lips.

"I thought I was in training." Avis was suddenly giddy, although she knew the tears were rising perilously close to the surface.

"Forget it. Tell me what happened. What did Lessine say to you?"

"Oh, the usual." The forced jocularity in her voice was startling, even to Avis. "That I should have agreed to coach Cheryl Cattier, that I was washed up as a dancer as far as he was concerned, and that he was the one who called the shots in my life, not me."

She paused to take a drink of the burning brandy, and then fixed wide eyes on Keith. "He said I never ruled my own life, even if I thought I did. He said now I had some jock running the show for me, trying to make me into what I wasn't." This wasn't entirely true, but Avis suddenly realized that part of her discomfort had to do with the fact that Larry, as usual, had touched on some of her own very real fears. "Is that right, Keith? Is some jock trying to make me into what I'm not?"

A bitter smile played across Keith's face. "Is that what you think, Avis?"

"I don't know what I think!" she said angrily. "That's why I'm asking you!"

He was silent at this tirade, leaving Avis feeling deflated and certain that it was true. If she didn't know what she thought, how could she trust Keith to know?

"What I mean is," she went on more quietly, "do you think he's right about me?" Her eyes were full of tears as the brandy loosened the wedge of anger that had been stuck in her chest.

"You mean, do I think you should have agreed to

tutor Cheryl? No, I don't." His voice was soothing, patient. "Do I think you're washed up as a dancer? No, certainly not." He reached out and pulled a strand of hair back from her damp cheeks. "Do I think that I'm manipulating you into doing something you don't want to do?" He shook his head sadly. "I hope not, but only you can know that, Avis. Only you can decide where your life is to go from this moment on."

Avis was really crying by now, and she shook her head in despair. "No," she sobbed, "he's right. He's the one who decides—about my dancing, I mean. And I don't know about anything else—I just don't know." She was crying too hard to speak clearly. "I don't know what's happening to my life, Keith. I'm scared!"

Keith did not reply, but leaned over and gathered her onto his lap as if she were a small child. He held her there, rocking gently back and forth and stroking her loose hair for a long, long time. It was only when Avis's tears had subsided into gentle hiccups that he began to speak, whispering softly against her hair.

"Avis, listen to me. Nobody makes you do anything in your life that you don't want to do. And nobody can keep you from doing what you really want, either. Do you understand that? Laurence Lessine thinks he can make you believe that, because it's in his best interests to have you believe it. But you don't for a moment believe that he can control your life, any more than you believe I can."

He shifted her around on his lap so that he could look down into her face, tear-stained and poignant. "Look at you," he whispered with a little smile. "Look at what you've done in your life. You've become one of the greatest dancers in the country at age twenty-eight. Do you think that was Laurence Lessine's doing? All he did was notice your power—as a dancer and a worker—and use it to make him and you famous.

There's no harm in that. But to think that he is responsible for what you have accomplished is to sell yourself far too short. You are a remarkable woman, Avis Considine, and your drive is as great as your talent. No one can make you what you are but yourself."

Avis snuggled closer and nodded, sniffling slightly. No one made her feel as small and as wanted as Keith Harding could make her feel and, even through her misery, she was bound to enjoy the sensation. "And what about what I'm about to become, Keith? I don't feel as if I have any control over that at all."

"You don't, not yet. It's too soon to tell. You may go back to dancing very soon—you may never go back." He dropped a kiss on the top of her forehead to take the sting out of this honest remark. "The swimming is something you are doing for the moment because it's working. What you do with it is purely your decision. Go on, or stop. It's your life, Avis. I'm just in it now . . . because I'm a very lucky man."

He dropped another kiss, this one longer and more tender, on the bridge of her nose. Avis felt the sadness and anger recede slowly. Keith was right, of course. Larry had not made her a dancer, and Keith would not make her a swimmer. There was nothing sinister about Keith's intentions, just as there had been nothing sinister about Laurence's intentions—at the beginning.

"I still think he did it," she said, looking up at him suddenly.

"Did what?"

"I think Larry was responsible for my injury. I think he may have had the marly floor cut shorter than I was used to. Nobody goes farther out into the wings in that performance than I do, so nobody else would have been hurt. Either he had the floor cut shorter than our usual floor, or he neglected to tell me that it was shorter. Either way, he is responsible." She spoke with complete certainty now. Larry's visit had made a suspicion into a conviction. She stared at Keith. "Do you believe me?"

He looked at her for a long time before nodding. "I think it's possible," he said carefully. "Now, what do you want to do about it?"

"Nothing." She settled back against his chest with a sigh. Suddenly it seemed enough just to know that Larry was responsible for her injury, not Avis herself. It vindicated her current situation, made it not of her doing, and therefore easier to bear. It was also easier to know that someone else shared her conviction, even if only marginally. She knew Keith was not as sure as she was, but it didn't matter. He supported her and that was enough.

"I don't want to do anything yet. First, I want to get well. Then we'll see what happens. Once I get very strong again, I'll know what I want to do." She smiled at him for the first time.

He smiled back. "I never doubted that for a moment," he said. "Your future is in your hands." He paused, and Avis saw the smile disappear briefly. "And what about the swimming?" he asked lightly.

Avis was suddenly aware of his body beneath the thin cotton kimono. "Swimming?" She reached up and put both arms around his neck. "Is there any other way to get strong, coach?"

He watched her face for a moment before giving in to her embrace with a small sigh. "I can think of a few other ways," he said, and bent his lips to her mouth.

Whatever remnants of bitterness, sadness, or anger Avis felt were wiped out with that first deep kiss. All was unimportant save the hunger she had felt for Keith, a hunger that had been building ever since their first and only night of lovemaking so many weeks ago. She wondered now, as she opened her mouth to receive his warm tongue, how she had managed to keep her need for him buried. It was so apparent to her now that it overshadowed the other driving needs in her life—to succeed, to be very good at what she did, to fulfill herself through dance. This was the fulfillment she sought now, and she sought it with an eagerness that would have shocked her had it been at any other time, or place, or with anybody but Keith Harding.

She tightened her arms around his neck and arched her body up against his, curling into the hollow of his lap as if she had been expressly made to fit there. Her lips moved across the generous surface of his mouth and face, reveling in the rough-hewn planes and crevices, in the sheer size of his features. She had a whole world to explore before her, and she was eager to see and experience it all.

Keith was aware of her hunger, although he kept his thoughts about it to himself. Whatever propelled Avis in her intense need for him also propelled his need for her. Although he could not have told her how he felt, was unwilling to tell her why he thought she needed him so badly at that moment, he knew that he could not restrain his own desires, which were intensifying by the second as Avis pressed her beating heart against his chest. He felt her tongue eagerly probing his mouth, and with a deep groan of abandonment, opened his mouth and his body and his heart to her.

If Avis felt his momentary hesitation and then the great release of his desire, she did not bother to comment on it. Now Keith was slipping her big shirt up over her firm stomach, exposing her small breasts to the cool air and the heat of his gaze. Avis stretched back against his arm so that he could slip the shirt over her head with the other hand. Then she lay back, reveling in the longing she saw on his face.

"A perfect little body," he whispered, wetting his lips with his tongue. "Perfect for dancing, and swimming . . . and perfect for love." He bent to her breasts and worked slowly to arouse the points of desire into hard, hot peaks. Avis threw both arms over her head and let them dangle off the edge of the couch. She was utterly abandoned to the circles of sensation Keith was drawing on her upper body with his lips, his tongue, his teeth. Then his hands moved to slip down her pants in one swift gesture, and she was reminded of the power that lay behind those gentle, articulate hands.

He lifted her back to a sitting position, straddling his lap. His robe had opened, and the touch of bare flesh against flesh aggravated them both to a fevered pitch. Avis thrust her hands inside the robe, and her mouth against his waiting lips. His beard and body hair were incredibly soft, worn fine by years in the water. His skin was smooth and cool, but the undercurrent of heat which rose from his groin was unmistakable.

When he shifted slightly and entered her, Avis was lost to all but the sensation enveloping her in ecstasy until she cried out, and heard Keith cry out with her. Their bodies, both physical machines trained to the peak of fitness, were transported to a level of delight that transcended anything they had ever worked for. Avis clung to Keith and shuddered against him in consummation.

They were lying on the floor on a generously padded oatmeal rug that was slightly scratchy but not at all unpleasant. Their limbs were hopelessly intertwined. Avis's legs were wrapped around Keith's bulk, their arms trailing upward like spent vines. Their eyes were closed, but both wore pleased, sleepy smiles, and Avis, although she did not know it, was purring softly deep in her throat. She felt the rise and fall of Keith's high chest beside her narrow one, slowing from a heavy accelerated rhythm to a calmer one. As his breathing relaxed, and his pulse returned to normal, she felt her own racing system slow down too. She began to concentrate on matching her breaths to his; he was her life source, her link to a future she did not know but no longer feared.

Keith, aware of her efforts to synchronize herself with him, smiled to himself but did not speak. Consciously, he forced himself to breathe more and more deeply, creating a gentle tide of hypnotic motion until, without even knowing how it happened, Avis drifted off into a deep sleep. She did not even wake up when he lifted her and carried her into his bedroom, covering her gently with a soft cotton blanket and sitting beside her to watch her peaceful, heart-shaped face for a long time before he slipped into the bed beside her.

Then he too slept.

Chapter Eleven

*T*hursday, July 10

Now everything has changed. In the past four weeks, it seems I have grown gills and fins. I spend all my waking hours in the water. Keith says it's the only way to build up the endurance I'll need, although I felt a lot stronger when I was working out on the Nautilus machines. But Keith says that the muscles you use for swimming can really only be developed in the water. He says that there's more to distance swimming than just being strong. He says it's a state of mind, and that's why I have to live and breathe swimming for the next three weeks.

He says, he says, he says . . . is that all I ever think about these days—Keith, and what he says and what he does? Yes, that's all. That and water, water, water . . ."

Despite the magic of their night of lovemaking, things seemed to return to normal very quickly for Avis and Keith. The day of the race was drawing closer, and neither of them was willing to jeopardize the months of hard training to reflect on the nights of unexpected

passion. There was only one thing to think about, and
that was the race.

Still, Avis suspected that Keith had an easier time of
it than she did. She could not easily erase the memory
of his kisses and his loving touch, even when they were
immersed in water. Keith acted as if their nights
together had never existed. He seemed able to separate
the swimmer from the woman with no effort at all, and
was so involved in working with the swimmer that the
woman ceased to exist for him.

Avis admired his ability to detach the personal from
the professional. She understood the need for it and
appreciated the fact that it made it easier for her to
concentrate on her work as well. But it had never been
easy for Avis to separate the tangled skeins of her life.
It had always taken a tremendous effort of the will, and
lately it seemed harder than ever.

Still, she had the swimming to think about, and
swimming was all-consuming, both physically and emotionally. She realized, as July came to a close and the
day of the race drew nearer, that she had not *really*
begun to swim until that time. At first she had swum
laps, concentrating on her stroke and building up her
strength and breathing capacity. But she had never
fully immersed herself in the act of swimming that
Keith demanded of her now. Laps, strokes, breaths—
all the techniques became irrelevant during those long,
endless hours spent in her watery world of silence and
sensation.

Avis grew adept at slowing down her thought proc-
esses when in the water, at letting the gravity of her
environment support her. Sometimes it took her several laps to complete a thought while the water dragged in
and around her, loosening the tensions, filtering the
debris from her thoughts. Her repertoire of music to

swim by grew; she was fond of Mozart, Mahler, and Joan Baez folk songs to get her through the hours.

Her body underwent a change in those final weeks. The muscles in her arms and legs began to stretch and smooth and lengthen, giving her a longer, sleeker look, despite the fact that she had gained almost six pounds. Her long, shiny black hair, which had always been her pride and joy, and which she had loved to wear in complicated chignons, was now routinely swept back in two utilitarian braids to accommodate her bathing cap, making her look younger.

The weight, in fact, had been much easier to gain than Avis had anticipated. Something about the nature of the exercise enabled her to gain, despite the fact that she was working as strenuously as she ever had in the dance studio. Partly it was because she was indulging her appetite to a greater degree than she had as a dancer, when every extra ounce appeared magnified a hundredfold in the studio mirrors. And partly it was because she was eating differently—Keith would go out for lunch while Avis was completing her stretching routine after the morning's swim, and he would return with something different every day: huge sandwiches piled high with carbohydrates and protein, big bowls of pasta or soup with slabs of whole-grain bread, or great plates of some exotic ethnic specialty full of spice and heady aromas. Avis ate it all without question, delighting in the satisfied look on Keith's face as he watched her clean her plate.

Then he would ply her with liquids until she thought she would float away. Ironically, with all the water around her, Avis was in danger of dehydration from so much strenuous activity, although she could never detect it herself. Keith especially liked to bring her milk-shakes, although he was never able to find a peanut-butter-flavored shake, much to Avis's secret relief.

But she took it as a sign of change that she did not object to Keith's diet, and that she allowed him to monitor her eating habits just as he monitored her waking and sleeping and all the hours in between. Unlike her relationship with Laurence, in which Avis had chafed at her lover's authoritarianism, she accepted Keith's control over her life without objection. When he forced her to hang on the edge of the pool for hours at a time, perfecting the loose-limbed, six-beat kick that was essential to distance work, or when he woke her before dawn to swim in chilly outdoor waters until her skin felt as if it could be peeled off like a wet bathing suit, she never once had a mutinous thought.

After her disastrous meeting with Larry Lessine, Avis had realized that the door to the National Ballet and her re-entry into the dance world was not going to be as easy for her as she had hoped it would be. She was convinced now that Larry had been responsible for her injury, which meant that he had really wanted her out of his way. And Avis was far too proud and stubborn to even consider going back where she wasn't wanted. Larry had probably counted on that to ensure her silence about his treachery. Like it or not, she had to admit that Keith was all she had at the moment.

Keith's presence in her life, unlike Laurence's, was never abrasive or cruel. Although he had never once mentioned their lovemaking, Avis knew this time that he had not truly forgotten about it. She was aware of a gentleness in his manner, a regard in his touch that betrayed his memory of the erotic passion they had shared. And she felt utterly confident in his hands because of it.

She was also coming to understand him more, and to appreciate the dedication with which he approached his work. She, too, shared that dedication, that total commitment to whatever she was doing, and sometimes she felt as if she and Keith were two sides of the same coin. She knew him intimately, and she knew him not at all, but it didn't matter because they were working together for the same goal. If she wondered at times why Keith had dropped everything else in his life in order to concentrate on training an untried swimmer in a minor amateur race, why in fact he was at the Sportscape Club to begin with, she never doubted that he had her best interests at heart.

She accepted Keith's control over her life without question. She wanted to win that race more than she had ever wanted anything in her life. Somehow, all her ambition to succeed as a dancer, ambition that had been developed and nurtured over years of hard work, was intensified in this three-month training period. In order to avoid the devastating possibility that she might never be able to dance again, Avis, with the single-minded compulsion that had marked her entire career, was able to focus herself on one thing and one thing only—getting in shape to win the MasterSwim competition.

Sometimes her obsessiveness was too much even for Keith. "Avis," he said one afternoon, sitting by the edge of the pool and watching the ferocious expression on her face as she practiced her six-beats and her alternative breathing exercises. "You have to be more relaxed when you work. The whole key to swimming distances is just to swim, not to devour the water in your path like some waterbound Valkyrie!"

Avis looked up, not amused by his imagery. "I have to work hard," she told him. "If I can't get it right, I won't be able to do it at all when the time comes."

Keith got out of his chair and slipped swiftly into the water beside her. Without saying a word, he placed one

hand on the small of her back and, by exerting mild
pressure there, and on a point just above her breasts,
he gently forced her into an upright position in the
water.

"Hey!" She looked at him in mild annoyance. "I
wasn't done with that set!"

But Keith was not put off. "Now you listen to me,"
he said severely, and Avis could tell from the way his
eyes turned a cloudy blue-gray that he meant business.
"Finishing this set or not finishing it isn't going to make
one whit of difference next week, and the sooner you
get that through your head the better off you'll be." His
voice softened when he saw the resentment disappear
from her expression, but the warning in his eyes
remained. "Look, Avis. You have to understand. You
can only do so much in the time allotted before this
race. Granted, you've had less time than most, and
granted, I've worked you harder than most, but that
doesn't mean you should work until you drop. To be
prepared for a swim like this you can only do so many
laps, so many training exercises, so many immersion
swims. On the day of that race, do you think it's going
to matter whether you've done six hundred laps or
eight hundred? Whether you've practiced alternative
breathing exercises a hundred times a day or a thou-
sand?" He shook his head and reached out to gently
push back a strand of wet hair that had escaped from
beneath her bathing cap onto her furrowed brow.

"All that will matter, Avis, when you get into that
water at Housefellow Lake, is that you swim, as fast as
you can for as long as you can. How you do it will
become totally irrelevant by then. What you know
now, you'll know then. It doesn't matter how many
more times you do it here in the pool. All that will
matter then is that you swim."

Avis shook her head. "That's not all that matters to

me, Keith—not anymore. I want to win that race next week."

Keith searched her face closely, and, watching him, Avis thought she saw a stab of sorrow flash across his features. "Why is that, Avis?" he asked, his voice suddenly soft. "Why do you want to win?"

Avis set her lips together, tasting the slightly sulphurous chlorine and salt that seemed to have stained her lips permanently. She wondered if it was possible that Keith didn't know the answer to that question. Then she realized that he must know, and only wanted to hear the words from her. "I want to win," she told him evenly, "because that's the only reason for competing."

He shook his head. "No, that's not true. I used to feel that way too, but I've learned that there are other reasons to play the game than just to win. There's the love of competition, the love of the sport, the love of doing something well regardless of where you stand in relationship to the rest of the field. You should understand that it's like your dancing. It wasn't important that you be the best dancer in the company, but just that you did your best, right?"

"This is different." Avis did not want to tell him about her secret desire to be the best dancer, a demon that she had been wrestling with for her entire career. "This is something I need for me, personally. It's different than dancing—I could never equate the two. But it's not a game. Not to me, it's not." She heard the bitterness in her voice, but she could do nothing to quelch it. "I need to win, Keith, don't you see?"

He didn't answer her at once, but regarded her with the same quiet gravity she had noticed before. Avis did not like that look, misinterpreting it as pity, which she could never abide. "What's the matter?" she asked defensively. "Don't you think I can do it? Don't you think I can win?"

"That's not the point," he began, but she cut him off, unwilling to concede her shaky point.

"It's the point for me," she said. "Right now, in my life, it's the whole point—the only point." She stopped and regarded his even, handsome features, cloaked now in his private regard. "I think you understand," she told him. "You used to be a competitor yourself, until you had to stop. Don't you remember how it was?"

Keith actually winced, but Avis was too caught up in her own argument to notice. "I remember," he said softly. "I remember all too well."

"Then you should understand." In the cool water, Avis suddenly felt a rush of fear. "Keith," she said tightly, "I can do it, can't I?" She looked up at him imploringly. "Tell me I can do it! You're my coach, damn it! Tell me I can win!"

A shadow of a smile, nostalgic and bitter, crossed Keith's face, but he nodded at once and replied confidently. "You can do it, of course!" His voice was soothing and encouraging, every syllable the coach's. "You've got the basics before you even start—a superbly conditioned body, strong shoulders, and well-developed muscle tone and lungs. You've been swimming long enough to have the necessary stamina, and God knows you've got the techniques down. You haven't shown any major area of weakness that I can see, as a matter of fact." The bitter smile reappeared briefly before he went on. "No, I'd say you were an excellent competitor, and that you have an excellent chance to win the MasterSwim Five-Mile Freshwater Swim." Now the smile softened. "And if not," he added with a twinkle in his eye, "there will be plenty of other races to choose from if we want them."

Somehow Avis was not satisfied by his words, despite the promise of other possible races. She had been hoping Keith would mention future races, since it was the only way she knew to bind him to her. But he had said "if," not "when," and there was that disturbing, faraway look in his eyes that made her feel uneasy. Did he really care about her future, about their future together?

She slipped back down in the water and began to work again. She could not let herself dwell on these disturbances. As long as Keith had voiced confidence in her chances, she would take him at his word. Keith was nothing if not sincere, and besides, what he said didn't matter. All that mattered at the moment was the upcoming swim. For now, swimming was everything to her. It had to be.

Then Keith noticed a slight swiveling in her hips when she kicked, and he became totally absorbed in helping her to correct the slight imperfection in her form, and seemed to forget all about their disquieting conversation. Avis, with Keith's hands firm around her narrow waist and his voice murmuring instructions and encouragement in her ear, soon forgot about her own doubts and fell back into the all-consuming attention to detail. Whatever Keith said was the law, and she had only to devote all her energy into translating his words into actions. He had once told her that he had never seen anyone as dedicated to listening as Avis, but she had not been surprised to hear it. She had spent her life learning by listening and watching, bent on absorbing the tiny details that meant the difference between a good dancer and a great one. Besides, Avis's ability to be an obsessive learner was something she considered a great asset, not a liability. If she had nothing else going for her at the moment in her life, at least she had that to fall back on!

It was a tribute to her ability to focus her attention on the details that Avis never let herself consider that she might have been in love with the idea of winning for the wrong reasons. And she tried not to dwell on the possibility that she had fallen a little bit in love with Keith, too. But in fact, her daily preoccupations were totally devoted to him, and her life was completely filled with his presence. Even her mind's eye was constantly conjuring mental images of him when he was not with her—Keith standing over her while she swam, Keith in the water beside her, Keith naked above her with a passionate smile on his generous mouth, his body hard and strong with desire for her. . . .

This last image was a source of great disturbance because, when she thought about it—and she was unable to avoid the subject for long—she realized that she had no idea what her relationship to him really was. Had he made love to her because he thought she needed it? It was true that both occasions had been sparked by an intense emotional trauma on her part. Or had he done it simply because she had been a willing, needy body, and there were few men who would bother resisting such temptation on principle?

She couldn't even begin to understand why she had wanted him so badly in the first place. Of course, he was a desirable man, but that had never been enough to get Avis to go to bed with somebody before, especially not someone who had been a virtual stranger at the time. Was it because she had needed a warm and loving body to affirm her desirability in times of stress? Or was there a deeper bond between them?

Avis could not allow herself to consider any of those possibilities. The race was too close to allow for such romantic indulgences. Still, she couldn't avoid the alarming frequency with which Keith's face wavered through her dreams like an underwater illusion, nor the fact that it was as a lover she saw him, not as a coach. He had owned her, body and soul, for the past two months, and yet she realized she did not even know where he went when he left her at her apartment door after a full day's training and a huge evening meal.

She knew he did not always go home, because she had tried calling his apartment, unable to stop herself from thinking about Keith and where he was. Twice he had not been home. Once he had answered the phone, and Avis, red with shame, had hung up.

Avis wished that she had someone to share her thoughts with other than Keith, especially since so many of her thoughts were about him. But she had lost touch with all of her friends in the past month. Her acquaintances at the dance studio seemed dim and faceless memories to her. Indeed, her entire life at the National Ballet, which had ended so abruptly just a few months before, seemed like a distant dream. She had even lost track of Beth's whereabouts since Beth left the company.

But the times when she wished for female companionship and confidences became fewer and fewer as August 3, the day of the MasterSwim, grew near. Avis and Keith were completely wrapped in a cocoon of water and each other, and Avis did not care, or dare, to attempt to rid herself of their mutual obsession with the race. The knowledge that the months following August 3 would be lonely—a time when she might not only lose Keith but also have to confront the loss of her new way of life—was something she could not allow herself to contemplate. So she worked, and listened to Keith, and swam . . . and swam. . . .

She did not swim on August 2—Keith would not allow it. "Are you kidding?" he said, when she appeared at the Sportscape Club for her usual early-morning workout. "Do you really think I'm going to let you get in the water today?"

"Why not?" Avis was genuinely surprised. She had worked hard at forgetting that today was the day before the race, and she had been expecting, hoping, for a business-as-usual workout. "I haven't been working too hard lately."

But Keith would hear none of it. "I've been tapering off your schedule gradually all week to allow you to build up some reserves of strength. If you think I'm going to ruin all that by letting you swim today, you're crazy. Today, we do nothing but rest—and eat, of course."

Avis realized then that Keith wasn't wearing his usual sweatpants over a swimsuit. He was in tight-fitting jeans and a thin-striped T-shirt under which his muscles bulged impressively. His hair was brushed back away from his face, and his beard had been newly trimmed. She felt a sudden and very strong rush of desire for him as he stood there on the far side of the pool, and she wondered briefly if by "rest" he might mean some time together in bed. But then she dismissed the idea as unsuitable for the day before a big race, and reminded herself that it was in times of stress that she tended to want Keith more than ever. It was not fair to Keith, or to her, and so she put the idea resolutely out of her mind and returned to the dressing room to put on her street clothes.

Still, she was glad she had chosen to wear a sundress that day—a simple yellow cotton shift that showed off her dark coloring and athletic limbs. She could tell the effect was not lost on Keith when she met him out in the lobby of the club, either.

"Well," he said, taking her hand and slipping it proprietarily through his elbow. "What do you want to do today? The day is yours, my dear—as long as you leave ample time for feeding your face."

"What are my options?" she inquired as they stepped out into the sunny August morning.

"Anything that you enjoy—as long as it involves a minimum of physical effort on your part, and mine, for that matter." He looked down at her and grinned suddenly. "Unfortunately, that leaves out nature's most fun activity, so we'll have to settle for second best. What'll it be?"

The fact that he had entertained the same notions as she had made Avis feel a lot better about her own erotic fantasies. She thought for a moment and then decided. "Movies," she said. "Definitely movies. I'd like to spend the day at the movies."

Keith grinned. "My thoughts exactly. I knew, beneath that dedicated, cultivated exterior, you were a closet movie junkie." They had turned southward, and Keith pulled out a pair of dark sunglasses and put them on. Avis was aware of second glances from several passersby as they walked arm in arm along the sidewalk, and she was sure the glances were for Keith. With her sundress, lack of makeup, and hair pulled into a high, cool ponytail, she felt like his kid sister more than his date. But then, she reasoned, she wasn't really Keith's date. He was simply taking care of her for the day, much like any older brother would do.

"The question is," Keith was saying, "what kind of movies? I'm partial to westerns and adventure flicks myself."

"I'm big on foreign films and romances," she told him.

He clicked his tongue regretfully. "There, you see. Nothing in common." He furrowed his brow. "Well, how about mysteries. I love Alfred Hitchcock, and there are always a few of his films playing around town."

"I like them too, but I've seen them so many times I know the endings, and that spoils the fun. How about a blockbuster? There must be a big first-run movie neither of us has seen."

"Probably, but most blockbusters don't start playing at ten A.M., and besides, that would only take up a few hours. I'm talking about a movie feast. You know, the kind where your eyes ache afterward."

"Oh, the kind where you lose yourself, right?" Avis giggled. She hadn't felt this relaxed in weeks. Whatever Keith was doing for her, he was doing it right.

"Exactly. And you eat so much salty popcorn that your lips swell up. Except you can't have popcorn—it's not an efficient food for swimming."

"Forget about the popcorn. The big problem is, what are we going to see?"

They both walked a few steps in silence and then turned to each other, uttering one word simultaneously.

"Cartoons!" The coincidence was so great and so ridiculous that they both burst out laughing.

"Terrific!" Keith said when he had recovered. "Ten million people in this city, and I find the one swimmer who shares my secret passion for animation. That's too much! Nothing in common, indeed!"

"And I happen to recall that there's an animation festival going on at the Thalia even as we speak. Early Disney, old Betty Boop . . . let's go!"

Keith grabbed her hand and they started to run, stopping only when Avis yelled after him that she would never be able to swim the following day if he kept up such a grueling pace. They arrived at the old repertory theater just as the first feature was about to begin, and trooped in amid the youngsters and old film fanatics like themselves to settle down for four hours of animated fun.

In the end, they didn't spend the entire day at the movies. They came stumbling out in the early afternoon after Keith decided that too much lunacy—not to mention too much laughing—would tap Avis's precious reserves of strength.

They had lunch at Keith's favorite Italian restaurant, a tiny hole-in-the-wall that turned out to be surprisingly elegant despite the fact that Avis, at Keith's request, was served an inelegant amount of pasta. Then they walked back across town and strolled idly through Central Park, taking refuge from the August heat under shady trees, near fountains, and finally in the Museum of Natural History, where they strolled through the cool dim halls full of dinosaur bones and Indian artifacts. By the time they emerged from the museum, it was early evening.

"OK," Keith said, drawing her close under his shoulder, "an early dinner and that's it for you today, young lady."

"Dinner? My God, I haven't even begun to work off lunch! And besides, I'm not a bit tired, Keith. As a matter of fact, I wouldn't mind another movie."

"Nope."

"Come on." Avis tugged playfully on his sleeve. "I'll even go see Hitchcock with you."

He covered her hand with his for a moment and then pulled it resolutely away. "Absolutely not. I'm your coach, and as your coach, I can order you to go to bed early. Believe me, you need the rest." He looked down at her and smiled. "And don't try any special powers of persuasion. I can be very tough when I have to."

Avis saw the flames of desire licking the calm blue-gray of his eyes, but decided she had better not push her luck. After all, she would only lose out in the end by not being able to compete well. She released her arm from beneath his shoulder, unaware of the disappointment in Keith's expression. By the time she looked up at him again, he was scanning the street for a suitable spot for dinner.

He chose a natural-food restaurant a few blocks away and ordered Avis a relatively light meal—a thin consommé, a small plate of steamed vegetables, and, of course, more pasta.

"Tomorrow morning I want you to eat a container of yogurt, that high-protein drink I gave you, and some vitamins. Nothing else." Keith waggled his finger beneath her nose.

Avis, who was struggling to finish eating the meal before her, winced. "Nothing else! As if I could force a single morsel more down my throat! Ugh! I'll never eat pasta again as long as I live!"

Keith looked up from his spinach salad. "You will if you want to race again."

Avis looked at him. He hadn't played the coach much all day long, and she was struck at how much she had enjoyed being with him. This was a totally different Keith from the one she knew—fun-loving, humorous, and completely at ease with her. There was no tension in him, no feeling that he had his own secret reasons for behaving the way he did. Avis suspected that this was the real Keith—not the driven, serious achiever she knew from their days at the pool, but the warm and easy man who had laughed through four hours of cartoons. She wondered why he had held that side of himself in reserve for so long; she had only caught brief glimpses of it until today. Was it something he preferred not to share with her because they had a professional relationship? Or did he usually share it with someone else?

Even if Avis had had the courage to ask, now was not the time. The race, she kept reminding herself—you've got to remember the race. Now was not the time to upset the balance of things. She finished her dinner and allowed Keith to convince her that they would take a taxi to her apartment, despite the fact that it was close by.

"You've had enough for the day," he said, helping her into the cab and then getting in next to her. "I want you home and in bed as soon as you get there, understand?"

"What if I can't fall asleep?" she asked. But she was beginning to feel tired already and had to resist the urge to lay her head on Keith's shoulder. "What if I'm too nervous to sleep?"

Keith laughed and, reaching out, pulled her head down against his chest. "You'll sleep," he whispered against her ear. "Believe me, you'll sleep." Then he groaned suddenly, and as if he could restrain himself no longer, he bent his lips down to hers. Holding her head in his hand, he kissed her tenderly, gathering her up into his arms as if she weighed no more than a baby.

"You'll sleep, Avis. You'll sleep, and tomorrow you'll win." He nuzzled his mouth against her neck, sending shivers of heat down the bare flesh of her chest and arms. "You see, you can do anything you want to do, if you work hard enough at it." He reached around with his free hand and tipped her chin up so that he could look into her eyes. "You can have anything you want—anything at all. Do you understand that? You just have to decide what it is you want."

There was a melancholy look in his eyes that Avis did not understand, especially since the rest of his features were alight with longing. "The same is true of you," she whispered. "You have to decide what you want, Keith."

They looked into each other's eyes for a long moment, and then Keith bent to kiss her again. But this time the kiss was not tender. It was full of longing, and so deep that it took Avis's breath away. Avis felt herself tumbling into the warm cavern of his mouth, tasting his breath, slightly cinnamon-scented from the tea they had drunk, and losing herself in the soft, springy forest of his beard. She felt his tongue pushing against the wall of her teeth and opened her mouth to invite him in. With a sigh, she nuzzled closer to him, feeling herself slip blissfully into a state of half-exhaustion, half-arousal.

The cab was slowing down, but Keith's hands were finding their way inside her dress bodice. Working delicately and discreetly, he began to fondle her small breasts into warm peaks of arousal. She pressed herself closer against him, feeling his strong thighs pressing against hers. More than anything, she longed for the touch of bare flesh against bare flesh, longed to press her needy breasts against the dense hair on his massive chest, to feel the hard push of his desire against the soft cavern between her thighs.

But suddenly Keith broke away. The cab driver had long since pulled up in front of Avis's apartment, and he was grinning at the couple through his rear-view mirror. "You guys better get out of here before you break a law," he said with a broad wink.

Avis blushed, but Keith just smiled. "I'm not getting out," he told the man. "The lady is."

"Keith . . ."

He shook his head and unfolded Avis from his lap. "No, I'll just go on to my place. You need to sleep, is that clear?" He tried to look severe, but his expression was still soft with longing.

"I'll never sleep," Avis declared. "Never."

"Oh yes, you will."

"What should I do if I can't?" she inquired, looking at him imploringly in the hopes he would suggest that she call him.

"If you can't sleep," Keith said, pushing her gently from the car, "then eat. I'll pick you up at six A.M."

Before she knew it, Avis was out of the cab, standing on the curb as it pulled swiftly away. She stayed there until the cab turned the corner. She was breathing shallowly, and wondering if the entire episode had perhaps been a water-induced hallucination. The entire day, she decided, had been unreal. Unreal, but delicious.

"That was a pretty impressive display," said a familiar voice behind her. Avis whirled around, startled, and came face to face with Beth. It was so incongruous, seeing her there when she was still suffering from the after-effects of Keith's torrid embrace, that Avis was momentarily unable to speak. She merely stared at her old friend until Beth, laughing a little uncomfortably, said, "Oh, come on! It hasn't been that long, has it? Don't tell me you don't recognize your oldest friend in the world?"

The sound of Beth's husky voice cured Avis of her momentary paralysis. With a muffled cry of delight, she threw her arms around Beth, nearly knocking them both over.

"Beth! Bethie, I'm so glad to see you! God, I've missed you so much." Even as she said it, Avis realized how true it was. Although she had not made much of an effort to get in touch with her old friend, she realized how much she had needed the friendship and confidence of another woman. She felt as if a lost part of her heart, not missed until that moment, had finally been restored. It was good to see a friend.

"I've missed you, too," Beth said, returning the hug with equal ferocity. "I feel like it's been years since we've talked." She pulled back and held Avis away in order to inspect her. "Where have you been all these months?"

Avis giggled. "Under water," she replied. "What about you?"

"Oh, here and there." Beth looked away for a moment, and then, linking arms with Avis, began to walk back toward the entrance to her apartment building. "Come on. I just left you a nasty note with the doorman, asking you if you'd dropped off the face of the earth. Let's go in and rip it up and go upstairs and talk."

Avis stepped under the awning of the building. "No, let's not go in yet. I'd rather walk. I suddenly feel like I have too much energy to be cooped up in one room with you."

Beth agreed, and so they set out down Columbus Avenue, jostling comfortably against the crowds of people out to enjoy the welcome cool of the early evening. "It's amazing, isn't it?" Beth asked as they strolled. "Here we are, wandering down Columbus just like we used to, looking at the shops and at the people. But so much has changed for both of us. We're the same, and yet our lives are so different."

Avis thought she detected a note of melancholy in Beth's voice, but she was too pleased to see her friend to dwell on it. "You're right," she mused. "But it's nice to know that things like friendships never change, no matter what we're doing with our lives."

"So what are you doing with your life?" Beth inquired. "I mean, aside from being underwater."

"Well, to tell you the truth, there's really not that much more to it than that, these days at least. I'm swimming in a race tomorrow. Would you believe it? Five miles!"

"I heard," Beth interjected quickly, but Avis didn't stop to inquire where she had heard it from.

"So mostly I've been training with Keith. It's been hard work, but rewarding."

Beth flashed her an impish grin. "If that was Keith in the cab with you, I saw how rewarding it can be," she joked.

"That was nothing, really. You see, tomorrow's the race, and I think he just wanted to give me . . . a little encouragement." Avis stopped and felt the heat of a blush warming her neck. She hoped Beth didn't notice. "Anyway, I'm working hard at it, and I'm getting very strong."

"Do you love it?" Beth asked the question so abruptly that Avis realized it must have been on her mind for some time.

"Do I love it? What do you mean?"

"I mean, is it as wonderful as dance? Does it fill your life the way dance does? The way dance *did?*"

Now Avis could not ignore the bitterness with which Beth corrected herself, nor the intensity of the look on her friend's face. She noticed that Beth was pale, and slightly puffy around the eyes. She did not look well, certainly not as good as she had looked when she was dancing. Avis was concerned all of a sudden, but she decided the question merited a serious reply.

"Well," she said slowly, "it does fill my life, that's for sure. And I find a certain kind of peace when I swim that's different from what I felt when I danced, but very special in its own way. Is it as wonderful as dancing?" She stopped and reflected. This was one of the questions she had refused to ask herself for too long. She had been afraid of the comparison. But now she realized that she would have to face the issue. "No," she went on slowly, "it's not as wonderful as dance. Swimming doesn't fill my soul the way dancing does— the way it did. But it's a step in the right direction for me. It's taught me that there are other things I can do in my life besides dance, other options if I can't dance." She caught Beth giving her a sharp sideways glance. "I don't know what will happen to me after this race," she admitted. "But I know I can do something besides dance, and that's important." She thought about Keith and felt a warmth through her groin at the clear and present memory of his touch on her skin. "Besides," she added with a smile, "there are other rewards." Keith, she told herself, was a reward. She hadn't felt this good about herself—and about Keith—in a long time.

But when she looked at Beth she saw that Beth was not pleased at Avis's fortune. She was staring straight ahead of her, and her mouth was pinched together in a way that meant she was struggling to hold something back. Avis knew her well enough to know that the revelation, whatever it was, would come of its own accord. So she touched her friend gently on the shoulder. "What about you?" she asked. "What have you found?"

"Nothing," Beth said flatly. "A big zero."

Although Avis had been expecting something negative, she was surprised by Beth's vehemence. "Nothing? I thought you and Frank had big plans for when you retired. I thought you were going to get married and start a school."

"We were. But of course, I didn't retire. I was kicked out, as you know, and dear old Frank, it turns out, can't handle the idea of life without a ballerina. He's still waiting for me to run back to Larry and get down on my knees to beg for character roles, comedy stuff . . . anything."

Avis was instantly sorry that they had not gone up to her apartment. These were not the sorts of revelations that could be shared on the street. But it was too late. Beth needed some comfort—now. "And what about you, Beth?" Avis asked softly. "Never mind what

Frank wants. What do you want to do with the rest of your life?"

"What does that matter?" Beth asked angrily. "I was brought up to be a dancer, and there's really nothing else I'm fit to do. Frank is right—I should have been content with what I had at the National. The fact that I don't like doing character roles has nothing to do with it. I should have done them, and gotten ready to do what every old dancer does—fade graciously into the wings without a fight."

Beth was perilously close to tears, and Avis reached out to squeeze her hand. "That's not true, Beth, and you know it. You can do anything you set your mind to do. What about that flower shop you used to talk about setting up? That's something you love and know a lot about."

"Flower shop, hah!" Beth scoffed. "I can't do anything without Frank's money, and he's not about to give it to a flower girl, that's for sure."

"If that's his attitude," Avis said stoutly, "then there's something wrong with Frank, not you." She was thinking of Keith, and how supportive he was.

Beth turned suddenly, her eyes blazing with anger. "There is nothing wrong with Frank! There's something wrong with us, don't you see that? You pretend that you're happy swimming around like a fish, but we both know you're full of bull! You're just waiting until you can dance again—if you can dance again! You're just hoping Larry will take you back, I know it!"

The evening was only mildly cool, but Avis suddenly felt icy cold, and goose bumps appeared on her bare arms. Beth was standing in the middle of the sidewalk and giving vent to all of Avis's most private fears. She wanted to put her hand over Beth's mouth, to run away—anything rather than stand there and listen to the venom which was pouring over her heart. But she was rooted to the ground by Beth's tirade.

"And look at me!" Beth went on, heedless of the curious stares they were drawing. "I'm thirty-five years old and I don't even know how to fill out an employment application card, let alone a bank loan. And who would back me to open a flower shop? What do I know about flowers? I'm just a dancer—a body for hire, too old to be hired for anything anymore. Don't you understand, Avis? We're freaks! You pretend you've got choices, but you're as panic-stricken as I am—I could tell as soon as I saw you. There's nothing for us to do once they're through with us. It's all we've ever been taught—ever been allowed to do! We can't be anything but dancers, even if we can't dance anymore!"

Avis's panic vented itself in anger. "That's a lot of nonsense," she retorted after a moment's stunned silence. "It's not true for you, and it's certainly not true for me. I've just been telling you that there are other options. Look at what I'm doing! Sure, I'd like to be dancing again, but at least I know I won't die if I don't!" She paused, hoping there was more conviction in her voice as she said this than she felt. "I'm doing something I've never done before in my life. Yes, it's scary, and it's hard, and I have doubts. But I love swimming, and I'm proud of my accomplishments as a swimmer, however small they may be."

"But you were one of the best, Avis—one of the best dancers around. How can you settle for meager accomplishments so easily? How can you settle for so much less?"

"It isn't necessarily less. There are other things in life besides being best." Avis thought of Keith's speech to her on the same subject, and recalled that she had not believed him then and she knew that Beth felt the same way now. "I'm doing what I want to do right now in my life, Beth," she went on in a hollow voice. She felt suddenly exhausted, and wished for the conversation to be over. "Believe me, Beth, it doesn't have to be dance for it to work, for your life to work."

Beth only looked at her, and Avis was stunned into silence by the sneer on her face. "Oh, really, Avis? Is that why you sent your boyfriend to snoop around down at the studio last week? Because you care so little about the world of dance?"

If Avis had felt a chill before, she felt her heart freeze up in fear now. The combination of Beth's angry expression and her unbelievable words made Avis feel temporarily queasy, as if the sidewalk had suddenly tipped up at her. "What are you talking about?" she managed to whisper hoarsely.

"Oh, come on, Avis. You don't have to fool me. It's Beth, your old friend, remember? The other reject from the National. You can tell me. What did you want him to find out? Who's taking your place in Larry's new piece? Who's the newest star? Whether Larry would consider taking you back? You can tell old Beth."

Avis reached out and grabbed Beth's wrist. "No," she hissed through clenched teeth. "You tell me. What the hell are you talking about?"

Beth winced and shrugged, clearly not believing Avis's profession of ignorance. "I happened to be down at the studio last week," she said with an air of exaggerated patience. "And there he was, your big handsome coach, hanging around and asking everyone a lot of questions."

"What kinds of questions?"

Beth rolled her eyes. "Questions about the performance at the Open-Air Theater. He seemed to want to know what happened backstage or something. He talked to some of the dancers and even to some of the technical crew." She sniffed. "He didn't talk to me, of course. Why bother?"

"Cut out the self-pity, Beth. It doesn't suit you." Avis snapped off the words, and Beth shifted uneasily, clearly uncomfortable with the sudden switch of roles. Now it was Avis who was ferocious, Avis who was the accuser. "What else did he say?" Avis asked. She could feel her heart hammering against her ribs, and there was a strange, metallic taste in her mouth—the taste of fear.

"I don't know what else he said," Beth replied sullenly. "He was asking some of the kids about the marly floor, I know that. And then Larry came out, and your friend said they had better talk in private, and so they went in to Larry's office. I didn't bother to eavesdrop, so don't bother asking."

Avis let her breath out in a rush. So that was it—she had heard the worst and survived. At least she was still breathing, albeit shallowly, and she could feel her hands trembling as they clutched the folds of her dress by her sides. "And that's all you heard? You don't remember any more?"

Beth's mouth tightened, and she took a step backward. "Sorry, Avis. I've played spy for you enough already. Besides, I'm sure you know better than I what went on. After all, your jock boyfriend must have reported back to you?"

Avis looked at Beth, feeling as if she was facing a complete stranger. All the intimacy and camaraderie they had shared before was gone. Beth was angry at Avis, and jealous of her ability to adapt, and whatever confidences they had shared in the past were now only fuel for Beth's bitter fire.

"As a matter of fact, Beth, no. I don't know what was said because I had no idea Keith even went to the

National. I still have no idea why he did it." But she did have an idea why, and what she thought didn't make her very happy.

"Oh, I think you do, though, Avis. You know what I think? I think you're trying to prove that your accident wasn't an accident. You're either trying to sue the company for neglect or you're trying to pressure Larry into taking you back in exchange for your silence." She laughed dryly. "If I were you, honey, I'd go for the cash settlement. You don't want to force Larry to take you back, not unless you want to be dancing character roles the rest of your life."

Avis shook her head slowly. She couldn't believe this was the same cheerful Beth, this vindictive woman who was using all her knowledge of Avis's weak spots to try and drag her down with her. Avis felt a wave of pity, and another wave of fear, because she knew that there was only a very fine line separating her from Beth.

Beth had shattered a carefully arranged patina of confidence and serenity only because she wanted someone to feel as badly as she did. It had worked, and Avis was furious about it. "Tell me, Beth," Avis said tightly. "What were you doing at the National when Keith was there? Surely you weren't just visiting for old times' sake, were you?"

Beth shot her a venomous look, opened her mouth to say something, and then thought better of it. Instead, she drew herself carefully together, tossed her long blond hair and, in her best dancer's stride, moved away from Avis, leaving her standing alone in the middle of the sidewalk.

"Oh, by the way," Beth tossed over her shoulder as she left, "be sure and let me know when you make the Olympic team. I hear amateur athletics can be very satisfying, especially for the older athlete."

With a last bitter look, she was gone.

Chapter Twelve

*S*unday, August 3 (1:00 A.M.)

I don't know who to be angrier at—Beth, Keith, or myself for getting caught in this situation. How could I have been so blind, so ignorant as to think that I could get through the race tomorrow without facing the truth about myself, and the truth about Keith?

I'm sure the only reason Beth came to see me was to let me know about Keith. She's bitter and vindictive, but that doesn't change what she told me. If Keith really did go to see Larry, and I have no reason to believe she would fabricate such a story, then everything I've ever believed about him is a lie.

What made him think he had the power to play God over my life like that? To go to the studio and actually confront Larry with what he knew were unprovable fears and accusations! Whatever chance I had to go back to the National is gone now. I've been betrayed by Keith in a way that I never was with Larry. I never trusted Larry to begin with, but Keith betrayed my trust.

So what do I do about it all? I'm sitting here in my one-room apartment in the middle of the night before a race that I had once hoped might reshape my life. I realize now how foolish I was to ever believe that, but the question still remains—where to go from here?

All the signposts are down in my life for the first time. There's no one at all to show me the way. I'm scared. I'm scared, and I'm hurt, and I'm angry. Oh, God, what do I do now?

For the first time since she had begun to keep a journal, Avis was unable to find relief in her writing. The questions kept plaguing her as she sat at her tiny desk in the dim light of predawn. She could find no answers, and no relief from their incessant rhythm. Why? Why had Keith gone to Larry?

Of course Avis knew why he had done it. Actually, it fitted with his image of himself as her coach, mentor, and general Svengali. He knew, especially after Larry's nocturnal visit, that Avis was upset about the possibility that Larry had been responsible for her injury. He probably felt that the question would gnaw at his swimmer until she was unable to concentrate on her swimming. So he had taken it upon himself to go and clear the matter up in her behalf.

Of course, that meant he had underestimated Avis dangerously. He had not realized that, with her tremendous powers of focus and concentration, she would be able to put the matter out of her mind. He had not given her credit for being as driven to succeed as he was. And in any case, if he hoped to set her mind at ease, why hadn't Keith reported back to her? Had he been afraid that the truth—whatever it was—would upset her even more than the agony of not knowing?

If that was true, then he thought even less of her than she imagined. To Avis, in her fatigued state, it also meant that all his attentions, both emotional and sexual, had been nothing more than the actions of a concerned, and not very conscientious, mentor. It had all been to make her feel better, to help her get through the night, so to speak.

Well, this was one night that she was not getting through so easily. Beth's revelations, about Keith and about Avis herself, had opened up Pandora's box. Now she could only sit back and watch the night go by, as all her fears danced around her like menacing shadows. She was not a swimmer; she never had been a swimmer. Swimming had only been a stopgap obsession, something to make her forget that she might never dance again. She was in no better condition than Beth—worse, really, because she hadn't yet faced the bitter truth about herself as Beth had. She was fit for nothing but dance. It was the only salve to her soul.

She had dared to hope, and even now it was hard to admit that she had ever harbored such a foolish fantasy. She had dared to hope that Keith himself might give new meaning to her life.

Only now did the true extent of her feelings reveal themselves—now, when it was too late. Keith was far more important to her than the swimming. Without warning, she had fallen in love with the man. But he had proven, by stepping into her life where he was not wanted, that he had no intention of stepping in where he *was* wanted. He had wanted to secure Avis's future as a swimmer, not as a lover.

But why? Why had he chosen her, and what did he have to prove? Avis knew very little about Keith's past, but she knew that he had some secret demons to exorcise, some private debt to pay off. He had never had any illusions about Avis, as a swimmer or as a lover. She was nothing to him but redemption, his way of proving something to himself or to the world. As she had been for Larry, Avis was nothing more than a commodity to Keith Harding.

And he was the world to her.

Once this MasterSwim was over, he would decide that he had had enough, that Avis was not his ticket to fame, fortune, or happiness. She was merely his ticket in the door. He would find another swimmer, someone with more training and more potential than an aging ex-dancer. He would be gone from her life—and then where would she be? Too late, she had learned the truth about Keith and about her love for him.

As dawn began to break through the windows, Avis began the arduous task of pulling herself together. It seemed to her that she had no choice. She had to swim at Housefellow Lake, and she had to win. All that was left was to win, to show Keith, and Beth, and Larry— and herself—that she was not just a tool for others. If she couldn't have Keith, at least she would have satisfaction.

The question was, would she be able to make the swim? Aside from the fact that she had slept sporadically, the events of the evening had called into question all her confidence. Keith had thought she could do it, but Keith was no longer to be trusted. *She* had thought she could do it, but that had been before her carefully constructed defense had been shattered.

Now it was not a question of thinking she could do it. She had to swim that race, and she had to win. Avis was accustomed to overcoming great obstacles, even her own fear. The more fiercely she wanted something, the harder she made herself work to get it. Given that equation, she thought wryly, she should have no trouble breaking records at the MasterSwim.

Surprisingly, by five A.M. she felt fairly well-rested and in control of her emotions. She knew the hardest part of the day would be the moment when she first faced Keith in the car, but she had determined that she would not be the one to bring up his trip to the National until after the race was over, until after she had won the race.

Carefully, as if following some elaborately choreographed scheme, Avis got ready for the MasterSwim. She showered and shaved the skin on her legs and arms with a new razor, until the skin felt new and silky beneath her touch. Then she lathered her body with a thick oil; she would use even heavier lanolin once she was at the race site to prevent severe sunburn and excessive dehydration. An early-morning weather forecast said the day would be cool and windy. Cool was good, as it would cut down on the sunburn, but windy was bad. Keith had told her that even a slight chop in the water could increase the swimmer's actual distance by half again, and a moderate chop might double her efforts. Avis packed her thinnest lycra Speedo suit— dark blue with deeply incised shoulders to allow her arms the greatest mobility.

She tied her hair in two braids and wound them tightly around her head, securing them with barrettes so that her bathing cap would fit snugly. She would have to wear goggles, too, even though she never liked them. Keith had told her that the natural bacteria count could render her temporarily blind before she was halfway through the course.

Her face in the mirror was pale but composed. There was no sign of the tremendous turmoil that she was suppressing carefully beneath the surface. She could not afford to let it show. Keith was astute enough to notice any small aberration, and she knew her composure would not stand up to any inquiries. She was determined not to let anything interfere with her concentration, not even Keith.

She made her breakfast and dutifully swallowed it all, despite a total lack of appetite. Then she packed her towels, ointments, bathing caps, and an extra suit. Last of all, she slipped on a terrycloth warm-up suit of pale blue over her suit.

Time was on her side. She had just finished zipping up the jacket of her suit when she heard the buzzer—Keith was downstairs waiting for her. Composing herself with an effort, she rode down in the elevator to meet him.

As soon as she saw him, Avis realized that there was something wrong with Keith too. He looked pale and thinner than he had the night before. He greeted her with a warm smile, and solicitously asked after her night's sleep as he helped her into the car, but he was too distracted to notice the shortness of her reply, or the circles under her eyes.

He got into the car and pulled carefully away from the curb. There was almost no traffic this early on a Sunday morning in August, so they were able to get out of the city easily and without any uncomfortable waits at traffic lights or in traffic jams. Keith seemed relieved to be able to concentrate silently on his driving, and Avis turned her head resolutely out the window and watched the city slip away.

The air was a good deal cooler than it had been in previous days, almost snappy with a hint of early fall. Avis was glad she had worn her full-length warm-up suit, but shivered at the prospect of the cold water. The swim was still a dream to her, an unreal event set sometime far in her future.

Now, as the sun rose higher and began to warm the dew, Avis found that she was beginning to look forward to the race. In times of crisis, Avis needed a task to take her mind off her problem. Now it seemed that the swim was not the crisis; the crisis was her life, and Keith, and her future. The MasterSwim was now the solution, the rebuttal to the sorrow she had felt and her only hope for salvation.

She began to feel a slight flutter in the pit of her stomach, and the anticipatory tensing of her muscles that she had always felt before going on a stage in an important new role. Her mind began to narrow itself in on the upcoming task, blocking out any thoughts but those of stroke and breath, technique and endurance. She found herself seeing the course of the swim in her mind's eye. Keith had posted an intricate map of Housefellow River Lake on the wall above his desk at the Sportscape Club, and Avis had been staring at it until she knew every nook and inlet, every gentle current, like the back of her hand.

She thought about the course now while Keith drove down the Jersey Turnpike, through the industrial cities of New Jersey and into the verdant green farmland. She thought of everything Keith had told her about the race—to start slowly and take at least thirty minutes to find her pace, to look for other swimmers, or look around to see where she was in relationship to the beginning and the end of the course.

She was so absorbed in her preparatory reverie that Keith had to call her name twice before she heard him. "Avis! Are you all right?"

She spun around to find him watching her closely, and she smiled slightly. In her current meditative state, she did not fear Keith's observant gaze. Nothing could penetrate her concentration.

"I'm fine," she replied. "Just getting my thoughts together, that's all."

He looked at her for a moment more, as if debating something with himself. Then, with a short little nod, he went on. "Right. Well, that's good. That's very good. But I want you to take a break from that for a minute and listen to me."

"What is it? Is something wrong?" There was the tiniest apprehension.

"I have something to say to you. It's a story, actually, but I think it's important for you to listen to it now."

He smiled, and a flash of his old humor lit up his tired eyes. "Besides," he added, "I think it will relax you."

Avis felt her nerves tighten. Surely, he was not going to choose this moment to tell her about his visit to Laurence Lessine? His timing could not be that awful! If he began to say things that upset her equilibrium, she would need to do something to stop him. She had to preserve her balance! She would tell him to shut up, or start singing Mozart very loudly. Or she would jump out of the car—anything to avoid a confrontation.

But Keith had already begun to talk.

"When I was a kid," he said, speaking in a gentle, reflective voice, "I used to dream about being a jet plane pilot. Like every little boy of my generation, it seemed to be the most exciting thing a human being could do—to fly higher and faster than anybody else in the world." Keith's eyes were on the road, but Avis could see that they were dim, focused on some faraway past that he now saw clearly before him.

"Unfortunately," he went on, "it turned out that I suffered from severe acrophobia. The first time I went up in a plane, I passed out." He chuckled softly. "It had something to do with my inner ears—the fluid wasn't right, or strong enough, or something. I was actually so distraught about it that my mother took me to a doctor. He said that I might be able to build up a tolerance to the reduced pressure by spending a lot of time in the water."

Avis shifted uncomfortably in her seat. She had no

idea where this rambling monologue was taking them, but she knew it was further away from her focus on the race than she cared to be. She felt a vague sense of discomfort, as though something that was about to be revealed would be embarrassing—for Keith, for her, or for them both.

Keith didn't seem to notice. "So," he said with a little sigh, "that was how I came to take up swimming. Completely by accident. A little late in life, as professional swimmers go. Only because I thought it would get me back to something that I dearly loved." He flashed her a canny glance. "Not at all unlike your reasons for swimming, don't you agree?"

"I suppose we have something in common," Avis offered reluctantly, knowing that to remain silent would be to invite closer scrutiny. "Of course, you were only a kid at the time."

"Twelve years old, to be exact. But as it turned out, I had quite a natural aptitude for swimming. I quickly caught up with the kids who had been swimming for years, and soon I was the fastest freestyler in the county.

"But I was not impressed with my own ability, even though my coach promised my parents that great things could happen for me if I stuck to it and worked very hard. I still hoped to be able to learn to fly someday, and I studied math, physics, and engineering in my spare time with the career as a jet pilot in mind." Keith paused and laughed. "I also studied music for years and years, because my mother, bless her soul, was not about to risk having a son who flew or swam for a living. She had always dreamed of my being a concert pianist, as she herself had been. That was how I eventually went to Oxford on a scholarship. Music and aeronautic engineering were two unusual skills to be studying together, and I suppose they couldn't pass up such a freakish scholar."

"That doesn't sound so freakish to me," Avis said. Despite her intention to remain as detached as possible from Keith's tale, she found herself being drawn in, both by his skill as a storyteller and by the similarities between his life and her own. She, too, had begun to dance almost as an afterthought—her best friend was doing it, and she just went along for the fun of it. She, too, had always taken time to study music; since her father had doubted that she would be able to make a living as a dancer, he had convinced her to consider a second career as a music teacher. She had soon outstripped all her classmates as a dancer, even her best friend who had hated her forever for her natural talent and determination.

"Perhaps not to you," Keith said, giving her a look that told her he knew exactly how well she must have identified with his story. "But when I started swimming competitively, I was thought of as somewhat odd. Anyway, the worst thing about me, as far as the other swimmers were concerned, was that I always won. As a matter of fact, by the time I won my slot on the Olympic swim team, I had the best win-loss record of any swimmer in their history. And of course, my teammates were not pleased about the extra attention I got. They felt, and rather deservedly, I suppose, that they should get the extra attention. After all, I didn't need much help to win, did I?"

They were coming up on the coastline, and Avis got her first scent of water through the opened window. Picking up her head like a racehorse, she sniffed expectantly at the air, aware that her heartbeat had just accelerated of its own accord.

Keith noticed. He had recovered from his earlier

distraction, and Avis was careful to keep her head averted as he went on with his tale. Although she felt good, she knew her face would betray her underlying strain if Keith looked hard enough.

"To make a long story short," Keith went on, "I got injured. It was a small thing, really—a stupid accident that should never have happened. I was preparing for a backstroke relay in a qualifying heat, and when I pushed off from the edge of the pool, I ran smack into a protruding starting box that had somehow gotten wedged into the water in the corner of the pool near my starting slot. The force of my push-off was so great that I cut right through to my collarbone, damaging several nerves and tendons in the process. All of that wouldn't have been so bad, but I didn't stop and get out of the pool. I went on and did a hundred meters of backstroke, which is the hardest stroke on your shoulders and upper back."

By now Avis had forgotten completely about the smell of water and the race, and was watching Keith raptly. He had the power to evoke a memory in his expression, and so she saw, very clearly, the pain of that injury and the compulsion which had forced him to continue. She also saw, in some carefully closeted corner of her mind, her own injury in the Odette pas de deux, and her own grueling but perfect performance despite her pain. She knew exactly what he had done in that pool years ago, and she knew exactly why.

Keith's voice was hard and gritty, but not bitter. "By the time they pulled me from that pool," he said, "the damage was done. I had irreparably injured my shoulder, and was told that if I ever swam again it would be a miracle." He paused for a moment to let the import of his words sink in. "My coach, of course, was all for trying for a miracle. But I had had enough. A month later, I was on my way to Oxford, and that was the last time I swam until I came back and started to work for Tom."

Avis opened her mouth to speak, but Keith cut her off with a warning finger placed on his lips. "By the time I came back to the States," he went on, "I had recovered. It wasn't until I came to visit Tom one day that it ever occurred to me what might have happened that afternoon so long ago."

"What? What might have happened?" Avis was sitting on the edge of her seat.

Keith turned and looked at her long and hard. "Someone caused that accident, Avis. Someone made me ram into that starting box. At the time I didn't know who, but I have a pretty good idea now." His eyes were fierce and bright.

"Who did it?"

To Avis's surprise, the fire died out of Keith's eyes and he shrugged. "It doesn't matter, does it? I mean, I can never prove it, so why bother? The point is, it's over. And I'm here, and so are you."

Avis felt a sudden chill. She had been so absorbed in the story that she hadn't realized until that moment how closely it paralleled her own experience in the Open-Air Theater. Keith had orchestrated the entire tale to bring her to this point. She felt thoroughly shaken and insecure.

"Why did you tell me that story, Keith?" she demanded after an awkward silence. He was watching her very closely, and he saw the accusation in her eyes. "I'm trying to prepare myself for this race, and you tell me a story that you know very well will upset me. Why did you do it?"

His expression was gentle, but his voice was urgent. "Because it needed to be told, Avis. It needed to be said before we get to Housefellow Lake." He had been slowing the car down as he spoke, and now he pulled it over and stopped in a forested rest area by the side of the road. They had left the highway, and there was nothing around for miles except the low, scruffy trees. Avis felt a stab of fear; she was trapped. Keith had turned so that he sat facing her, and she could tell from the deep light in his sea-colored eyes that what he was about to say was going to be difficult for him, and even harder for her to hear.

"I did a lot of thinking, last night, Avis. As a matter of fact, I didn't get one bit of sleep." *Neither did I,* Avis felt like telling him, but she kept quiet. "I made that confession to you about my past, not because I thought it was a good story, or even necessarily because I thought you should draw parallels between my life and yours, although God knows they're there to be drawn. I told you because I want you to know that people can do the right things for the wrong reasons." He paused and took a deep breath, and Avis understood how much what he was saying hurt him. "I've been coaching you to win this race for the wrong reasons, Avis. I think we're both doing it for the wrong reasons. And I think we're fooling ourselves, very dangerously, if we don't face up to the truth about ourselves, and about each other."

Avis knew what he was going to say before he even said it—he didn't want her to race today. Her first reaction was one of pure, cold rage. "Your story was very interesting, Keith," she said, making no attempt to control the venom in her voice. "It really told me a lot about you. I see what you mean about the wrong reasons. You're using me and the MasterSwim to prove to somebody that you know what went on. Is that it?"

A grim smile played across Keith's mouth, disappearing into the reddish recesses of his beard. "That's a rather dramatic interpretation of events, but yes, I suppose you could say I've been using the MasterSwim race to prove something to someone, even if that someone is only myself."

"But what about me, Keith? Did you ever stop to think about me while you were so busy vindicating yourself? Did it ever occur to you that I figured in your little tale of woe too? Where does this leave me, if you suddenly decided to get all high and mighty and confess that it was all just a game?"

"It isn't a game, Avis," Keith said with a warning note in his voice. "It has never been a game between us, at least not for me. I take you very seriously indeed."

"I'm sure you do," Avis said sarcastically. "You really respect my skills and my needs, don't you, Keith?"

"I try to." Now he sounded wary, as if he was trying to gauge what was to come. But Avis was too far gone in her anger to notice.

"You try to. Is that what you were doing snooping around at the National Ballet studios? Trying to respect my life, my integrity?"

Keith slammed the steering wheel with his palms, swearing softly. "Ah, so that's what this is all about! I should have known there was something wrong as soon as I saw you this morning." His eyes narrowed under lowering brows. "Who told you about it? Was it Larry?"

Avis curled her lip derisively. "Larry? No, it wasn't Larry, Keith. I'm sure you and Larry worked out a deal whereby he would stay well away from me. After all, he understands that you can't put a valuable commodity in jeopardy by upsetting her right before a big race, or a big role. You both understand the value of keeping the goods carefully packaged and undamaged, don't you?"

Keith looked at her and shook his head. "It doesn't matter who told you. I should have known you would find out from one of your old friends sooner or later." He seemed resigned and not the least bit embarrassed by his confession, which only made Avis angrier.

"I would have preferred sooner," she said bitterly. "From you. I would have preferred, actually, that you had not gone at all."

"It was not a question," Keith said, "of what you preferred."

"It wasn't? It wasn't?" Avis could feel her voice rising to the edge of hysteria. "It just happens to be *my* life we're talking about, Keith Harding. My past, and my future, and you've ruined it all. How dare you intrude on my life that way!"

"I went to see Larry and to talk to some of the people in the company because I thought the subject of your accident needed clearing up. I thought worrying about it might upset you too much to concentrate on the race." Keith chuckled dryly. "Of course, I realize now that I had underestimated your obsession. You don't have to face anything you don't want to, do you, Avis?"

"Thanks to you, I do now," Avis shot back. "Now I have to face the fact that I can never go back to dancing again. You've ruined my only chance to go back there; the one thing I had to hope for after this race was over. Now I can never face Larry and the rest of the company again. You've ruined my life, Keith. If I can't dance, my life might as well be over."

The force of what she had just said hit Avis like a physical blow, and she gasped, leaning back against the seat of the car. What had she just admitted? She had just stated the realization she had been trying for months to avoid—that dance was all that mattered to her, and that there was nothing else worth living for. It was a statement of loss and despair so powerful, and so honest, that it actually left her breathless for a moment. The air in the car was charged with the weight of her confession and all its implications. She and Keith sat staring at each other for a full minute, stunned by what they had just wrought. Then Avis buried her head in her hands and began to weep.

Keith was with her in an instant, gathering her up against him as he had in the taxi the evening before. He stroked her tightly wound coils of hair and murmured soothingly into her ear, dropping occasional kisses on top of her head. Avis was unable to pull away from him or to stem the flow of tears. Her body shook and her breath came in ragged gasps. She collapsed against Keith because she had no other recourse but to lean against the bulky comfort of his warm chest.

She did not know how long he held her, nor when he deemed it proper to begin to speak. But Avis knew that she could not yet think rationally about what had just happened. So she was forced to listen quietly to Keith, forcing her sobs to subside and nodding her head automatically.

"Avis, darling, please, you must listen to me. I'm sorry if I did something to upset you so terribly. Believe me, that was the furthest thing from my mind. I felt so helpless, and I knew that you felt desolate. Even if you never admitted it until just now, I knew exactly how you felt. I knew because I've been there myself, and like you, I took refuge in another obsession.

"But you have to understand that there are other ways of living your life. Moving from one obsession to another isn't going to solve your problems, Avis.

You've got to face what's happened to you head-on. One thing at a time." He reached down and tipped her chin up. "And we have to face what's been happening to us, too."

Avis blinked through her tears. "What does that mean?" she asked, her voice still raw.

He looked deeply into her eyes, as if searching for something. Then with a gentle smile, he shook his head. "Don't swim today, Avis. It's wrong for you— the wrong thing for the wrong reasons. I know how important it's been to you, how hard you've worked. But it won't help you face the rest of your life. We have to talk. We have to work this out. Together. You have to hear the truth."

Avis disentangled herself from his arms, her eyes still held by his. She had been waiting for him to say one thing, one sentence which would have rendered all the hurt, all the misunderstanding, unimportant and irrelevant. She had wanted him to say "I love you." That would have made it all right, and the MasterSwim would have been unnecessary.

But he had not said that. Instead, after forcing her to admit the sad secret which she had been holding inside herself ever since her injury, after forcing her to admit the lie she had been living during all those months of training, all he had said was "you have to face the truth."

Avis didn't want to talk. She had had enough words to last her a lifetime. Words, bitter and calculating words that hid or revealed the real reason for people's actions.

Swimming meant very little to her, except as a means to cope with the pain of rejection. Keith had used her, but she had used him, too. She had used him to get back at Larry, to get back at the other dancers who may have pitied her, and to hide from herself the awful truth: She did not want to swim—she wanted only to dance.

Now Keith wanted her to forget about the swim and talk some more. But Avis knew that it was too late. The words had not worked, and now she had only the water.

Keith must have seen the answer in her eyes, because he pulled back to his side of the car. "You're not going to back out, are you." It was a statement, not a question.

Avis stared straight ahead, out the window. "I'm swimming in that race, Keith. Please start the car now, or we'll be late."

He made no move to turn the ignition key. "You realize that you're jeopardizing everything by doing this. There's so much we haven't said. Why risk it all just because you feel you have something to prove?"

Now Avis turned to him, her dark eyes cold as stone. "What's the matter, Keith? Are you afraid I'll make you look like a fool when I don't win? Or are you afraid I *will* win, as you never had the guts to do after your accident?"

Keith winced at the stabbing words but did not respond. "I'm not thinking about me, Avis. I'm thinking about you."

"Well, stop thinking about me! I'm tired of other people thinking about me, making decisions for me, deciding whether I stay or go. This is my race, dammit, and I'm going to swim it!" Avis knew she was being irrational, but she was unable to stop herself. Once again, it had become a totem for her, the only constant in a world that was shattering.

Keith waited for a moment and then started the car. "You want to swim?" he asked through clenched teeth as he wheeled the car out onto the road. "Go ahead and swim. But I won't be there to watch you, Avis. I've had enough of this charade. You can go on fooling yourself forever, but not with me around to play nursemaid to your obsessions!"

"I don't need you to play nursemaid to me—that's just the point! I'm sick of other people running and ruining my life. If I want to ruin it, I'll do it myself! Now get me to that lake, and then you can do whatever you damn please!"

Chapter Thirteen

*H*e took her to the lake all right, although Avis wished several times during that hair-raising half-hour that she had walked. Keith drove brutally fast along the narrow two-lane highway, his eyes narrowed and his jaw set as he whipped the car around sudden turns with no thought at all for what might be approaching from the opposite direction.

Fortunately, they were on a fairly straight road which followed the shoreline except for occasional sudden turns. At those moments, Avis had no choice but to hang on to the dashboard and alternate between cursing Keith Harding and praying for her survival.

By the time they pulled in front of the dirt parking lot which led down to the bank of the river, Avis was tense and breathless, and she knew that Keith had purposely driven fast. There was still over an hour before she was actually due to be in the water, an hour in which she would have to work as hard to calm her frazzled nerves as she did to warm up her chilled muscles and bones. She got out of the car without looking at Keith and walked resolutely down the path. Part of her hoped that Keith would just start up the car again and leave her in peace so that she could collect her scattered thoughts. Part of her begged him to come after her, to spin her around by the shoulders and pull her close, to tell her that she was all wrong about everything, that he had done what he did because he loved her, and that the only thing he wanted was for them to be together.

Instead he sat in the car, and Avis could feel his eyes on her as she made her way toward the sparkling blue water that loomed through the trees ahead. His gaze penetrated the flannel warm-up suit like laser beams, and Avis had to resist the urge to break into a run. All the way through the thicket of trees to the race site, she expected to hear either the engine start or the door slam. By the time she reached the check-in area, she was sweating from the strain.

"I'm Avis Considine," she told the official who sat at the registration desk. She gave him her identification papers and registration form, which included information about her training club and coach. The official checked over the information and then looked up expectantly.

"And where is your coach?" he asked, looking around Avis as if he expected to see Keith hiding behind her back.

"He's . . ." Avis was suddenly at a loss to explain her situation. It had not occurred to her until that moment that she might need Keith to accompany her. "He can't make it just now," she finished lamely. "He'll be a little late."

"Well, we can't have that," the official said, shaking his head. "You've got to have a personal monitor. We can't be responsible for every swimmer in the water every minute. You've got to have someone watching you, or I'm afraid we can't let you swim."

Avis grabbed the edge of the table. Nausea swept through her stomach, threatening the morning meal.

"I've got to swim," she said breathlessly. "You don't understand. I've been training for this too long and too hard—there's too much at stake. I've just got to swim."

The man cocked his head quizzically. "Miss Considine, it's just a race. It's not the Olympic tryouts."

"I don't care about the Olympic tryouts," she said desperately. "That means nothing to me—this race means everything. You've got to understand. I can't let my coach ruin it all. He's . . . he's undependable. He said he'd be here by the time the race started, but he's just not . . . you've got to let me swim."

If Avis was aware of the tears that glazed her eyes at that moment, she made no attempt to brush them away. Instead she stared at the official with a mixture of beseechment and defiance. He blinked several times, slightly taken aback by the unexpected ferocity of the tiny dark woman who stood over him. Then his expression softened. "This your first race?" Avis nodded shortly. "I know how you feel. It's all or nothing—now or never, huh?" He reached out for her papers and stamped them with her official starting number, then gave her a plastic sheet with the same number to pin to her suit. "OK, Miss Considine, I'm going to bend the rules a little bit and let you through. But if your coach isn't here by the time you get in the water, we're going to have to pull you out. Your time wouldn't be official unless he was here anyway. Here you go, and . . . good luck."

He flashed a nice smile, which Avis returned gratefully. She felt as if she had just been given a reprieve. Her tension disappeared as she hurried over to the crowd of swimmers who were warming up by the starting area. The road ahead of her was clear, at least as far as the race went. She was convinced that once she got in the water there would be nothing that could stop her. The fact that her race time would be invalid unless

Keith showed—and he was hardly likely to do so—was irrelevant. All she wanted was a chance to get in the water and prove to herself that she could do it if she wanted.

There were over a hundred other people gathered in the starting area, which was a grassy slope that led to a wooden dock at a wide and shallow point in the river. Perhaps sixty of them would be swimming in the race. The rest were coaches and officials, many more of whom crowded the dock area and filled the four small motor launches that would ride alongside the four heats of swimmers. There were not many spectators, although as they had driven up to the race site she had noticed several groups of people picnicking at advantageous spots farther along the route. Nevertheless, the air of barely controlled excitement was in the air and it immediately affected Avis, who was familiar with the infectious currents that nervousness could produce. She chose a spot well back from the starting dock and began to stretch out slowly and methodically, forcing her mind once again to focus until she thought of nothing but the particular muscle she was working on and the water which spread out before her like a narrow blue ribbon.

Despite her efforts at control, when Avis heard the call for the first heat, her heart jumped into her throat. She was in the third heat—the next to last—and she knew that her nervousness would get progressively worse as the twenty-minute intervals between heats went by. Once Avis was ready to perform or compete, she liked to get right out there and do it. Waiting was the worst part; it gave her too much time to reconsider all the things she had hoped not to consider at all. All the memories she had made such an effort to banish from her mind came crowding in on her, in spite of her efforts to concentrate only on the swim.

Miraculously, no one tried to stop her when the third heat was called, and she moved to crouch in her starting position on the wooden deck. She knew full well that she had not totally overcome the panic which had been assailing her since her meeting with Beth the night before. She understood that while she was as ready as she would ever be in terms of physical conditioning and training, she could no longer fool herself into believing that her heart was in the race. The encounter with Beth and its devastating aftermath with Keith had been too much of a strain, even on her formidable powers of concentration. Now she could only pray that whatever physical ability she had would stand her in good stead. The one thing she would not do was back out. She almost hoped the kind official who had let her register would notice that her coach hadn't turned up, and that he would pull her from the race. Then she could say it had not been her fault. She could even blame it on Keith.

But there was another force operating on Avis, and she was as aware of it as she was aware of the wind chill which penetrated the extra layer of lanolin she had lathered on her skin. Avis felt she was fated to swim in the MasterSwim. There was too much at stake for her to abandon the chilly waters before her now. It was almost as if all the events of her life had conspired to see that she crouched there, in perfect pre-race position, with nothing before her but the water, nothing to look forward to but two hours spent in icy and exhausting effort, and no one at all to tell her it was worthwhile.

The report of the starting gun seemed ridiculously faint to Avis until she realized that she was hearing its echo through five feet of water. Her heat had begun, and miraculously given her distraction, her body had responded with the swiftness and precision of a Swiss

watch. She was in the water, and after the first breathless gasp she found that it was not as chilly as she had
thought it would be. She surfaced about eight feet out
from the dock, resisted the impulse to look to either
side and gauge where she stood in relationship to the
other swimmers, and took off with a steady stroke
downriver.

Stroke and pull, beat-beat-beat . . . it was amazing
how quickly she fell into the right rhythm, although she
knew it would be several minutes before she found her
pace. Stroke and pull and breathe . . . the very act of
swimming relaxed her. There were other swimmers,
but Avis's stroke was strong enough so that they
seemed as irrelevant as the faint chop on the surface of
the water. There was nothing to think about except her
stroke, her beat, and her breath, and she knew that
once she settled into her pace she would not even have
to think about that.

This is the reason, Avis thought dimly as she pulled
through the water, *that I chose swimming when I could
not dance. I am forced to totally immerse myself in what
I am doing.* No other activity afforded her the luxury of
total concentration.

Avis swam for what she thought was about twenty-
five minutes. She was aware of no other swimmers, no
disruption in the flow of water as it slipped past her
body. She began to feel the overall pattern of her pace
settling into her muscles, and the sensation of comfort,
of actually being at home in her watery universe, was so
great that she had to resist the urge to slow down. She
might as well have been in an easy chair as in six feet of
cool gray-blue water. She began to hum some Mozart
—the String Quartet in G Major—adapted to her
stroke so that the strong melody was slowed to an
almost lullaby rhythm.

It was hypnotic, there was no question about it. The

greatest pleasure was in not having to swim back and forth endlessly in a pool. Although she had swum in open water before, had swum in the Housefellow River before, she had never felt so strongly that she could just swim on in one direction forever. She was swimming away from the world, and that was all right with her.

By Avis's judgment, she had been swimming for almost an hour when the first pang of discomfort hit her. It was not so much physical as mental—a sense of uneasiness, as if troubled waters lay ahead. She lifted her head out of the water, but her eyes were dimmed and bleary from the long immersion and the lanolin which had gotten beneath her goggles. She could see nothing, but felt vaguely that there were other people nearby—swimmers, perhaps, or maybe one of the monitor launches. She thought she heard the low drone of an inboard motor, but her ears were filled with the silence of the river, and she was not sure what was real and what was fantasy.

The feeling of uneasiness grew. She tried to concentrate on Mozart, but she could not seem to make her stroke match the cadence of the music. Her arms felt heavy and her six-beat was erratic. She opened her eyes once or twice in the water and saw from the sun-dappled world around her that the sun must have come out at last. But the heat did not seem to penetrate the chill that had gripped her heart, and the blue color of the water reminded her of Keith Harding's eyes.

As soon as his name echoed through her mind, all pretense of enjoying her swim ended. She knew what was bothering her. Keith had been right; she was swimming beautifully, but she was doing it for the wrong reasons. She was swimming away from what she wanted most in the world. If she was really strong, she would be swimming in the other direction, back toward Keith Harding, to tell him that he had been right about everything. She was afraid to go back to the National Ballet because she had been afraid for a long time of her advancing age, her increasingly frequent injuries, and of the advent of nubile young dancers like Cheryl. She had been afraid that Laurence had sabotaged her career, but she was even more afraid that he hadn't, that it had been a stupid, senseless accident. She was afraid that what was true for Beth was true also for her, but even more afraid that, in trying to disprove Beth's accusations, she had turned away from the one thing that really did mean as much to her as dance—Keith.

Swimming was wonderful. It was an excellent sport, and she did it exceedingly well. If she wanted to, Avis could probably become a decent competitive swimmer. But she would be swimming to wipe out the memory of what was missing in her life, not to add something to her life. What she really wanted was to return to dancing—not in the total, all-out, all-consuming way she had danced before, but enough to satisfy her undiminished love for the art and joy of the dance. She wanted to swim, too, because she knew it had made her stronger as a dancer and as a person. But the compulsion to swim was no longer with her. She had only one compulsion left—her love for Keith Harding.

These revelations did not come all at once to Avis. They came slowly as she continued swimming, and they had the effect of easing the sudden onslaught of apprehension that had filled her before. She was confident now that she could swim, and finish the race. But she still felt the physical nearness of something other than water, and when she raised her head again she was momentarily disoriented. She even floundered a bit, thrashing and losing her stroke entirely. For the first time since she had begun to swim, she was afraid.

Her heart pounded rapidly and she treaded water, turning around and around in an attempt to get her bearings and avoid whatever it was that loomed near. Then, suddenly, she felt two arms hauling her up out of her watery confusion. Her first reaction was to cry out and try to pull away. The sudden contact was frightening, and besides, she was sure it was the race officials pulling her from the water because they had realized she had no coach with her. She still wanted to finish the race, and whoever held her had to hold on tight against Avis's strong protests.

But the man who held her was unnaturally strong. It was Keith, and he had no intention of letting her go. The struggle was brief—he had the leverage on his side, and an extra seventy-five pounds of pure muscle behind him. He got her on to the deck of the boat and laid her down on a thick white towel, kneeling beside her to shield the sun from her extra-sensitive eyes.

It took Avis a while to recognize him, and a while more to understand why he was there. But his smiling face, and the tender way he removed her bathing cap, stroking her long wet hair out in a dark fan around her head, was a better explanation than words could have offered at that moment. She tried to smile back to him, but the muscles in her face were stiff from the drag of the water, and she could only manage a weak grin. Her voice, too, when she tried to use it, sounded thick and faraway to her, although perhaps that was due to her waterlogged ears.

"What are you doing?" she managed to croak, but Keith silenced her with a kiss on her swollen lips.

"Shhhh. Don't talk. It's better if you just rest." He smiled and shook his head. "What do you think I'm doing here, you goose? I came back to get what's mine."

The possessive gleam in his eye told Avis exactly what he meant. "You should have let me finish—" she began, but he cut her off by thrusting a cup of warm liquid at her.

"Here, drink. This will restore fluids and body sugar. Now just hush up and let me rub some of this glop off you." She opened her mouth to say something else, but he shook his head. "I said don't talk. Can you hear all right? OK, then just listen. I'll do the talking."

Keith pulled another towel from a bag beside him and began to rub her skin gently. There was very little lanolin left, most of it having washed off in the water, but the rubbing felt warm and welcome, and she relaxed as the pleasure of his supple stroke increased along her legs and thighs. She couldn't see anyone else on the boat, although there was the dim sound of human voices nearby and she knew someone had to be at the wheel.

"It's one of the monitor launches," Keith said, noticing her looking around. "I commandeered the fourth heat boat by telling them I was your coach and I had just found out that you won the State Lottery."

"You what?" Avis tried to raise her head, but Keith pushed it back gently. "Relax," he said. "If anybody congratulates you, just thank them and grin." He winked. "After all, congratulations are in order, although not because you're a millionaire."

"Why are they in order?" Avis discovered that her voice was gaining strength and clarity, and that her sight was clearing by the minute. Keith, for instance, was no longer a blur, but a radiant mass in her field of vision.

"You'll find out in a little while. First, let's get you onto dry land and into dry clothes." He bent closer, and for the first time, she saw the concern written across his face. "You know," he whispered, "you were in no condition to go into that water today."

"I felt fine," Avis said, but she knew Keith was right. No amount of determination could have overcome the combination of a sleepless night and the toll of emotional stress that Avis had experienced in the past twenty-four hours. She might have made it, but then, she might not, and she had already decided that the race was not the most important thing in the world to her. Keith was, and at the moment the sight of him filled her with more contentment than a first-place ribbon could ever have.

Still, she was curious as to her progress. "How was I doing?" she asked.

Keith looked as if he had been expecting the question. "You were leading the pack for a while there. But then, suddenly, you seemed to flounder and lost your pace. That was when I knew I had to pull you out. I couldn't risk losing you, even to satisfy my urge to win. Or yours."

Avis understood what he meant. "But how far did I get? How long was I in the water?"

He smiled. "Twenty-three minutes."

Then she realized the extent to which she had fooled herself about the race. Only twenty minutes! She was silent the entire trip back to the dock, allowing Keith to minister to her and carry her up to the car, where he helped her out of her suit and into a warm fleece sweatsuit. Avis felt no embarrassment as he undressed her, shielding her from any possible passersby and bundling her into her clothes as if she were no bigger than a doll. There was no passion in his touch, but his hands were as warm and comforting as the intent expression on his face, and Avis began to feel better and better, despite the disappointing news about the race. She was not sorry that Keith had pulled her out of the water, but she would have liked to have been winning when he did.

Avis was ready to talk by the time Keith pulled away from Housefellow Lake. She wanted to tell him what had happened to her, how she felt about him, and that she understood why he had gone to Larry. She wanted to tell him that none of it mattered, as long as they were together. But Keith would not let her talk. He gave her a Thermos of thick hot chocolate and instructed her not to say a word until she had drained it. This was Keith the coach speaking, and Avis knew better than to argue with him.

The hot liquid was soothing, and tasted even better. By the time the Thermos was empty, Keith had pulled up along a deserted stretch of beach on the ocean side of the highway. The day had grown hot and sunny, and Keith pulled a blanket out of the back of the car and spread it out for them to lie on behind a sandy dune that faced the water.

"Now," he said when they were finally settled comfortably against one another. "Now let's talk."

"Me first," Avis said.

"Oh, no. Me first. I get to be first because I made the biggest mistake. I have more to explain than you do."

"OK," she conceded lightly. "But I'm not sure you're right."

"I'm right, believe me. Or rather, I was wrong. I should never have gone to the studio without your knowledge and consent. I told myself I was doing you a favor by looking into your accident for you, but the truth was, I was just protecting my interests. I wasn't thinking about Avis the person at all. I was thinking about Avis the potential competitive swimmer, and about Keith the coach.

"And, to be perfectly honest, I had another motive. I was jealous, Avis, jealous of your commitment to the ballet. I've never felt a total dedication to any one thing. Oh, sure, I attack everything I do as if it's the only thing in the world, but I envied that little cocoon of dance you and your friends had spun around your-selves. I envied your talent, your obsession, your utter infatuation with what you did. I even envied your relationship with Laurence."

"Oh, but that was over years ago!"

"Yes, but you were bound by ties that I could never understand or share. I've never finished anything in my life, Avis, don't you see that? Swimming, flying, music . . . But you! You've always been so committed. I wanted to turn your desire to dance into a desire to swim—for my own selfish reasons. And, God help me, I wanted to turn your desire for Larry into a desire for me. I wanted what you had as much as I wanted you. And so I tried to take over your life."

"Keith." Avis reached up and stroked his beard, which glowed in the strong sun. "You didn't have to go to all that trouble. All you had to do was ask, and I would have been there. Maybe not as a swimmer, but as a woman. I never knew how you felt, and I was too insecure about myself to tell you how I felt."

"I know, I know. But that was no excuse to do what I did. I can only say that I needed to be part of your life. Needed to try and understand what it was that held you so bound to the National. Finding out what had happened that night at the Open-Air Theater was only a part of it."

Avis shrugged. "It doesn't matter now. I realize now that I was probably wrong about Larry's being responsible for my injury."

"Yes. You were wrong."

"It was an accident. And I know now that should have been a sign to me that things were not going right—that I should have been slowing down, not dancing so many difficult parts. It was my own fault and not an accident after all. I shouldn't have blamed him."

"What?" There was genuine surprise in Keith's voice and, when he turned her around in his arms so that he could face her, there was surprise on his face. "Not an accident? But Avis! I thought . . . I thought you said Beth had told you."

"She told me you had gone to the studio, not what you had found out." Avis searched his face, confused. "What do you mean? Told me what?"

Keith shook his head. "You mean you still don't know? Avis, you were right all along! It wasn't an accident."

"Not an accident? But you said . . . Larry . . ." She felt suddenly dizzy.

"It wasn't Larry, Avis."

"Then who? Beth? Was it Beth?" The possibility hit her forcefully. Of course it could have been Beth! Beth, who was so angry, and so vindictive. "Beth?" She still couldn't believe it of her old friend.

"Not Beth." He was shaking his head slowly, gently, as if sorry to have to break the news. "It was Cheryl, I'm afraid."

"Cheryl? Cheryl Cattier?" This was the most stunning news of all. Avis could not believe that the sweet young girl who had been so in awe of Avis's skill would have had the courage or malice to purposely jeopardize another dancer's career. "Are you sure?"

Keith nodded sadly. "Oh, yes. Larry had already suspected something when I went to see him. As a matter of fact, he had been asking a few questions himself. It was Larry who figured out that Cheryl had cut the marly floor short. She had been rehearsing when the floor was being laid."

"But . . . Cheryl!" Avis was at a loss for words.

"I know, I know. She seemed too sweet to pull a trick like that. I don't think she did it maliciously, I think she just wanted you out of the way temporarily. Apparently, that role in Larry's new piece was very important to her. I guess she never stopped to think that you might get seriously injured. When Larry confronted her, she told him she thought you were invincible. That you might trip and get a bad review or something, but never that you would be unable to dance."

Avis turned away from him toward the jewellike sea. She didn't know whether to scream in anger or weep with pity. She was as sorry for Cheryl as she was for herself.

"Needless to say," Keith went on, "Cheryl is gone. She wasn't doing very well in the Bird of Paradise solo, Larry told me—probably a guilty conscience. That was why she came to ask for your help. Anyway, when he came to see you, he had hoped to get you to come back, although apparently that meeting backfired."

"Backfired? He behaved like a beast!"

"I guess he was jealous, too. He saw us together, and he realized that you weren't under his control anymore. He told me he saw then that you had found a new obsession. Swimming—and me." Keith smiled as he said this, almost shyly.

Avis turned back to Keith. "Then I guess he knew even before I did. Oh, Keith, if only I had been honest with you—with myself—right from the start. I thought I only wanted you physically because I needed someone —anyone—to ease my emotional pain. I didn't realize that needing someone is the best way of loving them. I thought I only needed you because I wanted to swim, because I wanted to get back at Larry and everybody who looked at me as a poor old has-been. What I really needed was someone to show me that I could offer plenty to this world without being obsessed by swimming or dancing. I could offer myself." Avis reached up and put both arms around Keith's neck. He had taken off his shirt, and she felt the soft expanse of his warm skin over the hard musculature of his shoulders.

"That sounds like an excellent proposition," Keith

murmured, lifting her sweatshirt so that his hands could curl up around her bare ribs.

"It's an offer you can't refuse," she replied, and then laid her lips firmly across his, blocking out any chance of further conversation.

Not that Keith had to be persuaded to stop talking and start making love. He made a short sound of surprise, strangled by the pressure of Avis's lips on his, but the sound quickly turned into a deep chuckle of delight, and ended with a low moan that betrayed his increasing arousal. Avis was on her knees, pressing her body against his and forcing him back against the sandy slope of the dune. Her body was still downy soft from the lanolin-and-water treatment it had just endured, and if her skin was slightly raw and her muscles slightly achy from her recent effort, the pain was easily surpassed by the pleasure she felt at being in Keith's arms at last. His hands were stroking up and down the length of her outstretched torso, stopping with increasing frequency to dally at her hardening nipples. His mouth had quickly responded to her demands, opening and delivering full measure of the heated hungry kisses that she had been seeking. His tongue thrust hard against the sides of her mouth, darting in and out as if to swallow the lower half of her face whole. His appetite was ravenous, and it aroused hers to greater heights than she had thought possible.

With one hand, Keith pressed against her shoulder and pushed her eager body back into an upright position. Using the other hand, he unzipped her sweatshirt and then, in the same motion, pulled her sweatpants down around her knees. He had only to lift her up slightly under both arms, which he did with no discernible effort, for the pants and top to fall easily to the blanket beneath them. Now Avis was totally nude, exposed to the sea and the sun and the August heat, and to the much greater fire that burned in Keith's aquamarine eyes.

"You are everything I ever wanted," he murmured, drinking in the sight of her brave body stretched languorously before him in utter defiance of any prying eyes that might be around. "Why did I ever try to make you into something you weren't?"

"Maybe you just wanted someone with a few more pounds on her frame," Avis teased, thrusting out one bare hip to accentuate what slight curve there was.

He laughed, but there was far more passion than merriment in his laugh. "You're all the woman I'll ever want," he said, gathering her to him slowly, so that he could savor every angle of her body as it bent toward him. "Even if you did lose those six pounds I made you gain."

"Once a dancer, always a dancer," she murmured, but then his lips were on her throat and her breasts and her belly, and she lifted her face to the blazing blue sky, unable to speak and unwilling to make the effort. Keith's hands easily spanned her waist and his thumbs dipped low into the sensitive declivity of her buttocks, sending an electric current through the base of her spine. His lips seemed to be everywhere at once, and her entire torso was melting into a single flame of desire. Externally, she seemed to be all in flames, and now all that she needed to make her happiness complete was to have him in her, to feel the heat consume her and to abandon herself to the complete commitment of loving him. Her hands, of their own accord, found the button of his jeans and pulled it open so that she could feel him straining against the cloth.

"This is the truth that we both needed to face," Keith whispered hoarsely as he raised himself up to remove the pants. "We knew all about commitment to a cause, to a goal, but neither of us was willing to admit that the commitment of our love for each other was all that we really wanted."

He had removed his pants and lay back down on the blanket, pulling Avis on top of him so that they lay flank to flank and cradled in the shadow of the dune.

"We've made love before," Avis murmured against his beard, "but why couldn't we see what was really going on? What I really want to do is spend the rest of my life with you. Whatever else I do with my time will only be an added joy, if we're together."

"Of course we'll be together!" Keith's voice was fierce. "Don't you ever even think anything else!" He wrapped his arms all the way around her with a groan. "Oh, my lovely water dancer. . . . I've never finished anything in my life, but my God, I'm going to make this last forever."

Avis was about to ask whether he was referring to their long-term relationship or their immediate situation. But then he was over her, and inside of her, and she knew that he meant both. The blazing sky and the heat and the light all seemed to coalesce into one fiery ball of passion at the core of her being, and she lost track of time and space, and the universe split apart and spun away and then was right again, because she knew that Keith Harding loved her and that he intended to make it last forever.

Epilogue

Monday, September 15

It's been a long time since I've written anything in this journal, and I suspect this may be the last entry. For a while, it was the only friend I had to share my thoughts with. Now I've found Keith, and not only do we share our thoughts, but we seem to have them together! I don't want to abandon this diary, but my life is so full now that I don't seem to have any time for it anymore.

I'm back at the studio, teaching for Larry, coaching a few promising young dancers, and helping to restage some of the old classics—even *Swan Lake!* Larry wants me to take on some solo roles this season, but I don't feel ready. I was away for too long, and besides, I'm too busy with the wedding plans to want to commit myself to a major role this winter! Perhaps in the spring, when I feel more secure about my dancing and when things have settled down for Keith and me. (Who am I kidding? Of course I'll dance some solo roles in the spring! I can't wait! But of course, that's because I know that when my career as a performer finally does come to an end, I'll have something to do with the rest of my life. I have Keith, don't I?)

I realized as I reread this journal that my love for Keith was there even before I was willing to acknowledge it myself. First, all I talked about was dance, or rather the lack of it. Then it was swimming, but increasingly all I seemed to talk about was Keith. His name jumps out at me from every page, hitting me over the head like a hammer. How could I not have seen the obvious—that I was in love with him right from the start?

But Keith says we're two of a kind, too wrapped up in what we think we should be doing to see any other possibilities, and too stubborn to admit those possibilities even when they do hit us on the head. As usual, he's right.

After our honeymoon, Keith is opening his own swim club. He wants to train young swimmers, but he's going to do it his way: rhythm training, weights, running. He even wants me to teach some basic ballet to his kids! He's got plenty of backers, and everybody says he'll be producing the Olympic teams in a few years.

I'll be at the studio, although Keith says he wants me to keep on swimming. He says it's great stamina training for dancers, and it's terrific for pregnant women too!

Just think all those little water dancers with smiling sea-green eyes! Life is so full of possibilities these days. I can hardly wait!

WIN

a fabulous $50,000 diamond jewelry collection

ENTER

by filling out the coupon below and mailing it by September 30, 1985

Send entries to:

U.S.
Silhouette Diamond Sweepstakes
P.O. Box 779
Madison Square Station
New York, NY 10159

Canada
Silhouette Diamond Sweepstakes
Suite 191
238 Davenport Road
Toronto, Ontario M5R 1J6

SILHOUETTE DIAMOND SWEEPSTAKES
ENTRY FORM

☐ Mrs.　　☐ Miss　　☐ Ms　　☐ Mr.

NAME _____ (please print)

ADDRESS _____ APT. # _____

CITY _____

STATE/(PROV.) _____

ZIP/(POSTAL CODE) _____

RTD-A-1

RULES FOR SILHOUETTE DIAMOND SWEEPSTAKES

OFFICIAL RULES—NO PURCHASE NECESSARY

1. Silhouette Diamond Sweepstakes is open to Canadian (except Quebec) and United States residents 18 years or older at the time of entry. Employees and immediate families of the publishers of Silhouette, their affiliates, retailers, distributors, printers, agencies and RONALD SMILEY INC. are excluded.

2. To enter, print your name and address on the official entry form or on a 3" x 5" slip of paper. You may enter as often as you choose, but each envelope must contain only one entry. Mail entries first class in Canada to Silhouette Diamond Sweepstakes, Suite 191, 238 Davenport Road, Toronto, Ontario M5R 1J6. In the United States, mail to Silhouette Diamond Sweepstakes, P.O. Box 779, Madison Square Station, New York, NY 10159. Entries must be postmarked between February 1 and September 30, 1985. Silhouette is not responsible for lost, late or misdirected mail.

3. First Prize of diamond jewelry, consisting of a necklace, ring, bracelet and earrings will be awarded. Approximate retail value is $50,000 U.S./$62,500 Canadian. Second Prize of 100 Silhouette Home Reader Service Subscriptions will be awarded. Approximate retail value of each is $162.00 U.S./$180.00 Canadian. No substitution, duplication, cash redemption or transfer of prizes will be permitted. Odds of winning depend upon the number of valid entries received. One prize to a family or household. Income taxes, other taxes and insurance on First Prize are the sole responsibility of the winners.

4. Winners will be selected under the supervision of RONALD SMILEY INC., an independent judging organization whose decisions are final, by random drawings from valid entries postmarked by September 30, 1985, and received no later than October 7, 1985. Entry in this sweepstakes indicates your awareness of the Official Rules. Winners who are residents of Canada must answer correctly a time-related arithmetical skill-testing question to qualify. First Prize winner will be notified by certified mail and must submit an Affidavit of Compliance within 10 days of notification. Returned Affidavits or prizes that are refused or undeliverable will result in alternative names being randomly drawn. Winners may be asked for use of their name and photo at no additional compensation.

5. For a First Prize winner list, send a stamped self-addressed envelope postmarked by September 30, 1985. In Canada, mail to Silhouette Diamond Contest Winner, Suite 309, 238 Davenport Road, Toronto, Ontario M5R 1J6. In the United States, mail to Silhouette Diamond Contest Winner, P.O. Box 182, Bowling Green Station, New York, NY 10274. This offer will appear in Silhouette publications and at participating retailers. Offer void in Quebec and subject to all Federal, Provincial, State and Municipal laws and regulations and wherever prohibited or restricted by law.

SDR-A-1

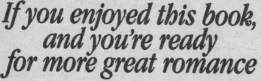

Silhouette Special Edition. Romances for the woman who expects a little more out of love.

If you enjoyed this book, and you're ready for more great romance

...get 4 romance novels FREE when you become a Silhouette Special Edition home subscriber.

Act now and we'll send you four exciting Silhouette Special Edition romance novels. They're our gift to introduce you to our convenient home subscription service. Every month, we'll send you six new passion-filled Special Edition books. Look them over for 15 days. If you keep them, pay just $11.70 for all six. Or return them at no charge.

We'll mail your books to you two full months *before they are available anywhere else.* Plus, with every shipment, you'll receive the Silhouette Books Newsletter absolutely free. *And with Silhouette Special Edition there are never any shipping or handling charges.*

Mail the coupon today to get your four free books—and more romance than you ever bargained for.

Silhouette Special Edition is a service mark and a registered trademark.

She fought for a bold future
until she could no longer
ignore the...

ECHO OF THUNDER

MAURA SEGER

Author of Eye of the Storm

ECHO OF THUNDER is the love story of James
Callahan and Alexis Brockton, who forge a union
that must withstand the pressures of their own
desires and the challenge of building a new television
empire.

Author Maura Seger's writing has been described by
Romantic Times as having a "superb.blend of
historical perspective, exciting romance and a deep
and abiding passion for the human soul."

**Available at your favorite
retail outlet in SEPTEMBER.**

ECO-B-1

Silhouette Special Edition

COMING NEXT MONTH

ONE MAN'S ART—Nora Roberts
To Genevieve Grandeau, love meant giving, sharing...trusting.
Grant Campbell was a loner. Could he, would he, allow
himself to be drawn into the life of this beautiful socialite?

THE CUTTING EDGE—Linda Howard
Brett Rutland's search for an embezzler brought Tessa Conway
into his life. For the first time, Brett was falling in love...until
his heart's desire became his prime suspect.

SECOND GENERATION—Roslyn MacDonald
Hollywood had taught costume designer Deanna Monroe that
there was no such thing as instant love. But Rick seemed to
defy Hollywood law, and Deanna was too charmed to realize
she could be heading for heartbreak.

EARTH AND FIRE—Jennifer West
Chalon Karras had once fallen in love with and married a rich
older man. Now Chalon was filled with grief over his sudden
death, and guilt at her growing passion for his dangerously
handsome son.

JUST ANOTHER PRETTY FACE—Elaine Camp
They met while working together on a film shot on location in
Egypt. Among the pyramids, assistant director Savanna Collier
and actor Teague Harris discovered the passion that made
Hollywood infamous, and treacherous.

MIDNIGHT SUN—Lisa Jackson
Because of a bitter family feud Ashley Stephens and Trevor
Daniels had tried to deny the flaming passion between them for
eight long years, but even fiery hatred couldn't keep them apart
forever.

AVAILABLE THIS MONTH

ALMOST HEAVEN
Carole Halston

REMEBER THE DREAMS
Christine Flynn

TEARS IN THE RAIN
Pamela Wallace

WATER DANCER
Jillian Blake

SWEET BURNING
Sandi Shane

THAT SPECIAL SUNDAY
Maggi Charles